The Merriest Misters

TIMOTHY JANOVSKY

ST. MARTIN'S
GRIFFIN
NEW YORK

First published in the United States by St. Martin's Griffin, an imprint of St. Martin's Publishing Group

THE MERRIEST MISTERS. Copyright © 2024 by Timothy Janovsky. All rights reserved. Printed in the United States of America. For information, address St. Martin's Publishing Group, 120 Broadway, New York, NY 10271.

www.stmartins.com

Designed by Meryl Sussman Levavi

Library of Congress Cataloging-in-Publication Data

Names: Janovsky, Timothy, author.
Title: The merriest misters / Timothy Janovsky.
Description: First edition. | New York : St. Martin's Griffin, 2024.
Identifiers: LCCN 2024016541 | ISBN 9781250338938
    (trade paperback) | ISBN 9781250338945 (ebook)
Subjects: LCGFT: Christmas fiction. | Romance fiction. | Gay fiction. |
    Novels.
Classification: LCC PS3610.A5796 M47 2024 | DDC 813/.6—dc23/
    eng/20240415
LC record available at https://lccn.loc.gov/2024016541

Our books may be purchased in bulk for promotional, educational, or business use. Please contact your local bookseller or the Macmillan Corporate and Premium Sales Department at 1-800-221-7945, extension 5442, or by email at MacmillanSpecialMarkets@macmillan.com.

First Edition: 2024

10 9 8 7 6 5 4 3 2 1

The Merriest Misters

For my fellow queer folk who love Christmas.
May we continue to make the Yuletide as gay as possible . . .

The Merriest Misters

YOU BETTER NOT POUT

QUINN

There's nothing sadder than watching a festive Christmas movie alone.

Scratch that, there's nothing sadder than watching a festive Christmas movie alone when your husband is upstairs doing work. Especially when you went through the trouble of picking out his favorite—*Elf*—in the hopes it would lure him from his office for the evening.

No luck.

I sit with my lukewarm hot chocolate, melty marshmallows sloshing around in my mug like reminders of my waterlogged dreams of domestic bliss for a special holiday season in our very first house.

When I was younger, before my parents divorced, my mom used to cover our entire fridge with Christmas cards from friends and family members from all over the world. They were the fancy, customizable ones you got printed at the pharmacy photo kiosk that showcase images of the whole family at Disney World in front of Cinderella Castle or posed in matching pajama sets before a fireplace—the family dog only half looking, angry to be tucked into people clothes for the laborious shoot. Every morning before breakfast, I would look at the husbands and wives in those cards and think, *That's what my marriage is going to be like. Picture-perfect.*

Then, I turned fifteen, realized I was gay, and suddenly those cards didn't represent the ideal future anymore. Maybe still for some, but not for me. Not, at least, until marriage equality and not until Patrick.

Patrick, who is upstairs drawing various types of toilets for a presentation at his architecture firm instead of watching *Elf* with his husband, his husband who made sure to steal extra packets of Swiss Miss from the teachers' lounge on his way out of work today.

I sit here joylessly watching as Will Ferrell tries to understand the complex crosswalks and door systems of New York City. There's a week until Christmas. I should not be stewing all by my-self in our garland-festooned living room. Today, I caught up on lesson planning during my prep period and put on an educational film at the end of the day, just to get a head start on grading. We promised tonight was movie night, so why has the kettle-corn bowl only had one hand in it all evening?

Okay, two. Two hands. Both of which were mine when I was shoveling away my sadness earlier since I'd been canceled on, but I can't be blamed for that. It's good kettle corn, straight from one of those decorative tins people love to gift around this time of year. Fresh and sticky and just the right amount of maybe-my-teeth-will-fall-out-this-time per chew.

For a whole of maybe twenty minutes, I'm angry. Then, Will Ferrell and Zooey Deschanel sing "Baby, It's Cold Outside" in the women's locker room at a department store that begs the ques-tion: Should this really be allowed in a family film?

Ick factor aside, I thaw, remembering when Patrick and I watched this movie together back when we were still dating. He started singing Buddy the Elf's parts. I started singing the Jovie parts. We weren't good singers. What we lacked in pitch, we made up for in volume, much to the dismay of our next-door neighbor, who banged a heavy fist on the wall and shouted, "This isn't *The*

Voice and, if it were, this isn't me hitting my button! Keep it down in there." We couldn't stop laughing.

Floating on the memories of a better, less stressful time, I go over to the teakettle, pour some hot water, and dump out the powdery chocolate. In my backpack, which I tucked in the hall closet, I find a candy cane one of my students gave me and stick it inside the red mug to stir. Patrick loves that extra hint of flavor.

With a small bowl of kettle corn and the cocoa, I go upstairs, treading lightly on the stubborn, rickety boards. This place was sold to us as a fixer-upper. I didn't realize that meant that with full-time jobs we'd need to be taking uppers just to get any of the fixing done in a timely manner. It's a mess, but according to the mortgage, it's *our* mess.

I'm trying to love it.

Just like I'm trying to love Patrick.

This Patrick, I should say. A Patrick that convinces me to forgo a honeymoon for a property investment and cancels movie plans last minute because he has to bring home the projects he didn't finish during the workday. I know he isn't getting paid extra for this overtime, even though we could use the money.

When I get to Patrick's office, I hear voices. He usually works in silence, so I know it's not a TV show or a podcast. He must be on the phone.

"It'll be great. Don't worry about it, Mom." The creaking means Patrick is pacing behind his desk. Damn, do any of these floorboards not have something to say? "I love you, too. I'll call again tomorrow once I tell Quinn. Sounds good. Good night."

I take that as my cue to enter with treats. "Tell me what?"

Patrick stands behind his desk, appearing haggard. His shaggy sandy-blond hair hangs lifeless, the ends of his bangs brushing the top rim of his wiry glasses. He's wearing one of his favorite sweater vests, unironically.

I think sometimes he wishes he were a dad in a nineties sitcom.

It's a dated aesthetic that works for him and gives him gravitas as an architect. Though, he thinks he'd look better with a mustache and curses his genes since he can't grow facial hair to save his life. "Are those for me?" he asks, nodding down at my offerings.

He makes space on his desk for me to set them down. "I thought I'd bring some of the fun up to you since you're so busy."

He scrubs a hand over his face. "These toilet partitions are a doozy."

I smile despite myself because Patrick Hargrave is not a man of many words and yet he still finds a way to slip *doozy* into casual conversation.

I approach his desk. From his printouts, notes, and sketches for the project, he's toying with everything from solid plastic to plastic laminate to stainless steel for the toilet cubicles. The sheer number of latch locks there are in the world makes my head spin.

"Looks like you've still got a lot to sort through," I say, rubbing a hand along his back as I always do. The wool of his sweater vest causes a slight, unpleasant static shock. "When's this presentation again?"

"Tomorrow." His shoulders slouch forward even more as he exhales.

It's selfish of me to wish that when he leaves the office he leaves behind his work, too, so we can be a couple again, like we were before we became a walking joint bank account, a talking marriage license.

Because this is his dream job. Just like teaching is—was?—my dream job.

That dream has started to feel more like a burden as of late, with budget cuts and class sizes doubling and my bulletin boards getting vandalized every other week. At times, I'm tempted to walk out the front door and never look back, like Nora in *A Doll's House*.

Dream jobs come with sacrifices. I have to support Patrick in his, despite his sacrifice being our time together.

He seems uninterested in discussing work any more, so I ask, "What were you talking to your mom about?"

"Uh, do you remember when their downstairs bathroom flooded a few months back?"

This is probably the longest conversation we've had this week, and even though we changed topics, it's still somehow about bathrooms. "Yeah," I say.

"Well, as a Christmas gift, my dad is going to get it redone."

"That's nice of him."

"Yeah, I thought so, too. They didn't ask me to do the redesign, but—" He slants his body away from mine, clearly not wanting my sympathy, even if I can see the color drain from his features. He shakes his head as if he can erase the emotion like a drawing on his iPad. "Their contractor wants to start right away—barring work on Christmas Day—which means the bathroom is going to be off-limits and the house will be a mess, so they can't host." Patrick's voice keeps going up at the ends of his sentences, which gives me pause.

"Okay, so what? Should we see what restaurants are open and reserve a table so we can plan to meet there?" I ask.

"It's so late. Everything is all booked up." Patrick smiles weakly. "I told her we'd host it here."

I gape at him. "You told her *what*? Without asking me? This place isn't any better than theirs, even with the renovation happening. They could be jackhammering there while we eat, and it would still be better."

"Come on," Patrick protests. "You know that's not true."

Patrick would've told you as much five months ago before we settled on this place and signed our lives away. It was Patrick's dream to design us an English-inspired farmhouse from scratch—someplace secluded, close to nature. Somewhere we could go on hikes and read books while drinking coffee on a charming porch. We'd each have our own office. The master bedroom would overlook a forest. But porches and master bedrooms with views even on already-built houses are expensive, so we shelved that dream for at least another decade.

"Are your parents still going to cook dinner at least?" I ask.

Patrick worries his bottom lip. "I sort of said we could handle that, too."

That anger from earlier? Oh, it's back. "And when exactly was the last time you touched an appliance in our kitchen that wasn't the microwave, the fridge, or the toaster oven?"

"Does the air fryer count?" he asks, obviously trying to defuse the tension with a joke.

"Jesus, Pat. Would it have killed you to run it by me first?"

"It's Christmas. You know how much Christmas means to my mom. I couldn't be the reason it was canceled," he says.

"Canceled? Your brother makes six figures and has a massive New York City apartment. Why couldn't he host?" I ask, arms folded, foot tapping. The anger comes out in all the clichéd ways with Patrick because I love the guy, but otherwise, he's largely oblivious.

"You know my parents would never drive into the city on Christmas. Besides, they'd never ask Bradley," he says.

"Because?"

"You know because. Because he's single. That's because." He huffs at me. "We're married now. We have a house now. This is what people who are married and have a house do. They host holidays. Why is this so surprising to you?"

I shake my head, thinking back on all the conversations we had about never being a typical married couple. About doing things our way. Only being in this for the tax breaks and the joint health insurance and the yes-you-have-legal-claim-over-this-human-being in life-or-death scenarios. What happened to that? "Hosting a holiday is not surprising to me. What's surprising to me is that my husband agreed to clean our house and cook an entire Christmas meal when he can't even pull himself away from his work for two hours to watch a Christmas movie with me." I wish I didn't sound so pathetic right now, but it's too late to gobble the words back up. Frankly, it was easier said than "I miss you" because it's impossible to miss someone sitting under the same roof as you every night, isn't it?

"Quinn, I didn't know it meant that much to you," he says, voice softening. "Just give me ten minutes, I'll bring all of this downstairs. I'll work in front of the TV."

I shake my head again, stopping him and feeling stupid this time. Work is more important. I could stand to have a little perspective. "No, that's silly. I'm being dramatic. Please forget I said anything. We'll make it work."

"We will," he agrees, offering me a conciliatory smile. "But right now, let's not worry about how and let's go watch *Elf*."

"I already watched half of it," I say, gently waving his idea off. Not feeling so argumentative. It's the holidays. Tensions are high. I don't want to be like my parents. I *won't* end up like my parents, that much is certain. Which means putting on a good face and being agreeable. Good spouses don't make unnecessary drama. "You keep working. Enjoy your snacks. I'm going to get into bed and google how to cook a ham."

"Are you sure?" Patrick asks.

"I'm sure." Though, as I trot off down the hallway, I'm secretly hoping step one for cooking a ham is: stick your head in the oven.

YOU BETTER NOT CRY

PATRICK

Disappointing my husband feels like grounds for inking my name on the Naughty List.

Quinn leaves my office with reassuring words. But I've made a mess of our night. I know that.

Probably could've gotten this bathroom nonsense done at the office today. But lately, I've been blocked. Creatively. Emotionally. Motivationally. So, all-nighter it is.

I pick up my pencil again. But I keep making mistakes. Erasing wrong lines and incorrect notes. The smudge marks grow larger and larger as my nimble fingers become tired. But I push through.

I sip the hot chocolate Quinn brought me. The tickling notes of peppermint from the added candy cane are perfection. Quinn is the most thoughtful man in the world.

Sometimes, I wish he could see that my care comes out differently.

Ever since I was young, I sought approval everywhere I went.

When I was in elementary school, I won a grade-wide contest to draw our dream house.

We had recently read a picture book about a kid who moves towns. He thinks up this fantastical house he could be moving to. Of course, when he gets there, it's just a regular old house. He's disappointed. His parents have to remind him that the memories they make in the house matter more than the house itself.

A sweet sentiment, sure. But my mind couldn't shake the way

he imagined a ski slope on the roof and an aquarium in the basement. Plus, it didn't help that my parents showed me the movie *Richie Rich* starring Macaulay Culkin—you know, the *Home Alone* kid—immediately after. It sent my imagination into a tizzy.

I ended up designing this futuristic smart house. All the teachers agreed it deserved the prize. My parents were vocally proud for once. And all the kids in school wanted me to design one specifically to their tastes. I was happy to do it, so I spent recesses drawing for the pleasure of my peers.

Words, I've never been great at. But drawing came naturally.

It wasn't until Spencer Haven—the class bully—asked me to make a house for him that I realized how much approval equated to success in my mind. When he asked for a drawing, he gave me little guidance. So I designed what I thought he'd like and when I gave it to him, he told me it was "trash."

I tried again.

"Garbage."

And again.

"Not even close."

To the point that I finally drew him a hundred different sketches over a weekend, brought them to school on Monday, and dropped them all on his desk.

"Here!" I shouted. "There has to be one in the bunch that suits you."

I got detention for making a mess. But Spencer never bothered me again.

In a way, it prepared me for the brutal feedback I got in architecture school and the disapproval from my parents over my career choices. So maybe I should send Spencer my thanks on Facebook one day. Wouldn't that be a laugh?

Through the wall, I hear Quinn struggling to start the shower. *Gurgle. Gurgle. Creak. Bang.*

I really need to get someone over here to check on these pipes. Add it to my barely touched to-do list.

Quinn's muffled plea makes it through the paper-thin wall. "Come on, please work!"

I go to stand then—

Slosh. Running water, finally. I let out a relieved sigh.

I'm hit with a fleeting thought. I should join Quinn in the shower as a sexy surprise. Watch as rivulets of water and soap slide down his freckly arms. Help him shampoo his curly, dark brown hair, which is long on the top and short on the sides. Kiss my way across his stubbly, deeply dimpled chin.

Whoa there. This is no time for distractions.

That's not what Quinn wants right now anyway. Even if we haven't had sex in a good . . . Jeez, it's bad when you can't even remember.

Our intimacy must still be stuffed in one of those brown boxes out in our mess of a garage.

Sex drought notwithstanding, I need him to see that I'm trying my hardest to be the provider I'm supposed to be for him. That's what husbands do. Specifically, that's what Hargrave men do.

Which is why I've taken on a moonlighting gig outside the architecture firm. I haven't told Quinn. Yet. He'd scold me. He'd worry. I don't need that. I need the money it's going to bring in, so we can turn this place into a proper home.

When our college friend Kacey Ortega came to me saying she wanted to use some of her backyard as a hub for her nonprofit— the one where she, as an out-and-proud trans woman, mentors queer and trans youth—I couldn't pass it up. One, because it's a good cause. Two, because it's Kacey. And three, selfishly, because I need my own designs out in the world if I plan to open my own architecture firm at some point in the future.

I make hasty adjustments to the bathroom presentation and shove it in my portfolio for tomorrow before switching over to Kacey's workshop. This is a true passion project. My design is something akin to a tiny home but with a good sense of space and workflow. There's an area for small group activities, shelves for a curated LGBTQ library, and long communal tables for volunteers to work at.

I need to get these plans squared away so I can send them off to Kacey. Because once I get them to Kacey, she's going to pay me part of what she owes me. I know there's not a ton of money in nonprofits. But she recently received a sizable grant and offered to pay. I would've done it for nothing because at my real job, it feels like I'm doing work that *means* nothing. And the people I work for make me *feel like* I'm nothing.

But I won't say no to a check.

I burn the midnight oil for as long as I can keep my eyes open.

Before I know it, I'm dozing over my drafting table. Drool spills out of the side of my mouth. My head fills up with dreams of sugarplums, bank misers asking for mortgage payments, and Quinn sleeping all alone in our bed. He looks so beautiful. Curled up and clutching a pillow to his chest.

I reach out to hold him.

But he disappears like a ghost.

6 DAYS 'TIL CHRISTMAS

I'm stupidly late for work.

I fly into a parking spot, grab my hastily packed portfolio off the passenger seat of my clunker of a Toyota Camry, and race inside the building.

It normally wouldn't be a huge deal if I were late. But, of course, this morning I'm one of the key presenters in our big client meeting.

Operating without coffee is hard for me, so my first stop is the break room. I pour a steaming helping into whatever mug looks the cleanest. I say hi to no one. But I do get the general sense people are whispering about my disheveled appearance. This wouldn't bother me if all of my senses weren't ramped into high alert.

I slurp as much scalding coffee down as I can. My tongue burns so badly that I can feel every angry taste bud.

I beeline for the bathroom, where I tame my hair into some semblance of presentability. As I unfasten my pants to tuck in my shirt, the door to the hallway swings open. My best work friend, Jason, stands there. Jason is tall, Black, and damn good at what he does.

"You know that's the sink and not a urinal, right?" he asks. He points right at my precarious pants situation while laughing to himself. "Does Quinn know you're wearing yesterday's clothes?"

I look down. Not only am I a mess, I'm a mess in yesterday's outfit. Salmon-colored button-up. Tan sweater vest. Wrinkled khaki pants. "This isn't a walk of shame."

"You don't have to explain yourself to me," he says. He disappears into a stall.

"I fell asleep in my office. I've got ten minutes to look like a human." I splash my face with water.

"And nine minutes to get those bathroom plan copies out to every chair in the meeting room," Jason says. His voice takes on a ghostly echo in the tiled, cavernous room.

"Oh, damn. That was my job?" I rush out before I hear his answer.

I throw most of my shit down at my desk, then try to wrangle the copier into cooperating. It has a mind of its own. And it is always out of paper. I load the tray, slip the drawing at the top of my stash into the scanner, and wait for that satisfying, robotic hum to begin.

Hrmmm. Music, absolute music.

Finally, one thing is going right.

I slide into the boardroom right as the clients are beginning to arrive. Satisfied with my performance, I slap down the papers with aplomb before taking my seat. It's only when the big boss, Calvin Carver—white, midsixties, thinning hair on the crown of his head that he combs in a way that's deceiving nobody—has called the room to order that I sip my coffee and nearly spit it out for all to see.

In my still-sleepy daze, I accidentally made a dozen copies of my sketches for Kacey's backyard workspace. Not the office building bathrooms we're meeting about. *Shit.*

At first, I think maybe nobody will notice. But then I feel Jason's elbow nudging me on my right.

When I look up, Calvin is glaring at me with the intensity of Krampus come to steal children's toys.

Jason, ever the quick thinker, begins scooping the papers up. "Leftovers from our last meeting. Leftovers from our last meeting." He keeps saying it to every old white man in a navy-blue suit crammed in here, so they don't think we're an incompetent firm that enters meetings unprepared.

Paralyzed by my mistake, I barely even register when Jason hands me the pages and says, "Go. Now. Quickly." He's saving my ass. But I can't help but read into his harsh tone.

The copier decides, this time, it's back to being my foe. It won't even turn on. I follow the power cord to the outlet hoping I just need to unplug it and plug it back in. But that doesn't work.

At least this time, it pings and tells me what the issue is: paper jam.

I have no time to get our head of technology over here to work his magic. Instead, I take it upon myself to open this sucker up and clear the clog.

By the time I'm racing back into the boardroom with the right copies, the meeting is halfway over. When it finishes and the office building people file out like zoo penguins at feeding time, Calvin pulls me aside and says, "My office. Ten minutes."

Another ten minutes of the worst cramps I've ever experienced.

We have one of those open floor plan offices. Even the more senior members of the firm have desks that are only separated by low dividers. I watch in dismay as the whisper network starts up. Numerous heads turn in my direction. My stomach becomes a snake eating its own tail.

Jason perches himself on the edge of my desk. He's loudly eating an apple. "Calvin's a hard-ass, but he's not heartless. He'll scold you. You'll be fine."

But when I enter Calvin's office, the temperature is far more frigid than usual. Calvin's hunched over his desk, rubbing his temples where his graying hair has also receded. He says nothing. I take the seat across from him.

Without opening his eyes, he holds up my sketch for Kacey's workshop. Jason must've missed one. "What is this?"

"Oh, uh." I've never been good about thinking on my feet. "Just something I'm fiddling with in my spare time. Nothing serious."

"Are you sure?" he asks. His black, beady eyes are intense. "Because I made a call to this organization—the Rainbow Connection Coalition—and the kind woman on the phone told me she hired you—Patrick Hargrave—as the architect for the project."

I should've been more explicit with Kacey about the parameters of our working relationship. Carver & Associates Architecture has a firm stance on moonlighting. While doing a job for a nonprofit isn't exactly a conflict of interest, it doesn't look great for me. Especially with my royal mess-ups this morning. "She's not paying me."

"That's not what I was told," he says. His frown lines grow their own frown lines. "Who am I to believe?"

I open my mouth. No words come out. I wish I could draw him an apology.

"Patrick, you're a hard worker, you're talented, and I think you make an excellent addition to our team, but teams need team players, not people who think they're superstars all on their own."

"Oh, I don't think that."

"Taking a moonlighting gig tells me otherwise." Calvin's wrinkly hands steeple in front of his face. He taps the point of his nose. Very serious. "On top of that, you used company supplies—the copier and the copy paper—to disseminate your work."

"That was an honest mistake. I swear to you." It's times like these I wish I didn't wear such strong prescription glasses. I'm sure he can tell my magnified eyes are growing watery. "I—"

I cut myself off. Defending myself is fruitless. I was running late and wasn't thinking. That's not a strong case for keeping me on. "I'm sorry."

"Regardless, Patrick, here at Carver & Associates Architecture, we have a zero-tolerance policy. Your general lack of attention over the last several months, your performance at the meeting today, and your disregard for policy mean we're going to have to let you go."

The words sound like an earthshaking explosion. "Sir, it was for a nonprofit."

"No matter."

"I needed the money for home repairs."

"Perhaps your next position will pay better."

"It's the holidays!"

"All the more time to spend counting your blessings."

I'm flabbergasted. I haven't been at this firm that long, but the blatant disrespect is unsettling. Even if I did make some major flubs today. I stand, stupefied, and begin to exit. Under my breath, I mumble, "Scrooge," but it doesn't make me feel better.

The door slams shut behind me.

Earlier, that wasn't a walk of shame. But this? Carrying a cardboard box full of my supplies out of the office with Jason by my side and an angry-looking security guard on our tail? Now *this* is a walk of shame.

MEET-CUTE IN A SANTA SUIT

PATRICK

A MEMORY

I never imagined, the weekend before Reading Period of the fall semester in my fourth year, I'd be doing a walk of shame across the Penderton University campus at six-thirty A.M. in a borrowed Santa suit, reeking of alcohol and bad decisions.

The crunch of my black leather dress shoes in the early morning frost sounds like cannonballs.

I trudge past the architecture building, where I spend most of my waking hours. And some of my sleeping ones, too. With my current workload, I'm stressed beyond belief.

So, maybe I should've imagined this exact scenario. Getting super drunk at the Supper Club Winter Wonderland Celebration. Being convinced to don the ratty old Santa suit that's been with the club for ages. Letting people take pictures while sitting on my lap. Going home with a long-haired freshman whose name I can't remember. Even though I left him less than twenty minutes ago. And his name was tacked onto the door I shut behind me.

Instead of heading back to my residence hall, I hook a left onto Prospect Avenue, or as we in the Supper Clubs like to call it, "the Street." I'm retracing my steps in search of my phone. It was nowhere to be found in what's-his-name's messy dorm room.

As I approach Olive & Ivy, the sixth house on the left, I notice another student standing outside. He's staring up at the austere, redbrick house with the gold, shiny 61 on the front door. He's a tall guy with a head of curly, chestnut hair. In profile, his chin juts out strong, and his right ear is large and pink at the top.

"Looking for something?" I ask when I'm close enough.

The guy startles. His prominent chin has a deep dimple in it. Immediately, I want to run the pad of my thumb across it. Memorize the adorable groove. "Sorry. Didn't mean to sneak up on you."

The guy's brown doe eyes double in size. "Oh, no. I must look like a creep. Sorry. I like to take early morning walks before the entire campus wakes up. I'm in the Teacher Prep program here, so it's good practice for when I'll have to set those four-thirty A.M. alarms to make it to my public-school job."

"A future educator, nice," I say. I stake my place on the sidewalk near him. I could've breezed right by and gone inside to scout for my phone. But his handsomeness and his musical voice are holding me here.

"I often walk down Prospect since I'm hoping to bicker next semester," he says. Bickering is the formal vetting process that consists of icebreakers and such that sophomores go through to become an official member of a Supper Club. "Also, all the clubhouses are so historical and pretty. I like this one the best. It looks like it's wearing a checkered belt."

I tilt my head and look up at this clubhouse with new eyes. He's right. Between the first and second stories, there is a stripe of diamond cutouts that resembles a checkerboard. "I've never heard it described quite like that. It was built in 1908," I say. Nerd-mode activated. "It's designed in the Norman Gothic style, which you can tell by the semicircular arches." His eyes follow my finger as it traces the outline of the windows.

"Are you a member?" he asks.

"I am."

A glimmer appears in his eyes. Maybe he sees me as an "in." Which is fine by me. I'd never say no to more cute, inquisitive guys in our club.

He asks, "They made you memorize all that?"

I laugh. "No, I'm studying to become an architect."

"An architect? I thought that was the kind of job men only had in movies."

A second, louder laugh spews out of me. "You sound like my parents." As soon as my own voice circles back to me, I stop laughing. I've revealed too much to a stranger.

"They don't approve?" he asks kindly. Inquisitive again. *So inquisitive.*

My gaze slips down to avoid eye contact. It's then that I remember I'm still wearing the Santa suit. This is already the worst first impression ever. I guess that's what allows the truth to tumble out. "They don't approve of anything that's not law, a topic I could not care less about." After a loaded silence, I add, "I'm Patrick, by the way."

"Quinn."

"Nice to meet you, Quinn." I shake his hand. That single touch somehow shocks me out of my hangover. My headache is less of a pounding sledgehammer and more like a rubber mallet. "Would you like a tour inside?"

His boyish features lift. "Really?"

"Really."

"Yes," he says before looking at his watch. The order of these actions should've been reversed, no?

"There is a catch, though."

His eyes shift. Probably wary of me. Who wouldn't be? I'm a strange upperclassman dressed as Santa and smelling of Smirnoff. I hold my hands up. "It's not a weird catch. I promise. I left my phone here last night and I, uh, don't exactly remember where I put it."

I should probably be offended when he snorts at me before saying, "Sure, yeah. I'll help you."

Inside, I lead cute, curly-haired Quinn through the original dining room and downstairs to the basement taproom. To fill the space, I tell Quinn about our affinity groups, which hold meetings weekly or biweekly in the clubhouse. Black and Ivy. Latin y Ivy. "Queer and Ivy," I say. I'm being deliberately leading. I glance back over my shoulder to catch his reaction.

"Cool." He smiles to himself. Eyes focused on the stairs beneath him. "I'd probably join that one." I turn back so if he does look up, he doesn't catch the unbridled glee that has cracked open my expression. My heart weirdly feels like a harp being plucked.

It's not until we're on the second floor, digging around in the TV room, that I get a bright idea. "Hey, do you have your phone on you?"

He pulls it out of the pocket of his well-worn, mauve-colored tweed coat. It's ratty at the elbows. "Yeah. Why?"

"Can I call myself on it?"

As the call connects, a ring emanates from the couch. I fish my hand between the cushions. That's when I remember that I came up here last night with the long-haired freshman to make out.

The memory embarrasses me. Heat floods my cheeks. I'm hit with two wishes. One, that I looked and felt better so Quinn wasn't seeing me like this. Two, that I hadn't found my phone just yet, so Quinn had a reason to stay.

But finals are coming up. I have nothing left to show him. I severely need a shower. And probably a strong swig of mouthwash to boot. Ultimately, I escort him back outside into the cold.

"Glad you found your phone."

"Glad you were outside to help me."

He nods. He smiles. It's charmingly crooked.

"Guess I'll see you during Street Week?" It's the official time when sophomores do meet-and-greets before bickering. I find it both hectic and fun. It would be even more so if Quinn was there.

"Definitely," he says. He wishes me good luck on my finals before turning to go in the opposite direction.

I'm overrun with this urge to call after him and suggest we renege on our obligations while the day is still young. We could spend the next twenty-four hours together getting to know each other like I want to.

But again, I have a mountain of work waiting for me back in my residence hall. There's also a new text in my inbox reading, Hey Santa. Where'd you disappear to? From the long-haired freshman I fled from this morning.

I don't take a chance or call after Quinn.

Instead, I make a U-turn, hopelessly pondering *what could have been* the whole walk back to my dorm.

IF YOU CAN'T STAND THE HEAT . . .

QUINN

It's after nine P.M. on Christmas Eve. I should not be at war with a ham.

"Can you believe I have to bake this ham the night before we even eat it?" I ask Veronica, my best friend and fellow second-grade teacher. She's on FaceTime with me as I try to make heads or tails of this maple-glazed baked ham recipe Patrick's mom sent me without much guidance. There are too many steps, and I'm scared I'm going to do it wrong and ruin Christmas like Patrick said. "I didn't read the instructions early enough to do this at a reasonable time. This is my longest break of the year, and I've spent it vacuuming, dusting, decorating, and now I'm making a whole damn feast. If this was a school night, I'd be winding down already. Instead, I'm cosplaying Ina Garten!"

I've already removed the rind on this ham, which involved a knife, some peeling, and a whole lot of cringing. This poor pig. My poor hands.

"Why can't you do all this tomorrow? It takes a few hours but it's not like you're slow-cooking it." Veronica is Jewish, so Christmas preparations are always confounding to her. Her family's Hanukkah celebrations are small—latkes, lighting the menorah, a gift or two—and her Christmases are spent watching all the pending Oscar contenders at the mostly empty movie theater with her mom. "I'm genuinely asking. I know nothing about ham. I don't eat it."

"Apparently if I want to *be a present host*, I should do it tonight so all I have to do is reheat it tomorrow and baste, baste, baste!" I find it hilarious that Mrs. Hargrave's handwritten instructions read so much like her speaking voice, right down to her love of repetition. "I feel so nineteen-fifties."

"It doesn't help that your house is practically that old," she jokes. On the other end of the call, she's crocheting an olive-green beanie for the woman she likes who tends bar at our favorite haunt, the Loose Nail. We'd usually be there on Christmas Eve sharing a pitcher and wings while a drag queen in a Mrs. Claus costume sings "Santa Baby," but alas.

I roll my eyes. "I just pray this prehistoric oven finally preheats before I lose my mind."

Over at the stovetop, the sugar in my glaze has finally all dissolved. I grab a brush and start painting my ham, which reminds me of doing art demonstrations with my students. "It's not about perfection," I always say. "It's about expression."

I take that attitude into this meal. It'll be Christmas. Nobody is going to criticize my cooking.

Well, maybe Mrs. Hargrave, but she'll pull me aside quietly in the kitchen to tell me. I would never consider Mrs. Hargrave homophobic. She is wholly accepting, planned most of our wedding, and vocally slaps down the haters she went to high school with on Facebook. However, I think she has some regressive ideas of who I am to Patrick.

"Are you sure you don't want to come for Christmas dinner?" I ask Veronica, who is so engrossed in her hat-making that she's probably forgotten we were on the phone. We're those kinds of friends—comfortable in the silence we share. Work trauma bonds are the kinds that can't be broken. "I'm making a ton of sides. Well, trying to. There won't just be ham."

"I'm going to pass on that, thanks. I have a hot date with Cate

Blanchett and a refillable tub of popcorn." She winks at me, pushing her brown curls—almost as unruly as my own at their current length—out of her face so she can see what she's doing better. "But I have faith you'll smash this heteronormative bullshit with a thirty-nine-and-a-half-foot pole."

"Thank you," I say. "Though I really could be using this time to figure out how I'm going to teach a class of thirty kids without an aide come January. Did you see that email from Principal Masterson?"

For this, Veronica sets down her crochet hook. "Do not remind me of the hell on Earth that awaits us after this break. Try as we might, no one can truly prepare for the apocalypse."

"Drama queen." I turn away for a second to shout at the oven that has annoyingly not yet reached 320 degrees, even after a reasonable amount of time has passed.

"You're one to talk. You're yelling at an inanimate appliance! And you're the co-advisor of the Oakwood Elementary School *drama* club," Veronica huffs, resuming her work. Her camera feed is a tangle of thick yarn.

"Oh, lord. That's a problem for post–New Year Quinn." Yet another obligation taking up space on my already full plate.

"You know, if you're stressed about it, you're allowed to say no to things. You can always bow out gracefully," she says.

"No, I can't. Mrs. Birch needs me. She can't handle directing all those kids and the production elements by herself." I glare at the oven, hoping my sharp eyebrow might scare the heat into jumping up. "I'm just feeling the second-year burnout, that's all, and this district keeps throwing us curveball after curveball."

"My, my. Sports metaphors? Are you sure you haven't left the gas on too high?"

"V, please. You know I have a complicated relationship with baseball." I would add *and my dad* but that is not the kind of intrusive thought I need to be having while making a Christmas ham for my in-laws. "I know I'll survive, but after the wedding picture

situation and my evaluation . . . I don't know. I see the kids struggling from the lack of individualized attention already. What's going to happen when it's just me? I'm only one person with two
hands. Evidenced now by the fact that I should be sautéing green
beans, but I can't put this ham in this damn oven yet!"

"Where's your other half, your second pair?" Veronica asks of
Patrick.

"Outside hanging lights to please his parents," I say, a wormy
feeling invading my gut. "He worked from home all week, which
isn't usual for him. Then today, when I got back from the grocery
store with all this stuff, he rushed outside like being in the same
room with me was going to give him hives."

"You think he's avoiding you?" she asks, concerned. She's always one step ahead of me conversation-wise.

"Maybe," I say, mulling it over and pouring myself a glass of
red wine. "Maybe not. But he's definitely keeping something from
me. I can feel it."

"Why don't you ask him?"

"Because I have a whole-ass ham to worry about. I can't go
starting conversations I don't have the time to finish." I don't mention that we barely even talk about the weather these days.

"Be careful where you place your verbal commas," Veronica
says, unable to stop being a teacher ever. "Sounded like you said
ass-ham. A ham made of ass."

"You're an ass-ham!" I joke, and we both laugh, but the levity
doesn't last long enough. In a more somber tone, I ask a question
that's been on my mind for the past few months. "V, how do you
know when a relationship isn't working anymore?"

She sets her crocheting down for good this time and stares
right into her phone camera. "What's going on?"

"Nothing. Not really." Her narrowed eyes distill her disbelief,
and I quickly rescind my negation. "It's just that this isn't new behavior. Yeah, it's more avoidant than normal, but ever since we
bought this place— No, maybe it was earlier. Actually, it was defi-

nitely earlier." I trill my lips in frustration over the timeline in my head. "Ever since we canceled our honeymoon, we've barely had any time together. It's like we put on these wedding rings and stopped seeing each other."

"Oh, Quinn," she says in a sympathetic tone that makes my skin crawl. I'm not looking for pity. What do I have to complain about? I have a job, a husband, a house. Every which one of them is giving me a migraine right now, but still. By all metrics, I should be thriving, not complaining. "Does Patrick feel the same way?"

"If he does, he hasn't said anything. Most nights he takes his dinner up to his office while he does more work, and I take my papers into the living room to grade, and the next time I see him, he's in bed asleep." Half the time, I stand there for a second and wonder what he's dreaming about. His designs, probably.

Maybe if I were a blueprint he would pay better attention to me.

Veronica shakes her head. "I hate to say it, but you're basically stating the thesis of my parents' divorce."

"Please don't use the D-word." That's what my mom called it when my parents were going through it. She'd say, "I'll be in my room. Gotta call the D-word lawyer again" or "This D-word is being dragged out too long by that D-bag. I wish he would settle already." I never knew if she was doing it to be funny for my benefit or if saying the word in full was too painful for her. Either way, it stuck.

"I'm not saying that's what's going to happen with you two," Veronica clarifies. "All I'm saying is a pattern becomes a habit and a habit becomes resentment and resentment leads to nothing good."

The sound of the front door scares me. My heart jumps into my throat with worry. I tell Veronica to hold on as I venture down the hallway and into the foyer, but nobody is there. "Pat?" I call to no response. It must've been the wind. The lightest breeze and this house groans. I shrug and take a deep breath.

"It's probably just me," I say to Veronica when I return, shoving aside any thoughts to the contrary. "It's all in my head. It'll be fine."

Just like I made a promise to Patrick with our vows, I made a promise to myself that I would never end up like my parents.

But maybe divorce wasn't the part I was supposed to be worried about. It was falling out of love with the one person I envisioned an entire life together with.

A text banner hovers over Veronica's skeptical expression.

> **Patrick:** Can you come outside for a minute and help me with the lights?

The oven temperature is still not where it needs to be, so I can step away from this kitchen and close this can of worms I never should've opened in the first place. It'll probably do me some good.

Sure, I type back. Be right there.

5

A BEAUTIFUL BEGINNING

QUINN

A MEMORY

Alongside a semi-blurry photo of a billboard advertisement for a company unfortunately named E.R.E.C.T. Architecture, I type out a text to one of the last numbers in my outgoing calls list: I guess architect isn't just a job in the movies after all.

I'm in the passenger seat of Mom's clunky car on our way to the Christmas tree farm. I told her dozens of times over the phone that she should go without me or buy a fake one from the store that we could put up together when I got home on the twenty-second of December for winter break, but she refused, which is why it's Christmas Eve and we're about to pay premium prices we can't swing for waiting so long.

A response to the photo doesn't come until we've already got the exorbitantly expensive spruce into our house and the rickety tree stand we dug out of a beat-up box.

Patrick: LMAO

I'm disappointed at first by the lackluster message until a second text rolls in.

> **Patrick:** They couldn't have arranged their initials in any other order? That's a terrible name for a business!!!

I type back, Or a genius one. Nobody is ever going to forget it!

> **Patrick:** THEY'RE MAKING A MOCKERY OF MY CHOSEN PROFESSION!!!!!!

I didn't expect him to be such an effusive exclamation point user. It's dorky, but adorable. I've been obsessing over whether to text the handsome, shaggy-haired guy in the Santa suit ever since we met outside Olive & Ivy. Now I'm unabashedly grinning at my phone, happy I did.

"Who are you texting?" Mom asks, setting out some ornaments.

"Nobody," I say, quickly locking my phone and leaving the text thread for later when I'm in my room, alone, and my blushing can't be dissected or judged or frowned upon.

Patrick and I end up texting all throughout winter break. When the spring semester starts and Street Week rolls around, I know Patrick's favorite color (jade green), his favorite TV show (*The Office*), and that his first crush was the high school–aged lifeguard at the pool club he frequented with his family.

In March, I bicker for Olive & Ivy and get in. I thank Patrick profusely, even though he insists he had nothing to do with it.

"Everybody loves you. Stop thanking me!" he says when I have my first meal (an exquisite chicken piccata) at the clubhouse as an official member.

Loves. That word in his slightly raspy voice plays on repeat in my brain for countless sleepless nights.

From then on, I spend more time at the Olive & Ivy clubhouse than I do in my own dorm room. I most look forward to Thursday nights when we have members-only meals around a theme like

Asian fusion or *An Evening in Paris* because Patrick never misses one, and we always sit together.

Aside from the Queer & Ivy affinity group, I join Bach & Ivy, a group dedicated to watching *The Bachelor* and all its subsequent spinoffs live each week from our TV room. I even go so far as to create blank brackets for us to fill out, so we can all place weekly bets on who is going to make it to the final rose ceremony.

Through some goading, I convince Patrick to join us. During the first episode, he's grumpy, looking at his phone for half of it. By the third, he's the most riveted, vocal viewer of the bunch.

It probably helps a little that some of the dates take place at various historic castles and estates, places of architectural interest, or as Patrick calls them, "Building porn." Every time he says it, I blush.

Despite our closeness and the sheer amount of time we spend together, nothing more than a friendship materializes between me and Patrick, even when I have dreams of him as the Bachelor and me as one of the gay contestants vying for his affections.

I'm too scared to make a move for the metaphorical final rose. What if I ruin everything?

But then, on a sunny Saturday in April, something shifts.

TruckFest is happening on Prospect Ave. Lining the road are food trucks and tents from local vendors. All the money raised is going toward local nonprofits like Meals on Wheels. I was a lead organizer for this event. There's a good turnout, yet it feels like Patrick and I are alone amidst the crowd.

We're sharing yucca fries and sipping Japanese sodas when Patrick looks at me differently. Not bad differently. Almost like I'm an abstract painting and he's finally made out the shapes amongst the colorful chaos.

"Do I have something on my face?" I ask, grabbing for a napkin.

"No," he says, glancing away shyly. I've seen him sullen, but

I've never seen him *shy*. "I've just been working up the courage all afternoon to ask you to be my date to the spring formal."

My heart beats so frantically I'm afraid it's going to dig a hole right through my sternum. "Really?"

"Really," he says. "I like you, Quinn. A lot. Almost as much as the Bachelor likes any blond-haired personal trainer named Christine."

An unflattering laugh rips out of me, but I don't care.

"Thank God you laughed," he says bashfully. That's another emotion I haven't seen on him before. I think I like it. "I've been practicing that line all week."

I say, "I like you, too. Of course I'll be your date."

A lopsided smile takes over Patrick's face. "Cool."

"Cool," I echo, feeling like I might float away.

I pick up a yucca fry from our shared paper basket. The tension between us, however, hasn't diffused. "Is there something else?" I ask with my mouth full.

He nods. "I've also been working up the courage to, uh, kiss you?"

My breath catches, and I nearly choke, but I save it at the last second. I wipe my lips on the back of my hand and act courageous enough for the both of us. Because his kiss is all I've dreamed about since we met on this very sidewalk four months ago. He tastes like melon and salt and everything I've ever wanted.

More, actually. More than anything I ever imagined for myself.

BROKEN HEARTS AND BREAK-INS

PATRICK

1 DAY 'TIL CHRISTMAS

I stand outside in the cold waiting for Quinn. The only thought in my mind is: *Quinn knows I'm keeping something from him.*

I overheard him say so to Veronica.

It's been five days, and I haven't had the heart to tell him I got fired yet. It's not that I usually keep big news from my husband. Just this.

Oh, and Kacey's workshop.

But that's it, I swear.

It's just that things have been rocky between us for a while now. Getting fired for taking on a moonlighting gig isn't just rocky. It's an avalanche headed straight for our relationship.

Veronica said the word *divorce*. Quinn couldn't possibly be considering that. Could he?

Especially after hearing that, I figure it's best to save the news of my unemployment for after Christmas. Give us one perfect holiday, then bring on the wrecking ball. That seems like the kinder option. In the meantime, I've dedicated my work time to googling how to open my own firm. Scouring the net for freelance jobs. Putting the finishing touches on Kacey's plans.

Kacey is the lifeline I need. While the money is sparse, it's not nothing. Also, I'm getting a little bit of severance from Carver & Associates, which will float us. Quinn will know when he needs to

know. He'll be understanding about it. That's the hope I'm cling-
ing to.

Before I left the Carver & Associates parking lot after getting
let go, Jason leaned into my open window and said, "Remember
when we were kids and we believed in Santa sight unseen? Just
know there's the right opportunity around the corner for you if
you believe hard enough." As I drove off, "Believe" by Josh Groban
came on the radio. There was a little comfort to be found in that
glorious man's soothing baritone.

Right now I choose to focus on the joy of turning on the Christmas lights beside my handsome husband. Because everything else
is too upsetting and uncertain.

Quinn steps outside. He hasn't bundled up properly, so I slip
off my red-and-green scarf and hand it to him. His neck gets cold
quickly. He thanks me, wrapping it around himself.

He looks up at our two-story house with a hint of hopefulness in
his expression. Twinkle lights always get a dazzling smile out of him.
If I were to draw that smile, it would be a lighthouse on a dark shore.

I sorely need that guiding light tonight.

I grab the extension cord and the nearest plug. "Let's do it together." I keep the receptive end.

"Since when do you choose that position?" he half-heartedly
jokes.

I blush. But he can't tell because it's dark. And my cheeks are
probably already pink from the cold. "Don't spoil your Christmas
gift now."

He snorts loudly. Rolls his eyes at me. "Santa must've gotten
my letter this year."

"He's known to make the wishes of good boys come true." Our
banter always makes me feel better.

"Oh, I've been good, have I?"

"Very, very good." To wipe away everything I overheard and to
ease Quinn's doubts about us, I lean in and kiss him.

Quinn's lips always taste the slightest bit like the peppermint

ChapStick he's loved as long as I've known him. The kiss is quick. It's cold. But his lips remind me how uncontainable our love is. Is it interminable, too?

God, I hope so.

"I love you," I whisper to him. Say it with my whole heart. I won't let that go. Not without a fight. "Now let's see this sucker shine."

The plugs come together.

Our home glows. Yellow and bright and lovely. It gives me hope. Warms my heart.

For about a minute.

And then everything flickers, dulls, sparks, and stops working.

"Huh?" I don't know why, but I jiggle the cords. That's when I notice the lights in our windows are out, too. "Shit. I think I tripped a breaker."

"Well." Quinn follows the line of the extension cord. To another extension cord. To a string of lights. On and on like that all the way to the outlet. "I don't think you're supposed to do this."

"I feel like my dad did it all the time."

Quinn sports a crestfallen frown. "Maybe call him? See if he can come and help?"

"It's"—I check my watch—"almost ten P.M. He's probably getting ready for bed." I don't know that for certain. But I avoid calling him when I can. He raised his boys to be self-sufficient. Letting him down the night before Christmas is the last thing I need.

"Shit," Quinn mutters to himself.

"What?"

"The ham," he says. "Can't cook it now unless I want to figure out how to light the stove and do everything by candlelight like I'm a Dickens character. Guess it's going in the fridge until tomorrow. Hopefully it keeps. I'll just have to be a bad host on Christmas."

"What is that supposed to mean?" I ask. I'm genuinely confused. Quinn is so good with my family. Especially since his isn't around much anymore.

"Never mind." He starts walking up the steps toward the door. Before he disappears back inside to deal with the uncooked ham, he asks directly, "Are we happy?"

I'm taken aback by this massive question. He just told Veronica that he probably wouldn't pry. "Yeah, of course. Why wouldn't we be?" Every muscle in my body constricts. Even my toes in my boots curl up and go rigid.

"Because . . ." His sentence disappears like the cloud of his breath.

"Because?" I ask promptingly. Even though I don't want to hear the answer. The answer is only going to destroy me.

"Because we don't feel like us these days." His arms flap at his sides. It's apparent that a lot of frustrations are coming out all at once. "We feel . . . *old*. Settled? Bored?"

"What are you even—"

"I don't know! I'm just asking . . ." He takes a long, loud inhale. "What is all this? What are we even doing? I don't like to cook. You don't like to decorate. We don't like to host things. We could barely afford this house, but we bought it anyway and now we're miserable. We hate it!"

"I don't hate it. You hate it?" I ask. Then, I realize how silly that was. That's clearly not the most important part of what he was saying. "It's Christmas Eve, Quinn. What is this all about? Where is this coming from?"

He shakes his head. "I don't know. I don't know what page you're on right now, but it's clear we're on different ones." Somehow, his words ring in my head like he thinks the page he's on is better.

"Well, I'm sorry I can't flip through the book of life faster for you." I fold my arms across my chest. I'm angry and hungry and tired and speaking too fast for my brain to catch up. "I'm sorry I didn't read your mind to know you hated this house. I'm sorry I didn't know movie night meant so much to you. And while I'm at it, I'm sorry I got fired from my job. Maybe you *should* divorce me." I kick at the icy, dead grass. The toe of my boot creates a divot. Only a million more kicks and maybe it'll be a hole big enough to bury myself in.

Quinn's face falls and his hands drop to his sides. He takes an almost fearful-looking step forward. "What are you talking about?"

"I overheard what you and Veronica said."

His head shakes. Almost imperceptibly. "No. Not that. The part about you getting fired from your job. When?"

My eyes refuse to meet his out of shame. "Five days ago."

"Five days ago?" I expect loud anger for withholding this from him. All I get is barely audible disappointment. It's far worse in my book. My whole body goes numb in a way that has nothing to do with the cold.

"Say something?" I ask pitifully.

Quinn clears his throat, looking away. The sound of us cracking apart is embedded in the words he says next. "I'm exhausted. We can—We can talk about all of this after Christmas but right now, I'm going to bundle up and sleep in the guest room so I can get up early and finish cooking."

"Quinn—"

"Don't, Pat," he says shakily. It breaks my heart. Him sounding this way. "Just don't. Not tonight."

Quinn shuts the front door slightly too hard and the 43 that denotes our house number pops off. It hits the cement landing with a clatter. Dammit. One more thing to add to the never-ending list of fixes.

Two, if you count Quinn and me.

After unplugging the cords, I go down to the basement and fiddle with the fuse box to the best of my ability. I need to keep moving so I don't fall apart over all this. We're still hosting Christmas. Can't do that without power.

It takes me an hour and a YouTube video, but I get it done. I'm sure Quinn is happy the heat kicked back on. He hates being cold while he sleeps. Even when he cutely hogs every blanket we own no matter the temperature.

What if this is it? What if we never sleep in the same bed again?

To rid myself of those questions, I head into the garage. I'm on the hunt for outdoor-friendly power strips since, from what Quinn said, it seems we're going ahead with pretending our marriage isn't falling apart for the next twenty-four hours.

I've barely been in the garage since we moved in. It's a veritable minefield of things we didn't know what to do with. At the time, instead of labeling the boxes, we assumed we'd remember where we put everything. Now I'm beyond upset with myself as I dig through stuff we probably could've gotten rid of in a yard sale.

In my hunt, my hand lands upon a shiny, weathered piece of paper. It's the Christmas card we made and got printed at CVS the year we moved in to our first apartment together. Quinn was student teaching, and I had just gotten hired at Carver & Associates.

There's a romantic optimism in our expressions.

The next year, we got engaged a month prior, so our holiday season was consumed with wedding planning.

This is our fifth Christmas together, first as a married couple, and I don't feel the Christmas spirit at all. I feel nothing but dread, actually.

I got fired. I lied to my husband. He's talking about divorce with his best friend. I put us up to the impossible task of hosting a perfect Christmas dinner at the last minute.

Maybe we aren't happy after all.

Looking at my watch, I realize it's already past midnight. The lights are a bust. I need at least a wink of sleep to regroup. Figure out how I'm going to make it up a million times over to Quinn. Prove to him that we are worth fighting for after he sounded so defeated.

Irritated with myself, I abandon the hunt for extension cords and head back inside where somebody is fumbling around in the kitchen. I'm about to call out Quinn's name when a low grumble that sounds nothing like Quinn thunders through the house.

In the hallway, the front door is unlocked. Could someone have broken in? My heart starts to race.

As I inch into the kitchen, the shadowy form of a tall, round man looms on the periphery. He's munching on something. Squinting, I see that Quinn appears to have left out a plate of cookies and a glass of milk for Santa—something silly and cute he's always done since we've lived together, even when our apartment didn't have a chimney. Even sillier and cuter is that he'd get up earlier than me, race downstairs, sip the milk and bite the cookies, so that when I got up, I'd think Santa had been there. Quinn would even go so far as to sign some of his gifts to me as FROM SANTA in a loopy scrawl.

In front of me, the intruder struggles to lift the glass with his mitten-covered hand to wash down his snack. But when he finally does, the milk goes flying into the air. "Ew, fuck. What is that? Oat milk? Disgusting."

I grab for the nearest object. Adrenaline and fear mix and surge through me. Someone has broken in—someone rude, at that—and I won't let him ruin our Christmas or get to Quinn.

Though, he's dressed all in red. So perhaps he wanted to get caught. It's not exactly an all-black catsuit that I might not have seen at this hour in this darkness.

With vigilante-mode activated, I heave a frying pan from the drying rack as the burglar samples the third cookie on the plate. I stand up to my full height and command with ferocity, "Put the cookie down and nobody gets hurt."

The man turns and steps forward.

Frightened, I let out a scream that's bordering on a squeal.

I close my eyes.

And then I swing.

Clang.

Thud.

"Crap!"

A WAKING NIGHTMARE

QUINN

CHRISTMAS

The stress of Patrick's massive confession mixed with playing host-with-the-most tomorrow when our electric is out has seeped into my dreams and turned them into freaky nightmares.

The sound of my name being called repeatedly pierces the veil of my subconscious. I wrestle myself awake only to notice that I might've landed in yet another nightmare, *Inception* style. The shadowy outline of Patrick hovers over me, and even through sleep-crusted eyes, I can tell he's holding a large, metallic object up at his side in a menacing way.

This is it. I'm about to be *Dateline*'d. I thought that was only a straight people problem.

My hands fly up to protect myself. "Please don't hurt me!"

"What? Oh. Sorry." Patrick drops the frying pan—I mean, I *think* it's a frying pan; I'm not keen to lean over and inspect closer. The object hits the carpeted floor with a muddled ring. "I didn't mean to scare you."

"Mission failed," I say, hand clasped over my speedily rising chest. I try to sit up, placated in the knowledge that my husband hasn't come to turn me into the subject of a future true crime podcast, but newly unsettled by the way Patrick flops onto the side of the bed in the guest bedroom with his features scrunched. "What's wrong? What happened?"

I'm hot in my long-sleeve T-shirt and hoodie, and the night-light I put in here when we had overnight company last is on across the room, casting a dim honeyed glow across the floor. The power must be back on. "Did something happen with the breaker in the basement? Was there a family of rats down there?" Patrick hates animals with long tails that scurry. I don't know why exactly his first choice of rodent repellent would be cookware, per se, but Patrick has done weirder things.

"No, I—" He cuts himself off, shaking his head.

"What?" This bed-in-a-box mattress dimples as I scoot up onto my knees. I would normally run a hand along his back, the comforting gesture he probably needs most, but I can't bring myself to touch him. Not after our conversation outside.

What would I do if one of my students was in a sleep-deprived panic spiral? "Big inhale, hold your breath, count to seven, biiiiiig exhale. Good, very good. Now, tell me what happened."

Finally, Patrick looks at me, marginally calmer but fear still helixing in his expression. "I think I killed a man."

I shoot back from him, twist the knob on the bedside lamp, and look him over in the light. There's no blood on his hands. The frying pan—okay, good; it *was* a normal frying pan—isn't dented or misshapen in any way. The only evidence that this could be the truth is the stupefied way Patrick stares off into the middle-distance barely breathing, eyebrows converged like he's trying to figure out a complex math problem.

"Pat, I think maybe you got shocked by the electrical cords earlier." I need to rationalize this, so my heart rate slows and I don't freak myself out more. "Or you're overtired and imagining weird things. Hell, I was just dreaming about a pig with your mom's voice."

That snaps Patrick out of his stupor. "Did you just call my mom a pig?"

"No. That's not the point. Why don't you forget the lights and go to bed? You're imagining things." He's delusional right now. Running on fumes, clearly. I guess that can happen when you lose your job and have no idea how you're going to pay a mortgage on a house with only one meager, stretched-to-the-max income.

"Quinn, I'm serious. I think I killed a man. I think I killed . . . *Santa.*"

"Santa?" I ask, hoping I've misheard him.

"Claus."

I surprise us both by laughing raucously at the seriousness with which he says this. "Pat, Santa Claus isn't real." I put out the cookies and milk every year as tradition, and Patrick gets up in the middle of the night to create the illusion that Santa's been to our apartment, but this is taking it a step too far. "If this is some kind of weird joke you're trying to pull so I won't be mad at you, it's not going to work."

He jumps up, possibly offended by this. "Come with me, I'll show you."

Obviously, he's not going to give up this sleep-addled charade until I oblige, so I do the only thing a trying-to-be-patient husband can do when his spouse is losing his marbles in the middle of the night: I shove on my slippers, pick up the frying pan to put back in the cabinet in the kitchen, and begrudgingly humor him by following along.

"If this is all an elaborate ruse because there's some special Christmas present waiting for me under the tree, I swear to—" I don't finish that sentence because there's a red lump of velvet in the shape of a man sprawled out across our floor, unmoving.

"Holy shit!" Fear grabs hold of my legs. I can't step any closer. "Who is that?" The confusion in the set of Patrick's brows is not reassuring in the slightest. I take stock of the long white beard, the portly belly, and the scuffed black boots with the shiny buckles. No wonder Patrick thought he killed Santa Claus. This man looks like he stepped out of a picture book.

"I don't know. After I got the power back on, I went out to the garage in search of power strips and when I came back in, he was in here eating the cookies." Patrick rakes his hands furiously through his long, slightly greasy hair.

This is not good. Our marriage is on the rocks, our mortgage is going to drown us in debt, and now we may be criminals.

Regaining a small sense of courage, I approach the breathing lump with caution, then nudge the man's shoulder with my slipper. "Hello, sir? Wake up. We need you to get up now." The man doesn't respond. "I knew we should've set up an alarm system!"

"I don't think now is the time to discuss that," Patrick snaps, pacing behind me. "Do you think we should call the police? Do you think we were the target of some Christmas-specific robbery ring where men who look and dress like Santa hit unsuspecting houses?"

While anything is plausible at this point, something about that isn't adding up in my mind. "What kind of crook stops what he's doing to taste-test cookies?" I inspect the plate covered in crumbs.

"Maybe he was going for verisimilitude." I shoot Patrick with as much skepticism as I can muster. "What? Don't look at me like that. It makes sense. Who would believe an emergency call about a man in a red suit breaking into their house and eating cookies on Christmas Eve? It's not all that different than when you get up in the middle of the night to eat them so it seems like Santa's been here."

Confusion flicks me in the forehead. "I don't do that. You do that."

"I do, what?" Patrick asks, nose crinkled. "No, I don't do anything. You put out the cookies and then sneak out of bed and eat them."

"No," I say, annoyingly slowly, partially for him to understand and partially for my own benefit. "I put out the cookies and *you* sneak out of bed and eat them."

"I have never in the history of our relationship snuck out of bed on Christmas Eve to—"

Our bickering and possible magic-based revelation are stopped by a groan from the floor. Down there, the man has shifted slightly. Another groan escapes from between his lips hidden inside that nest of white hair.

Panic provokes me. "He's waking up! What do we do?"

"How should I know?" Patrick, boots squishing on the linoleum, trepidaciously approaches the man that has now begun to shake himself awake. "Hello there. Are you all right? I didn't hit you too hard, did I?"

My heart is thudding so loudly. I'm hovering behind my husband as he approaches Maybe Santa with apology laced in his voice. "It's okay. Don't be alarmed."

"It's a man. Not a rescue dog," I chide.

"I'm trying to be reassuring."

"He broke into our house!"

"He could be Santa Claus!" Patrick whips around to look at me, eyes wide. He already believes it to be true. I can tell. He's always had a childish sense of wonder about him. An optimism that the world held zany truths within its folds.

"He could be anybo—" I don't get to finish that statement because behind Patrick I notice the man sit up far too fast for someone who was just knocked out cold and, in the dim light, it looks like he's trying to reach for Patrick's ankle.

Santa Claus or not. Fight or not. Nobody touches my man!

Without thinking, barely even remembering that I'm holding the frying pan at this point, I swing and connect with something hard.

Clang.

Thud.

"Double crap!" Patrick yells.

THE GREATEST GIFT OF ALL

PATRICK

A MEMORY

Quinn picks me up from the lot near the upperclassmen residence hall where I've been living in a single room. But, in truth, it's been more like a double room. At least based on how much of Quinn's stuff populates my desk and drawers and the number of nights Quinn and I have happily squished together on my twin XL bed, talking until all hours of the night.

When I open the passenger door to Quinn's decade-old sedan, there's a colorful bag overflowing with tissue paper waiting for me. A tiny Mylar balloon that says HAPPY BIRTHDAY on a stick pops out of the top.

"Should I open this now?" I ask as we back out of our spot. I have no idea where we're going.

"Go for it." Quinn's got Christmas music playing on the radio. The whistle notes and the bells in the background make me feel festive and in the birthday spirit.

As we merge onto a main road, I pull out of the bag a LEGO set of the Guggenheim Museum. It's a building by Frank Lloyd Wright that I've always admired for its use of rotundas. It's such a thoughtful present that I could cry.

I reach across the center console and squeeze Quinn's arm. He gets me. He really gets me. "Thank you."

"I figure we can work on it together and then display it in your dorm room." He takes his eyes off the road for a second to look at me. My heart teeters toward him. We've been friends since January and officially dating since April. They've been six of the happiest months of my college career. Maybe even my whole life.

"Surprise!" Quinn says, two hours later, when we step out of the car.

Before us is an unusual place called Casola's Christmas Village. It's a farm outfitted in lights aplenty. It has North Pole–esque displays that incorporate the nearby lake, trees, and walkways. Quinn remembered me saying, over the summer in the blaze of July at the Jersey Shore where we'd meet for soft serve and kisses under the lifeguard stand, that Christmas is my favorite holiday. I'm touched that he listens so closely.

"I also figured it was appropriate given what you were wearing when we met," Quinn says. I guess I hadn't made that bad of a first impression back then as I thought.

We spend several hours exploring, taking silly photos, and eating snacks. At some point, we visit Santa's Post Office, where high school students dressed as elves hand out sheets of paper to everyone. We partake in the tradition of writing a letter to the big man himself. On my sheet of paper I write my wish succinctly with a large yellow No. 2 pencil:

I wish to love Quinn Muller forever.

It hits me in that moment that I do, after only six months of dating, love Quinn. I can't deny it when it's clear as day on the paper in front of me.

I love his passion for mentoring children. I love his eclectic taste in music and movies. I love that he says yes to things no matter how busy he is or how out of left field they might be.

Later as we stroll across the Kissing Bridge, Quinn inquires about what I asked Santa for this year. Instead of telling the truth, I make a joke. "My degree. Finally!" He laughs before we stop, and I kiss him.

After exploring Santa Claus Lane, we decide it's late. We've had our fill of holiday cheer and hot chocolate. We climb back into the car and drive the two hours back to campus. Surprisingly, the whole way, I regale Quinn with tales of birthdays past. Gifts received. Cakes eaten. Tears shed.

Somehow, Quinn Muller has unblocked me. I can't, for the life of me, shut up once he's gotten me started. That's why I barely notice when, on a pitch-black back road not far from campus, a deer jumps out in front of Quinn's car.

I grab for the handle above my seat. Brace myself.

Quinn does everything right. He doesn't swerve into the other lane. He doesn't panic or scream (too much). The deer, struck and injured, runs off limping.

We're alive. We're safe. Just a little breathless.

Even so, Quinn's frozen.

I ask if he's all right to no response.

It's me who calls the police to report the accident. Me who gives our statement. Me who takes the wheel again once the officer departs. Quinn, still shaking, hugs his coat to his chest and doesn't speak.

On the drive back, I worry that Quinn's upset with me. I was talking too much. Too loudly. I was probably distracting him.

In the six months we've been dating we've never had so much as an argument. This incident is new territory. I've messed up everything.

It's not until we're back in the parking lot by my dorm building that Quinn unbuckles his seat belt and, assuaging my darkest fears, fiercely embraces me. His face smushes into the meat of my shoulder. "Thank you," he says with resounding relief.

"Of course." I run a hand soothingly through his curls. His hair has quickly become my favorite texture in the world.

Gingerly, he inches back, looks up at me with watery eyes, and says, "Pat, I love you."

The LEGO set was perfect. But this is the greatest gift he ever could've given me.

"I love you, too, Quinn." I kiss away his tears before kissing his newly smiling lips. "I love you so, so much," I say again just to ensure he heard me. Loud and clear.

UP ON THE ROOFTOP

PATRICK

CHRISTMAS

Quinn is sheet-white and frozen.

I snap in front of his face. Trying to get him back to reality.

This is *reality*, right? Because it certainly doesn't feel real.

It takes twenty minutes, but we finally get the man onto the living room couch and (mostly) upright. His head is dipped. His lip is a little busted. Quinn's swing wasn't that strong. I think it scared the man more than it hurt him. The frightening thud was purely from the man's sheer mass.

But he's definitely not playing dead. He's conked out.

Which means we're not any closer to answers.

"I'm sorry," Quinn mutters frantically. It's the seventh time he's said it. "I thought he was going to hurt you."

"It's okay. I only knocked him out the first time because I was afraid he'd hurt *you*."

Our eyes connect. This would be a sweet moment in our tattered relationship if a man who may or may not be Santa Claus wasn't partially passed out and maybe concussed on our (now that I consider it) *ugly* suede couch.

Quinn worries his lip. "I know I've asked this a million times, but what do we do now?"

"Wait until he wakes up, I guess." I heave out a breath that barely registers over a sudden, noxious pounding up on the roof.

"What was that?" If I really dial in, something lighter and jinglier floats underneath the pounding. "Are those bells?"

One after the other, we rush out the front door and onto the icy lawn. I pitch my gaze upward and, sure enough, my wondering eyes are graced with the sight of a massive red-and-gold sleigh. Eight fearsome reindeer are tethered to it by reins bedecked with bells.

"Seriously? That was reshingled before we closed!" I cry, noticing the damage that the weighty flight vehicle is causing. "Are you seeing this?" Bemused, I turn to look at Quinn. He's on his knees. In the grass. Balling up leftover snow from a storm a week ago and shoving his face in it.

"I'm dreaming! I'm going to wake up! I have to wake up!"

I grab Quinn by the arm. "Stop! You're going to wake the neighbors!"

I scan the street. The houses aren't very close together. But I'm surprised to find that no one has rushed outside to see what the commotion is about. The one time it would be helpful to live near nosy people.

"Wake the neighbors? We killed Santa Claus." Quinn sounds as undone as I felt when I wandered into the bedroom earlier.

"We didn't kill anyone. He was breathing. He was just passed out. Come on. Let's get back inside before we both freeze to death."

Listening to reason or at the very least too cold to protest, Quinn nods and follows me.

Back in the blasting warmth of the house, still unsure what to do, I'm stopped in my tracks by the sound of clomping boots. Not mine. And not Quinn's, either.

At the inlet to the hallway, Santa Claus stands with one hand on his slightly bruised lip. The other holds the frying pan out in front of him.

"Don't come any closer!" he cries in a higher-pitched voice than you'd expect from the storied big man. "I'm warning you."

Instinctually, I step in front of Quinn. I hold my arms up in evident surrender. Quinn mirrors me. "Okay, okay."

"Fuck! You really busted my lip!" Santa or Not Santa shouts.

"That's not a very Santa-like word to use," Quinn whispers behind me. I shush him. He's only going to escalate the situation. This man is already red-faced and steaming.

"I know this was a good gig for a while, but I can't handle it anymore. I have had it up to here with this holiday horseshit!" The pan-that-started-it-all clatters to the ground and with the same hand that had been holding it, Santa audibly snaps his mittened fingers.

A tornado of gold sparkles whips around him. The red suit and the white hair all fall away until, before us, where Santa once stood, there's only a tattooed man with scraggly hair and a stubbly face who couldn't be more than thirty-five. "I quit!" he yells up to the ceiling.

Around his feet is a cloak with a halo of gold dust wiggling around it. It captures my attention until the man walks toward us with intent. Jabs a finger in our direction. "It's your problem now."

The man exits the house. Disappears into the night.

A frantic beat goes by before Quinn yells, "What the hell was that?"

"I don't know," I mumble, awestruck. My heart sputters.

This whole night is bending my mind into a glass pyramid that's refracting my thoughts like colorful light in a thousand different directions.

I'm inexplicably drawn to the left-behind cloak. It glimmers there on our floor like it's transported here from another realm. So bright I might even mistake it for a fallen star. As if hypnotized, I inch closer.

"Pat, what are you doing?"

"I just want to get a better look." Why is this glowing piece of fabric somehow calling to me?

"What if it's cursed or something?" Quinn asks, voice pitching up into a scared place.

"We can't just leave it in the middle of the floor!"

"At least go get your gloves!"

"I'll be fine!" I'm bending over. Leaning into the light. Sensing an unexplainable warmth.

Right as I begin to reach for it, someone who is unquestionably not my husband shouts, "Don't touch it unless you're willing to take the job!"

AN ELF APPEARS

QUINN

I'm staring at an elf.

At least, I think he's an elf.

I guess it's insensitive of me to assume but there is a short (though not that much shorter than me) white man wearing a pointy green hat on top of a mop of messy black hair with pointy ears sticking out the sides.

"Don't touch it unless you're willing to take the job!" Patrick snaps up and looks back at me. All I can do is point at our new visitor who is still standing in his own tornado of golden glitter. Slowly, it swirls to nothing.

"Who are you?" I ask because my husband is clearly too stunned to speak, still crouching centimeters away from the glowing cloak that lies crumpled on our floor. Who knows where that's been? I teach second graders. I know the dangers of touching lost items, just rewind to my last three head colds.

"Bart. I mean, *Ho*bart Holly, head elf." He shimmies up to full height, shoulders back, smile tight. He wears velvety deep green overalls and leather boots with pointed toes. "All my friends call me Bart."

"Nice to meet you, Bart," Patrick says, extending a hand in the professional way he's been programmed to do.

"I said *friends*." There's a firm edge to his otherwise singsong voice.

The shade of it all! Patrick retracts his hand awkwardly, so I step forward, needing to pronounce some agency here because Patrick is fumbling. "Hobart, excuse my husband. He didn't mean to offend you by assuming we were all friends here. We obviously just met. Listen, we're having a very bad night, and we're a little stressed out."

Hobart sighs. "You're stressed out? This is my first Christmas as head elf and Santa has just quit on me!"

A rational, less tired version of myself would question everything that's going on here, but right now, either Patrick and I are having a joint hallucination or this is really happening. Strangely, *this is really happening* seems to be winning out, so I aim for the easiest answer I can get. "To clarify, that man who just walked out of here is Santa Claus?"

"*Was* Santa Claus," Hobart clarifies.

"I'm going to need more than that from you, buddy," Patrick says.

"I said my name is *Hobart,* not Buddy." Hobart crinkles his face in cartoonish disgust, leaning away. "As if I would ever be as careless as Buddy. How could you mistake me for *him*?"

I shake my head. These two are sorely ineffectual communicators, which makes sense given how Patrick kept his unemployment from me for five whole days. Could he not have asked me to unplug the vacuum for a minute so we could talk? How hard would that have been?

"How rude!" Hobart adds.

"Hobart, I apologize for my husband again, but please focus. We don't know any Buddy or anything about your beef with him. All we know is that Santa broke into our home, transformed into a grumpy much-younger man, and then left his sleigh on our roof and his cloak on our floor, so what do you mean that he *was* Santa Claus? Who's Santa Claus now?"

"No one," Hobart says with head-of-his-class snootiness. "That cloak is enchanted. Its magic masks the wearer as Santa or his cultural equivalent in other cities and countries and continents across the world. What you see is what you believe."

"So there could be more than one Santa Claus?" Patrick asks.

Hobart tsks. "Don't be ridiculous. There's only one cloak. Whoever wears it has the job. The magic bonds to you."

Enchanted cloaks? Magic bonds? I can't wrap my head around any of this.

"How was that guy able to walk right out of here if the cloak is bonded to him?" Patrick asks, sounding nearly intrigued and excited. It's the same voice he uses when he's walking me through his budding ideas for a new project.

"We really don't have time for me to explain the complex magic system of the North Pole to you," Hobart says, producing an ornate golden pocket watch from the front of his overalls and cringing at the time. He shakes his head. "I need you two to make a very important decision very fast."

The banging on the roof interrupts us again. The sound is so loud I fear those flying reindeer might come falling in on us at any second. Hobart taps his fingers on his chin, clearly antsy. "Decision? What sort of decision?" Patrick asks.

Hobart nods. "Put on the cloak or cancel Christmas."

"You're joking." I look to Patrick, who is possibly seriously considering this. "He has to be joking, right?"

"I'm afraid I'm not joking. On Christmas Eve, if the enchanted cloak gets taken off, time stops for exactly one hour." Hobart toys with that golden pocket watch, which has a similar dusty golden aura to it as the cloak that's still balled on the floor. "If nobody puts it on by the stroke of sixty minutes, then the reindeer are rerouted back to the North Pole and the rest of the gifts go undelivered."

"Why don't you put it on?" I ask, voicing the obvious.

"I'm an elf! There are rules! Which again, I don't have the time to get into right now." His eyes sparkle with sudden pleading. "I only have forty-five minutes to get one of you into the cloak, prepped on sleigh navigation, and off to New York or we're done for."

I can't believe the entire fate of Christmas is hanging on our shoulders. Why us?

Well, I guess there's an easy answer: because my husband nearly made an omelet out of the last guy.

"We'll—" Patrick starts to say, probably about to step up and play the hero. I love that he wants to be a reliable helping hand, but what kind of husband would I be if I just let him bond with an enchanted cloak without talking it through first?

"Sidebar!" I shout. "*We'll* sidebar. First. Give us five minutes to discuss this." I'm marching toward the stairs as I whisper, "Our room. *Now*."

ADVENTURE AWAITS

PATRICK

Santa. Is. Real.

It doesn't matter at all that Quinn just sounded frustratingly like Calvin Carver when he said "Our room. *Now*."

I'm too awestruck to care.

When we make it to our bedroom it's as if all my senses have sharpened past their peak. The world is candy-cane crisp. Everything from the framed photos of us in college displayed on the dresser to the overstuffed built-in bookshelves with Quinn's novels and my coffee table books is in high-definition. Like my glasses' prescription got an upgrade.

Normally, when I stumble into our room at this hour after a late night of working on some project or another, the queen-sized bed calls to me. Right now, I've never been more awake.

"We have to do it," I say. The warmth and lure of the enchanted cloak we've left in the foyer sizzles in my fingertips still.

Quinn is half-heartedly making the bed. "Pat, listen to yourself. You're out of your mind. The only things we have to do are fix up this house, cook a ham, and be ready for your parents to arrive by three P.M. tomorrow. Whatever else happens is not our business."

I empathize with Quinn in this moment because I know I threw us in the deep end by agreeing to host Christmas. And I know he's under immense stress at work. And I *know* he's unhappy with me for not telling him I lost my job. But . . . but . . .

"It's *Santa*." The words ring in my own ears as childish. I suppose that makes sense. All my wildest childhood fantasies have been confirmed tonight. If Santa Claus and elves and the North Pole exist, what about the futuristic dream house I concocted in grade school? Is there magic in this world that could make that real? If not that, then what about the more realistic one I'd imagined for Quinn and me? The charming porch and the stone exterior and claw-foot tub?

What about what I wrote in that letter to Santa on my twenty-second birthday?

I wish to love Quinn Muller forever.

Maybe the universe is giving me a gift. A surefire solution to the problems we've been facing.

"What are the odds that we agree to host Christmas, and I get . . ." I stop myself short. No sense reminding him of my unemployment status right now. It deserves its own conversation. Once this is settled. ". . . All messed up with the lights, and I was awake for this to happen. Think of all the years we've slept through it. All the years we were convinced the other was eating the cookies. Doesn't this feel fated?"

"No, it feels outrageous."

"Think about your students." I didn't want to have to pull this card. But he's making this difficult. "What if that guy that just quit never made it to their houses and they wake up tomorrow present-less like those poor Who children in *The Grinch*?"

"The moral of that story is the presents *don't* matter."

"Maybe in a perfect Seuss-world, but come on. If you were a child, how would you feel if you woke up on Christmas morning knowing Santa hadn't been there?"

Quinn's eyes cast downward. He blows out his cheeks. This is the same way he got when I proposed to him. Even the same way he got when I was trying to convince him to invest our money in this house that has a defunct clock built into the wood paneling and faucets that will, no matter how many plumbers come check on them, not stop leaking.

Maybe I hate this house, too.

"Didn't you just say we felt old and settled and boring?" I ask.

"No. I said *bored*. There's a difference." He retreats from me. "There's no way in hell I'm boarding a magical flying sleigh. Too many things could go wrong." Quinn lives in the present. You have to when you're a teacher. Balancing today's lessons with the various ailments and interruptions of seven-year-olds. I, as an architect, have to choose to live for the brighter future. Innovation. Pushing the envelope.

"I understand," I say. "If tonight, I can help make tomorrow a magical day for children all over the globe, then I have to put on that cloak and go." I reach out to grab his right hand. I run the pad of my thumb across his wedding band. "But I really want to go with you."

That's what I'd said in my vows. Which took me ages to write. When I stood up in front of our friends and family, on that day at sunset on the Jersey Shore, I told Quinn that in every adventure life brought me, I wanted to be able to look to my side and see him smiling there. This is no exception.

"I'm sorry, but this is all incredibly ridiculous, I'm so freakin' tired, and I just don't trust you right now," he says, taking his hand back.

My chest hitches. I'm hurt by his words. But I'm more pissed at myself for losing his trust. "I get it." I pause to consider what I say next. "I guess I'll, uh, see you when I get back?"

"Yeah, I guess." His voice is exasperated. He sits down on the bed and faces away from me.

I close the door as I exit the bedroom, so I'm not tempted to look back at him. Because if I do, I know I'll stay. I'll drop to my knees at his feet and ask him what I need to do to make this all okay again.

But there's a time-sensitive mission at hand that feels destined for me. I can't let that pass.

Back downstairs, the cloak is still there but Hobart isn't.

"Hobart?" I shout into the room. He probably has some kind of magical hearing. I'm proven right, even if I still jump from the shock when he materializes in front of me, surrounded by his bright cloud of gold.

"You called?" He's clutching his pocket watch like it might explode at any second.

"I'm in," I say.

He looks around. "Just you, then?"

My heart aches for Quinn. But what can I do? Christmas can't be canceled. "Just me."

"Okay then. It's time. Put on the cloak."

The moment I have permission, the tingling takes hold of me until I'm clutching the fabric of the cloak. I wrap it around myself and disappear into a haze of golden glitter. It feels as if, simply by my putting it on, it's changing my molecular makeup. The glitter is spiraling in between my cells.

My body grows fuller. And taller. Power surges through me.

Then, the gold dust stops swirling, falls, and shoots itself into the palms of my hands.

"That's it?" I ask. I guess I was expecting it to take longer.

"That's it. Transformation complete," Hobart says. "How do you feel?"

"Good. How do I look?" I ask.

His mouth shifts to one side. "Scared out of your mind. But! No time for that. To the roof we go!"

TAKING CHANCES

QUINN

My husband, an elf, and eight flying reindeer are on my roof right now.

I haven't moved from my spot on the bed since Patrick left the room, and their footsteps pound forcefully right above my head. Whispers of their voices creep in. Hobart is instructing Patrick on flight patterns, rein usage, and which buttons on the dashboard do what. He's even introducing the reindeer to Patrick one by one.

I can't believe I'm missing this.

No, scratch that. What am I thinking? This is all so outlandish that I'm shaking.

Patrick is the openly trusting one in our relationship. The kind of guy who floats off on ideas, chases whims. No wonder he's taken this all as fact.

When we first started dating, he showed me this wacky drawing of a futuristic house that won him first prize in some elementary school competition. His mom kept it preserved in a plastic sleeve. His design ran on technology we're light-years away from and, presumably, magic. I don't think he ever outgrew the desire to live inside a fantasy, so it makes sense he wants to go off and get himself bonded to an enchanted cloak.

I must be losing my mind.

I adore Patrick's trust in a brighter tomorrow, but sometimes I feel like I have to be practical about today for both of us, which means even if I'm upset with him, I can't stop looking out for him. That part of me doesn't have an off switch.

I'd be a wreck if anything happened to him tonight and I wasn't there. His parents would certainly never forgive me for it. How would I even explain it? *Oh, I'm sorry, your son disappeared into the night with someone who claimed to be an elf.* They'd have me medically examined!

For that alone, I refuse to stay here stewing while my husband goes off on a world-spanning, once-in-a-lifetime adventure. He can have his head in the clouds all he wants, but somebody has to keep his feet on the ground.

Well, as on-the-ground as they can be while in a freakin' flying sleigh!

"Here we go again," I mutter to myself, wiggling into a pair of underwear, jeans, and a puffer coat.

Without Hobart's magic, to get to the roof, I have to pull down the ladder to the attic, which I'm barely tall enough to reach. It takes me three jumps before I hook the string with my left middle finger and the grate comes sliding at me with unwieldy force.

The rungs on the ladder are wobbly, so I grip the sides as best I can and hold on for dear life.

The attic is a spooky place that we never go in so it's full of cobwebs and smells pungently of disuse. I power through with my sleeve over my nose, crank open the nearest window, and attempt to climb out.

That's when I hear hooves all moving in unison above me.

"Wait!" I shout, but I know they can't hear me over all the noise. "Wait for me!"

I try to haul myself out headfirst, but my glove can't get a good grip on the edge of the roof. The reindeer are kicking snow that's rolling toward me, hitting me square in the face. I spit it out, about to give up completely when a hand clasps my forearm and tugs me upward with impressive strength.

Once I'm on the roof, I'm being stared at by a confused Hobart and—

"Patrick?" I ask, mostly to myself. He's at least a foot taller and 150 pounds bulkier since I saw him in the bedroom. He dons the iconic red suit and hat. Patrick always wanted to grow facial hair, but I'm certain he didn't want it the color of freshly fallen snow, unfurling all the way down to his knees, blowing to the left with the wind.

When Patrick steps closer and I get all this blasted snow out of my eyes, I can, if I really stare, see *him* beneath the spectacles and the round cheeks, beneath the red velvet and white trim. It's the baby-blue eyes, mostly. They say the eyes are the window to the soul. In this case, they're the last remnants of my husband. At least the husband I had an hour ago.

That cloak casts one hell of an illusion.

"What's going on? We're on a tight schedule. We don't have time for delays!" Hobart says, giving me a rankled look.

"I'm coming with you," I say confidently.

"You are?" Patrick asks, beaming.

"I don't want you to go alone," I say.

"Okay. That's fine. Right, Hobart? That's fine?"

"Whatever gets us in the air fastest is fine by me. Get in!" Hobart is already boarding the sleigh again, impatience ricocheting off him.

Hobart's keeping company with the giant sack of presents that, despite the laws of physics, is not weighing this machine down. Patrick and I file into the front seat. I did not get the safety briefing, so I fasten my seat belt, say a silent prayer, and let Patrick take the wheel.

Patrick flips switches and pushes buttons, but at the end of his little routine we're not moving. "What's happening?" I ask.

"You have to say it," Hobart says to Patrick.

"Again?"

"Yes. Every time or they won't move."

Patrick sighs and clears his throat. In full voice, he shouts into the night, "On, Dasher! On, Dancer! On, Prancer! On, Vixen!" When each reindeer's name is called, it goes from standing motionless on four legs to floating in the air. "On, Comet! On, Cupid! On, Donner! On, Blitzen!"

"What about Rudo—" The rest of my words get sucked back into my mouth as we shoot off at hyper speed into the sky.

THE FIRST STOP

QUINN

I will not look over the side. I will not puke. I will not look over the side. I will not puke.

We are soaring sky-high (I'm trying hard not to think about just *how high* we are), and the turbulence and Patrick's jerky control have me reaching for the barf bag, which Hobart hands to me, just in case. I am not built for this kind of accelerated excitement.

Patrick is trying his best to steer this reindeer-led flying machine but it seems set on defying his every command.

"Why does it drift right when I turn left?" Patrick asks, sounding annoyed. A new fear clips up into my head: *What if we capsize? Would we fall out and back to Earth? Are there parachutes on this thing?*

"The magic is still fritzing. It has to get used to you."

"Can you tell it to behave?" he asks.

"Not how it works," Hobart says.

Patrick huffs, drawing my attention away from the vast, inky sky and toward him.

It's still disorienting to peer at Patrick and see a jolly-looking elderly gentleman.

Hobart has assured us as soon as he removes the cloak, the spell will break and I'll once again see his twenty-six-year-old self—blond hair and wiry frame and no-need-for-a-shave cheeks.

Strangely, there is something sort of attractive about the way he looks right now. Not that I ever found myself pining after Santa in Coca-Cola ads or in those old stop-motion specials, but I do find myself appreciating a more wizened man every now and then. Admiring their laugh lines and their distinguished streaks of gray. Daddy issues notwithstanding, it's allowing me to see Patrick from a new perspective. The cloak shrouds him in a different light.

"Coming in for our first stop," Hobart announces.

Apparently, the previous Santa had hit all of New Jersey already, so we sprang off to a New York suburb. We land bumpily on a random roof in a quiet neighborhood.

"Ready for your first drop-off?" Hobart asks.

Patrick rubs his hands together. "Ready! What do I do?"

"What do *we* do?" I ask, standing. I've come all this way, somewhat conquered my fear of heights, and nearly thrown up a couple times. There's no way I'm letting him go do this alone.

Hobart crinkles his brow. "It's customary for Santa to go by himself."

"Yeah, well, I'm sure it's customary for Santa not to quit in the middle of his once-a-year shift, too, but I'm here."

"Fine, but stay close," Hobart says. "The enchanted cloak's magic can only extend so far. It's a bit like Wi-Fi. If you step out of signal range, you're on your own. So, let's get started!"

Setting aside Hobart's cryptic warning, we grab the presents designated for this address. On the flight over, Hobart instructed that we had a few tasks once we were inside:

1. Find the Christmas tree.
2. Lay out the presents.
3. Respond to any notes left by children.
4. Sample the cookies and milk.
5. Bring up any reindeer feed.
6. Get back to the sleigh before being caught.

It sounds simple.

It's not.

One at a time, we float down the chimney chute Mary Poppins–style. A self-moving sack of gifts is right behind.

It's mystifying, being inside someone else's home in pitch darkness. We're traversing a minefield of epic proportions as we decide which way to turn.

"This feels illegal," I whisper to Patrick, who is already leading the charge toward the Christmas tree. He must be following the weak goldish glow coming from around the corner.

"We're spreading joy. That's basically the least illegal thing you can do. Besides, we're leaving stuff not taking stuff." He's got the present-sack slung over his shoulder now, and he carries it with remarkable strength. Would I have been this burly had I put on the cloak?

There are rhythmic snores coming from a nearby dog bed. I panic at first, but then settle on my next step. The dog must be a deep sleeper, or the magic makes it so it can't see or hear me. Either way, I rush past, not wanting to test my luck. I don't do dogs. Not one bit.

In our quest, I nearly run into a breakfast nook, too taken by a kitchen ripped straight from a Nancy Meyers movie. It has marble countertops, high-top stools, a fabulous farmhouse sink, and tasteful hanging light pendants. I sigh, inspecting the state-of-the-art oven that probably preheats by proximity, reads your mind, and adjusts for the right temperature.

"I actually might *want* to cook if we had a kitchen like this," I whisper.

Patrick snorts in response.

"What was that?"

"Nothing."

"No, that wasn't nothing. That was a snort. Why?" I ask, not giving an inch.

"Because, hours ago, you had a breakdown outside our house about how you won't cook."

"No, I said I *don't like* to cook, but I might if we had a nice, working kitchen like this one and it wasn't thrust upon me or expected of me," I say.

"Who's expecting it of you?" he asks, switching the sack of gifts from one shoulder to the other with ease.

I do my best Patrick impression, pretending I'm walking through the front door and setting down my portfolio by the coatrack. "Hey, babe, what's for dinner?"

"Is that supposed to be me?" he asks, having the nerve to sound offended.

"No, it's not supposed to be you. It *is* you. Every night. As if I haven't just had a long, stressful workday, too." I know what he's about to say before he says it. "And offering to make sandwiches every blue moon with lunch meat and rolls I went out and bought earlier that week doesn't count as doing your share."

Patrick's eyes bulge. At first, I think it's because he's upset, but then I track his gaze lower and to my left. There's a clanking behind me, the patter of paws, and then a low, menacing growl that causes fear to spring up into my throat.

"Quinn, don't move."

SANTA SAVES THE DAY

PATRICK

Behind Quinn, there is an unfriendly-looking rottweiler with its teeth bared and its back arched. We have invaded his territory. He's making sure we know it.

"Quinn, don't move."

Quinn freezes on the spot.

The cloak gives me powers. It should keep us shielded. Hobart said as long as Quinn stayed close, he'd be protected, too. How can the dog see us now when it didn't even flinch as we passed it before?

Then again, how could I backhand the last guy with a frying pan?

Shaking away the question, I focus on my newfound night vision, which allows me to notice that one of the ceramic canisters on the counter to my right is labeled DOG TREATS.

"Distract him," I say.

Quinn widens his eyes at me. "First you tell me not to move. Now you tell me distract him. How do you expect me to do both?"

"Quinn, please listen." I hope I'm conveying the seriousness here. "When I say go, jump up onto the counter ledge there. I'm going to grab a T-R-E-A-T from the jar over here. I will rush to the sliding door over there and chuck it into the fenced-in yard."

Quinn shakes his head. Sticks to his spot.

"You have to trust me, okay?" *I just don't trust you right now.* Quinn's words from earlier pierce me again. The same way his terrified eyes do right now. I push through the hurt. He needs me too much. "Keep looking at me. I got you. I won't let anything happen to you. On the count of three. One. Two. *Three*."

I lunge to the right. Thankfully, Quinn goes left. The dog predictably follows Quinn with a bark I hope doesn't wake the whole house. Then, the dog hears the clang of my hand in the familiar jar. At the back door, with a handful of biscuits, I struggle with the lock but get it open in enough time.

Whoosh.

Cold air invades the warm house. I chuck the treats onto the deck and shut the door behind the dog.

Quinn's still atop the counter. He watches me with wide eyes. I offer him help down. Through my thick mitten, I can feel Quinn's hand quaking. "You're okay."

"I was bitten as a kid," Quinn says, voice wavering.

"I remember." We had a lot of conversations about adopting a pet when we lived in our first apartment. Quinn would entertain a cat, but dogs were always out of the question. His skittishness was founded in real trauma that I'm seeing now in real time.

"It was a rottweiler."

That part I didn't know. *How could I not know that? Did he tell me and I forgot?* I guess it explains why he's avoidant of Veronica's astoundingly friendly black Lab, Luca, but he's never gone sheet-white stationary like that around him.

Quinn closes his eyes and sags against me. Closing the gap between our bodies.

The golden bubble around me glows brighter with the contact. I sense myself getting stronger. As if the magic is responding to our nearness. To the way Quinn smells and breathes and lets me support him.

"Do you want to go back up to the sleigh?" I ask him. He hasn't pulled his hand away from mine yet like he did earlier. It's strange to see how dwarfed his hand is, cradled in my black leather mitten. My hands, since the cloak transformation, feel more like massive, brawny bear claws. I'm not quite adept enough to maneuver them properly, but they're just the right size to comfort Quinn it seems.

"No." He snaps up straight. Takes his hand back. I wish he hadn't. I don't know how long it'll be until he trusts me enough to let me that close again. I swallow the upset as my golden aura dulls slightly. "Let's keep going," he says.

When I enter what must be this family's living room, I'm greeted by this gorgeous, real tree adorned with lights and ribbons, ornaments and candy canes. It brings me back to Christmases of my youth. Every year-round picture frame and trinket in my house had a Christmas counterpart. On the day after Thanksgiving, like clockwork, Mom would painstakingly transform our home into a winter wonderland. When she was finished, not a single decoration would be misaligned or out of place. The Hargrave brood runs on perfection. I wish I inherited that gene.

I move closer to this family's tree with the sack of gifts. I recall the sad fake tree Quinn put up in our house this year—Target's cheapest—decorated with basic, impersonal ornaments. None of the homemade, crafted-with-love creations littering the branches here.

Our starter house was meant to be a home. But maybe I wasn't putting in the work to make it anything more than four in-need-of-some-TLC walls and a shoddy roof.

"Why don't I set out the presents and you can go get a head start on those cookies?" Across the room, on a small end table, there is a decorative plate with three cookies on it. Beside the plate are a sweating glass of milk and, from this distance, what appears to be a white envelope.

Quinn nods. "Maybe the sugar rush will right me."

I set out the presents one at a time. I'm careful to arrange them in a way that is pleasing. I want the kids in this household to rush downstairs and for their eyes to immediately light up with joy.

Once I'm finished, I walk over to where Quinn is nursing a red-colored cookie with white chocolate chips in it.

The scrawl on the envelope on the table is childlike and in crayon. The note inside, this part written in pencil, reads:

Dear Santa,
Thank u for bringing me the rainbow unicorne stuffed animal
for X-mas last year. It is my most favorite thing that I have. I
know some kids at skool tease me about Pinkie, but I don't care.
I think rainbows and unicornes are nice and 4 every1. They r
pretty and magical. One day, I want 2 b pretty and magical 2.
        Thank u for making my x-mas dream come tru.
Love,
Tyler
P.S. I don't need any gifts this year
P.P.S. but if u brought Pinkie a friend that would be kool 2. I'm
pretty sure I was good. Thanks.

A little laugh hiccups out of Quinn.

"What is it?" I ask.

"Kids today are just cool." He smiles to himself. A mini surge ripples through me. Akin to the shock I got when I tripped the house breaker with the overload of lights.

"This is amazingly sweet," I say, getting a tad choked up. As a kid, I was plagued by the way Toys "R" Us stores and catalogues were bisected by pink and blue coloring. Other boys my age wanted action figures and sports equipment. I wanted the biggest Crayola pack possible and unlimited pieces of construction paper. "I'm glad I—Santa, I mean—could help this kid."

Hours ago, I would've considered Santa nothing more than a wish-granting fabrication. But this note is proof that Santa can provide more than just gifts. He can provide affirmation. Maybe even confidence. That's worth more than any toy in my book.

"You have to write him back," Quinn says.

I shrug. I wasn't daunted by flying a sleigh, but this feels insurmountable. "You know I'm better with drawing. Why don't you do it?"

Quinn picks up the pencil. From the furrow of his brow, I sense a swell of responsibility rising through him.

I observe as he writes:

You're very welcome, Tyler.
I think Pinkie will be thrilled by the new addition to your friend
group, but always remember that loving what you love and
being yourself are the greatest gifts there are.
Magically yours,

Quinn passes me the pencil. "This part's all you, Mr. C."

As if the pencil is possessed, I inscribe the Santa Claus signature onto the piece of construction paper. It's practically calligraphy. When I'm done admiring it, I fold the paper up and slip it back inside the envelope.

"I don't know how you do that. You always find just the right words for every situation," I say.

I can tell the compliment makes Quinn bristle a bit. We're having high-octane fun, but there's still tension between us. I pivot.

"One last bit of business to attend to." I pick up one cookie. The first bite is blissful. Chocolatey, gooey, and with a hint of peppermint. "Damn that's good."

Quinn washes his down with some milk from the glass. "Just think, we're basically about to embark on a cookie tour of the entire world." His tone is airier, as if the cookie has sedated him a bit.

"It's the honeymoon we never had. We always said we wanted to travel widely," I say, eyebrows going up when the faintest shadow of a second smile appears on his face.

"We're even getting to fly private!" Quinn says.

"Without pollution, I might add!" Hobart appears out of thin air. Breaks into our conversation. "What?" He grows defensive at my skeptical, shaken look. "Just because I live in the North Pole doesn't mean I don't read the news."

"I wasn't suggesting—"

Hobart holds up a hand. "Are we finished lollygagging? We've got whole continents left to hit! Unless you want to disappoint people all over the globe, let's go, go, go!"

Grabbing the baggie of oats for the reindeer fleet, I follow Hobart and Quinn back to the sleigh. Amped up for a long, exciting evening.

A SURPRISING OFFER

PATRICK

On the roof of a house somewhere in snowy Canada, I'm sad.

The sleigh is finally empty.

After an entire evening of outrunning frisky pets, hiding from inquisitive kids, and taste-testing cookies on both sides of the delicious spectrum, it looks like our work is complete. Geographically dizzy, we've delivered gifts all over the world. Defied time, space, and all other such logic I thought to be proven fact only this morning.

My worldview is cracked open.

For the first time in a long time, I'm vibrantly alive. And it's not just the cloak's power. It's this surging sense of purpose that fizzles in my fingertips. And the way Quinn played my teammate all evening.

I'm hoping this experience has eradicated any worries about our future and any unnecessary thoughts about divorce. Though he is still keeping distance between us in the front seat, I can tell his resolve has melted a bit. His sleepy eyes keep flicking toward me with contentment, not upset. That's a start.

"All right, sleigh. Take us on home." Hobart's command comes from the back seat. He's stuffing away his pocket watch and sending an alert to the elves back in the North Pole. Without the massive gift sack, he can sprawl out. He lies supine with his hat brim tugged down to cover his eyes.

"What a night," I murmur. Mostly to myself.

Quinn does a sluggish little nod into the fabric of the seat. He's tuckered out. His eyes are struggling to stay open. I can't wait to get home and curl up in our bed beside him. If he doesn't migrate back to the guest room, that is. If he lets me hold him like I used to. Like I want to.

If our brains don't remember this wacky experience in the morning, I have a strange premonition our bodies will. That my muscles are locking in all these preternatural sensations. This night will live between my bones. Vibrate forever around my cells. It's a part of me.

A part of me that I wish I didn't have to let go of so soon.

Some minutes later, I check out the GPS and alarmingly notice that we're heading north.

"Hey, Hobart, I think we're going the wrong direction." I can't fully turn around to look at him because Quinn has dozed off. His head lolled onto my shoulder. I like the comforting position too much to risk waking him.

"Uhhhh . . ." In the several hours I've known Hobart, he doesn't seem like the kind of man who's ever at a loss for words. The sky continues to grow lighter. Oranges and yellows paint broad brushstrokes around the arc of the Earth. It would be beautiful and mesmerizing if I weren't suffering nervousness.

Abruptly, the sleigh and the reindeer, as if they sense my severe confusion and are in cahoots together, slingshot back. We whoosh through some sort of portal.

All I see is color. All I feel is floaty.

Then, there in the distance is the sort of village you have to see to believe. It's a snowy enclave that's backed by the northern lights. They dance to the tune of a song that rises through the otherwise quiet night. As we fly closer, I can tell it's singing. A horde of voices grows stronger as we approach an unexpected destination.

Quinn stirs awake at my side. "Where are we?" he asks, groggy.

The speckled landscape comes into sharper focus. A-framed buildings with snow-dusted roofs. Windows glowing with the most uplifting amber light. A massive decorated tree presiding over a town square. Dozens of rambling cobblestone streets creating a maze.

We whizz by towers and turrets and a large chalet up on the hill with its own chairlift.

"I think we're in the North Pole," I say. It's both exactly as I imagined it as a child and somehow even more magical. "Hobart, what are we doing here? You told us we were headed home."

"Yeah, about that," Hobart says. "*My* home. We have some business to attend to."

"Business?" Quinn asks. He sits up and tries to fix his messy hair. "What kind of business?"

"I think it's best the Council of Priors tells you about it."

The sleigh does a victory loop around the centerpiece tree. Below, elves of every kind raise their glasses while singing a song with indistinguishable lyrics over the roar of the sleigh. They dance and smile. I guess I'd be this jolly, too, if I only had a few days off a year and this was one of them.

My unemployment status wallops me at the worst moment.

We pull into a stable in what is surely the main workshop given its massive structure and several wings. We are helped down by a gaggle of elves congratulating us on a great run.

At the end of a lengthy hallway lined with painted portraits of Santas past, there are bright red Tudor-style double doors with rounded tops and wrought-iron, ornate handles. Hobart leads us inside a capacious room. It has dark stone floors and a cathedral roof. There are several chairs at the far end occupied by imposing-looking people. Anxiety jolts up my spine as we're instructed to walk the rolled-out strip of plush red carpet and stop in front of them.

"The cloak, please," Hobart says. He holds his outstretched arms to me. I feel around for a zipper or a drawstring. "Just snap."

With the flick of my fingers, the Santa mirage dematerializes into a cloud of dust and forms the enchanted cloak again. It lies pooled around my feet. I pick it up shakily and hand it to Hobart. Are we in trouble with a legion of magical beings right now?

"Welcome, Patrick and Quinn," says the man closest to the center. He's Black with tight-clipped gray hair and round eyes. "My name is Chris. The North Pole and the world at large thank you for your service this evening."

I don't know what else to do so I bow. Awkwardly.

"You're welcome?" Quinn says. He sounds as wobbly as I feel. "Sorry, but, um, no offense. Who are you?"

My eyes scan down the line as Quinn speaks. There's a Black woman with her hair in a dark green bonnet to Chris's right. Beside them is a younger white couple. She has blond hair and he has a shaved head. I slowly recognize each of these couples from the quick glimpses I got of their paintings in the hallway.

"We are the Council of Priors," Buzzed Head says. "We have all served as Santa and Mrs. Claus at one point or another and have decided to retire here to act as a governing body. We preside over the village and ensure the seamless passing down of the Santa position."

A brown-skinned woman whose feet don't quite reach the floor with wavy hair wearing a flowing green robe says, "We have brought you here to call on you, once more, to make a decision about the fate of Christmases to come."

Quinn's eyebrows shoot up as he looks at me. Totally stricken. "Christmases to come? I thought this was a one-night thing."

I find Hobart in the assembled crowd. He is emphatically not meeting my eyes. Clearly, he left out a key component earlier. I can't tell if I should be worried or excited. "I'm not following, either."

The woman that appears to be the youngest—the pale blonde—pipes up next. "Basically, the Santa role must be filled by the stroke of midnight on Christmas Day or the following year's Christmas is in jeopardy. Are you in or out?"

Chris speaks again. He's calmer than his blond counterpart.

"What Ashley is trying to say is that we are in a bit of a bind. We've never had a Santa quit mid-run before. Most Santas, when they're ready to move on, do their final Christmas and have a predecessor already in place. Kyle, the gentleman you *met* earlier this evening . . ." It's all too clear what he means by *met*. Knocked out. Angered. Forced to quit. Damn, we're in so much shit. I'm a chaos magnet. "Well, he and his wife never quite gelled with their roles here and didn't notify the council that they'd be departing after only one Christmas, which means we had no forewarning or time to find suitable replacements."

"We wouldn't ask you if it weren't absolutely necessary," says the woman in the bonnet. She wears an almost pleading smile to match.

My fingers vibrate with purpose once more. I realize that this is the same fizzy feeling I got back when I started at Carver & Associates, when I began architecture classes in college, and when I created all those dream-house drawings for my classmates back in elementary school. I always laughed it off when someone referred to their job as their *calling*. But what if this is what they meant? A physical impulse to act. Could I—Patrick Hargrave of sound mind and queer heart from suburban New Jersey—be Santa Claus?

Yes, chimes a little voice inside my head. It's a voice I recognize but haven't heard in some time.

"And what would I be doing?" Quinn asks. He sounds nearly annoyed. I know that tone well. It's come out more than a dozen times over the several months since we bought the house. Every time something new has broken or gone bust.

"Well, you'd be Mrs. Cla—" Ashley peers around to the others (there are eight of them total) in puzzlement.

"Darling," says the oldest white woman in the bunch. She has wispy white hair and age spots on her hands. She reminds me of my Nan Hargrave. She's got gumption, I can tell by her assured posture. She sits next to a man who looks like the closest to Santa without needing the cloak. "If you'll excuse us, in the uncountable years this operation has been going on, we've never had a same-sex couple in these roles before. Emmanuella, you were in politics in your past life, any ideas on what we could call Quinn?"

Emmanuella, who has been anxiously braiding her long wavy hair, doesn't even glance up as she says, "How about the Merriest Mister? Like the First Mister, but merrier!"

"Oh, that's wonderful!" White Hair says. She claps her hands together in delight.

Chris speaks again. "Rest assured, should you assume the roles, everything will be provided for you, from housing to clothing to anything your heart desires. Your lives in the normal world will be put on pause."

"Put on pause? Paused, how?" I ask. The fizzing inside me has moved from my fingertips into my elbows. It edges gradually toward my shoulders.

"Careers, payments, et cetera. We take care of everything while you're away," he says.

Ashley adds, "It's a bit like when you have student loans and work for a nonprofit."

"Think of it as forbearance," Emmanuella says.

"For your whole life," Buzzed Head says.

An albatross of bills lifts off my shoulders. No applying for unemployment. No paying our mortgage with that ridiculous, variable interest rate. No worrying about repairs or pipes or shoddy wiring.

What's less settled and bored than a major move to a magic village?

"At least for one year," says White Hair's presumed husband. "There's a trial period. Some Santas stay on for the long haul like me and Colleen or Yvonne and Chris. Others work for a year or two and then retire like Ashley and Samson. Others return to their regular lives like Emmanuella and Jorge almost did. It's what suits you, the community, and the needs of Christmas the best."

This austere room, their thrones and stares. It all should feel so stiflingly formal. And yet this feels more like a golden ticket to wide-open freedom. An adventure for Quinn and me to go on. Together. To leave the constraints of our life behind for a little while and play new roles. Fun, jolly, completely unexpected roles.

"We understand this is a huge decision," Yvonne says, reaching out a hand to her husband, Chris. "It will come with sacrifices including not leaving the North Pole once you've committed."

"Jeez," Quinn utters.

"Of course we don't expect an answer right this second." Chris squeezes his wife's hand. "Go home, get some rest, enjoy Christmas with your family and friends, and talk it over. We look forward to hearing what you decide."

Part of me wants to jump up and say yes immediately. Thank them for this amazing opportunity. But I can sense Quinn's uncertainty beside me growing larger.

Instead of making any rash decisions in the moment, we let Hobart escort us out and back to the garage area where we parked the sleigh earlier. The reindeer have been untethered. Probably brought to their stables for food and rest.

Beside the sleigh we rode in tonight, there is a smaller sleigh. Nearly a sidecar. It only has two seats.

Over the rev of the magical flying machine whirring to life, Hobart says, "I'm sorry I didn't tell you the full scope of what was happening here. I'm new at this job. Unprecedented times call for desperate measures. I hope you can forgive me." The tops of his pointy ears go pink.

Perhaps seeing Hobart as he sees one of his students—overwhelmed but trying his best—Quinn steps forward and hugs Hobart. "It's okay. Thanks for keeping us safe tonight."

Hobart is stiff at first. His arms stick out forward, held at the elbow in apparent shock. But then he relaxes into it and wraps his arms around Quinn. He hugs me next, then helps us settle inside the flying contraption.

"It's a small but mighty machine. You'll be home in the blink of an eye." I try not to cringe when he slaps the front of the machine, and something not-good-sounding clangs inside. "Sorry, again. Hope to see you both soon."

As Hobart backs away, the coordinates he punched in lock and load on a screen. The machine, without any coaxing, does a half circle as two barn doors open automatically. Strapped in with harnesses and seat belts, we clasp hands and hold on tightly.

For the gazillionth time this evening, we launch off into the sky, and perhaps a brand-new future for us.

MEET THE PARENTS

QUINN

The future is impossible to ignore when there's a giant banner hanging in front of me reading: PENDERTON UNIVERSITY . . . EMBRACE THE FUTURE. Those words in that font stir my worry.

"Magna cum laude," I say, nervously flipping through the commencement program. Bradley, Patrick's brother with the perfect hair and the law degree, sits next to me. We arrived around the same time and despite having never met us in person, he walked right up to me and chatted amiably with me as we found our seats. "It's really impressive."

"I was summa cum laude, but yeah." He sips from a mini bottle of water we were handed on the way in. We're in the Penderton stadium in uncharacteristic May heat. The football field is lined with rows upon rows of folding chairs in front of an end zone–spanning stage. Mr. and Mrs. Hargrave haven't shown up yet. I'm trying not to pick at my fresh manicure. I want to make a good impression, and making a good impression means having perfect nails that match our university colors—red and white.

Mom was supposed to be here, but she's never made a habit of showing up when and where she says she's going to, so I wasn't completely surprised when she called and started rambling about a dead car battery.

A little while later, Mr. and Mrs. Hargrave enter our section looking as if they've just stepped off the golf course at the country club. Sweat-wicking polo and hat for him. Head-to-toe white linen for her. I stand to greet them, feeling damp and underdressed in a silky, billowy blouse and drawstring trousers that I bought in the women's clearance section at a boutique.

"Quinn, it's wonderful to finally meet you," Mrs. Hargrave says, kissing me lightly, once on each cheek. She takes stock of my outfit but speaks nothing of it.

"Put it there," Mr. Hargrave says, wrapping my much smaller hand in a too-strong shake.

They say their hellos to Bradley, settle into their seats. Mrs. Hargrave produces a tiny, battery-powered fan from her ginormous bag. It sputters to life with a whirr, though I'm not sure it's doing much since we're sitting in direct, scorching sunlight.

"Bummer your mother couldn't come. Such a bummer," Mrs. Hargrave says, pulling out a compact mirror, presumably to see how shiny she is. "It's unfortunate we didn't know sooner. Patrick's Nan would've loved to be here."

"She's nearly ninety. There's no way she would've sat out in this." Bradley shrugs off his blazer jacket, so effortless. Patrick has always depicted him as the golden child, supremely polished. I thought he was exaggerating, but Bradley doesn't even have pit stains or a dewy forehead.

"I'd have brought her a hat. She'd have been fine." Mrs. Hargrave snaps the compact shut to punctuate her point. Already I can tell that she's no-nonsense. Mom's antithesis in nearly every way. "Oh well."

"Sorry," I say meekly, already feeling like I've done something wrong. Like I'm wrong. Wrong for not saying something sooner. Wrong for Patrick, maybe.

She pats my closest knee placatingly, and then the ceremony starts.

Any discomfort sedimented inside me crumbles away when Patrick marches in, long gown swishing as he walks. And, much later, when they call Patrick's name to receive his diploma, the four of us stand and cheer for the gods.

"I'm so proud of him," Mrs. Hargrave says, looking over at me with tears rimming her blue eyes that match Patrick's. She holds Mr. Hargrave's hand tightly. I wonder, for a moment, if Patrick's angsting over his parents' disapproval is more of a self-inflicted pain than a by-product of their true feelings.

"Me, too," I say, smiling. It's nice, this connection. This feeling of being one of them, having a person tying us together.

Afterward, Patrick joins us and kisses me. My head spins from how brazenly he does this in front of his family, and how sure he must be about me and our relationship.

An hour later, when we arrive at his house, Patrick takes me up to the second floor (a novelty to me!) and to his childhood bedroom with its blue walls and blue carpet and blue bedspread. It screams "a boy lives here!" Right down to the participation trophies for every sport imaginable lining the top of a bookshelf. I had some of those once. They got shoved in a box and forgotten about as soon as my dad left.

"Congratulations," I say to Patrick, looping my arms around his back. I know how hard he worked for five years to get his dream degree.

"Thank you. I hope my parents weren't grilling you too hard," he says.

"They didn't really have a chance to—"

"Quinn!" comes Mrs. Hargrave's voice through the cracked open door. "Would you mind coming downstairs and giving me a hand?"

"Mom—" Patrick starts to say.

"No." I place a hand on his chest. "I'll go. You need to get changed. I'll see you out there."

"Okay," he says before a quick kiss. "Thanks."

Back downstairs, Mrs. Hargrave sends Mr. Hargrave and

Bradley out back to assist with the tents, the tables, and the chairs. I begin to follow them, to offer some extra muscle, but she stops me. "Oh, no, Quinn. They'll handle that. I need you here."

If she's insinuating something, I don't question it because we have a nice time chatting, getting to know each other. I wash my hands and begin slicing cucumbers for the veggie platter. The one the caterer sent over was, in her words, "unpresentable." It looks fine to me, but again, I don't question it.

"I'm so glad we could finally meet face-to-face. Patrick has told me so much about you." She's popping cherry tomatoes into a plastic container. "He really likes you."

"I really like him, too." I hope I don't come off as uncomfortable. I'm not in the practice of talking about my feelings, at least not the positive ones. That's not how Mom and I operate.

"And moving in together, that's a big step. A big step, indeed," she says. Her eyes shift sideways toward my face. Her burgundy lips turn up into a coy smile.

Shocked, I nearly cut off a finger because I'm not looking carefully at what I'm doing. "What?"

She obviously thinks I only misheard her. "Patrick showed me the photos of the apartment in Penderton he's thinking of renting. It looks lovely. I'm sure you two will be very happy there."

My heart skips into overdrive. I assumed he'd move home while he figures out his next steps like most other postgrads. This is the first I'm hearing of a hypothetical apartment for us. I rearrange my face so not to show that.

"Word to the wise," she says, giving me a conspiratorial look from beneath extra-long eyelashes. "Hargrave men are tough nuts. There are three cardinal rules to keep them happy. Three. Be agreeable and flexible. Don't interfere with their work. And always keep their plates full." She hands me a small plate loaded with veggies, then winks. "You'll thank me later."

After bringing Patrick the plate, I go through the motions of the party.

I drink plentiful flutes of champagne and meet aunts and uncles whose names I file away for safekeeping, waiting for the right moment to get Patrick alone so I can ask him about what his mother let slip. I don't know how I feel about it yet, but I'm erring on the side of elated that there's a future for us.

Throughout the duration of the party, Patrick shows me off proudly. Dances with me, barefoot in the grass, to music we're too young to know the words to.

It's not until the cake plates have been cleared, everyone having eaten different portions of Patrick's face pressed onto too-sweet buttercream, that I catch him alone, horizontal on a lounge chair beside their in-ground pool, staring up at the darkening sky. We're both on the drunker side of the tipsy continuum. There's a green bottle of champagne with gold foil flakes falling off it, sitting half-drunk on the ground beside his chair.

"Recuperating?" I ask. I kick off my sandals, roll up the legs of my pants, and dip my feet in the pool. The cool water feels good on my hot, sticky skin.

"Sort of." Patrick groans before getting up to join me. "How did you handle it all?"

"Pretty well," I say, meaning it. I'm not used to big family shindigs. It was always just Mom and me. Against the world. For better or worse.

The thought of my mom reminds me of his. "But your mom did say something interesting earlier."

He smacks his lips knowingly. "This is about the apartment, isn't it?"

"It's not *not* about the apartment."

He takes his phone from his pocket and pulls up a rental listing to show me. "I toured it. It's nice."

"It is." I scroll through the pictures.

"In my mom's defense, I told her I'd ask you last week, but time ran away from me."

"I get it." The more I scroll the more I see us there, in those rooms—sleeping there, entertaining there, growing together there.

But then, I get scared for a whole new reason. At Penderton, we were in a bubble. Our relationship existed in a vacuum. As of today, we are citizens of the world. Yes, technically, I may still be a student come August, but I'll be spending 85 percent of my time in a school classroom, not the lecture halls of Penderton. Whether we like it or not, an era of our lives is ending.

He places a hand on my thigh. "I think we should do it. While I apply for jobs, I think we should live together. You said you were feeling weird about the suite-style housing Penderton assigned you to with randoms."

"I am." The scariness of this step coils into anxiety. I wish we could stay as we are, right now. No differences. But, staring too hard at the water rippling around my feet in the pool, I suppose that's not possible. Time marches forward. I need to pick up my knees and start moving, too.

"I think we should do it." Patrick's tone is convincing, and his palm is warm, nearly creating an impression where it sits on my knee like the permanent impression he's already placed on my heart.

"But what about my housing deposit?" I ask.

"I'm sure they'll refund you. We'll figure it out."

"I'll be busy a lot with student teaching."

"That's fine by me. I'll need to be focused on working on my portfolio and applying for jobs anyway." He squeezes my leg. "I *want* us to do this."

Hacking my way through the dark reservations that grow like weeds around me, I take Mrs. Hargrave's advice. I choose to be agreeable and flexible. Even if it might upset Mom. Even if I'm not 100 percent certain it's the right move for me. I'm 100 percent certain Patrick is the right man for me. And that's enough. "Okay."

"Okay?" His smile is so heartwarming that it quells my worry.

"Yeah. Okay." I nod my head, pitching into him. My handsome

guy. My partner. This will be good. "It'll be a brand-new adventure for us."

"Okay!" he shouts, arms stretched to the sky. Leaning back, he grabs the half-drunk champagne bottle and swigs from it before offering it to me. "Now we have even more to celebrate! Let's get drunk."

I kiss him then say, "You don't need to tell me twice."

THE MORNING AFTER

QUINN

CHRISTMAS

Can you have a hangover from magic?

I shoot out of bed with a tension headache when I notice what time it is on the octagonal clock. That clock has followed me from my college dorm room to our first apartment and now to this house. This house that looks much dingier and shabbier since I saw the immaculate North Pole in all its storybook glory.

I did see the North Pole last night, didn't I?

It couldn't have all been some hyperrealistic dream.

Patrick is curled in the fetal position on the other side of the bed, snoring lightly and rhythmically like a white noise machine.

There are no hints of the portly, jolly man he was magicked into last night. No white whiskers sprouting out from his upper lip or enchanted cloak hanging in our doorless closet. (The door fell off in my hand when we moved in. It's a whole thing.)

Instead of focusing on last night's adventure, the repairs we may never get around to, or Patrick's big admission about what went down at Carver & Associates, I set my mind on that uncooked ham hogging up the fridge.

It's Christmas Day. At this point, it's going to still be in the oven when the guests arrive, but my mother-in-law's disappointment is a rickety rope bridge I can't quite cross at this hour.

I throw on my robe and slippers and pad downstairs, feeling

like I did in college at the tail end of finals week, utterly drained. No amount of coffee in the world is going to be able to cure me of this or give me the amount of energy needed to prepare a Christmas-worthy feast.

When I enter the kitchen, I stop dead in my tracks.

"What in the love of Martha Stewart?" I ask myself. The kitchen has been transformed. Newly decorated, it's almost unrecognizable.

It's nothing like the luxuriousness of some of the kitchens we traipsed through last night while delivering gifts. The dated, faded wallpaper still needs replacing and that terrible oven still mocks me from across the room, but everything else is spotless and decked out to the nines.

The oval-shaped kitchen table has a red, patterned tablecloth draped across it with a runner down the middle and a decorative candle centerpiece. A sweet, vanilla bean fragrance floats on the air like someone was baking sugar cookies in here moments before I arrived. There are serving trays, bowls, and tongs set out on all the counters.

I wander through the kitchen, awestruck, and into the dining room, where never-before-seen tables stand with equally new Christmas-themed dining sets laid out in front of each non-wobbly chair. Beside every plate is shined golden cutlery and right above are priceless crystal glasses.

Our previously defunct fireplace is a roaring hearth that sends lapping waves of heat throughout the room. The rinky-dink Target tree I'd put up forlornly all by my lonesome has vanished. In its place stands a real, fragrant spruce so beautiful and impeccably decorated that it must've been stolen from the set of a Hallmark Christmas film. Either from relief or happiness, tears spring up into my eyes.

Taking it in, I sit down in the nearest chair and notice a tiny, folded card standing up on its own.

Dear Patrick and Quinn,
Merry Christmas! While you were out delivering gifts, we had
our elves fly here and prepare your Christmas Day celebration.
Consider all the decorations, foods, and fixes our gifts to you
both for your heroic work.
Magically yours,
The Council of Priors
P.S. We look forward to hearing your response, either way, this
evening.

I take a deep breath as my heartbeat slows to a steady rap.

"It was all real," I whisper to myself.

I can't tell if this is reassuring or breakdown-inducing.

On one hand, I don't think Patrick and I have had fun like last night in a long time. We were laughing and chugging glasses of milk and feeding each other cookies like we were judges on the Food Network. Even the less-than-ideal parts—nearly getting bitten by that rottweiler and plentiful chimney-less houses—were solvable riddles on our ridiculous quest.

On the other hand, Patrick not telling me he got fired is still a high-flying red flag. We never used to keep things from each other, especially not something as important as losing your job. While I'm sure it was hard and I can only imagine how distraught he was, I wish he had confided in me and let me comfort him. Isn't that what a husband is supposed to do? He didn't even give me a chance to be there for him.

Despite it all, we have a massive choice to make. This trumps moving in together, getting married, and buying our house. This means leaving behind our lives, our families, for a full year, to what? Play dress-up and make toys at the Earth's northernmost tip? Preposterous.

Only, it isn't.

Last night, I could tell from Patrick's questions to the Council of Priors that his interest was more than piqued by the offer. He sounded genuinely excited by the prospect. I can't tell if the gurgling in my stomach right now is from nerves, anxiety, or a lack of breakfast.

On that note, I make my way to the fridge. I shove aside the cooked green beans, the finished ham, and a dozen other dishes I would not have had the time to prepare myself. I grab a yogurt from the back, a spoon from a drawer, and read over the reheating instructions on a handy card left in perfect cursive by one of the elves.

A half hour later, I have to practically peel Patrick out of bed. I shower for longer than normal, relishing in the spray even if the water pressure leaves a lot to be desired. At the closet, I ponder over what to wear.

In college, I experimented a lot with my wardrobe.

Piece by piece, year by year, comment by comment, I disposed of those remnants of experimentation. Those remnants of *me*, really.

It started with Mrs. Hargrave commenting on a pair of costume pearls I wore to Mr. Hargrave's sixtieth-birthday party at a homey Italian restaurant in New Brunswick. I was coming out of the restroom when I overheard: "Does he need to be wearing those fake pearls? Uncle Luke and Aunt Aggie won't shut up about them. This dinner is supposed to be about your father."

"I'll talk to him," Patrick had said in the mollifying tone he often used with his mother. It was deeper than his normal speaking voice. I often wondered if he realized he was code-switching around his parents the way he sometimes did with Uber drivers or particularly bro-y bartenders.

That night, I wanted to say something. The heated bubbling inside my chest told me I *had* to say something.

Instead, I pivoted, unclasped the magnetic necklace, and dropped it in the trash in the bathroom before returning to the table.

Patrick gave me a funny look, his mouth full of spaghetti. After he swallowed, he asked, "What happened to your necklace?"

"It broke," I lied. "How are the meatballs?"

We never spoke of it again.

Then, I became a teacher, which is essentially like putting yourself in front of the Fashion Police twenty-four seven, except nobody is an arbiter of taste, they're all concerned about the dress code. About "the students."

So even though my hands are reaching for the silky red blouse with the tie around the neck and the sheer, puffy sleeves that Veronica gifted me, I put on my family-approved Christmas outfit, which consists of a cable-knit sweater and constrictive slacks.

While I'm fixing myself in the mirror, there's a knock at the front door. Downstairs, I don't even need to look through the peephole to know who it is.

My in-laws have arrived. *Thirty minutes early.*

I swing the door open, sporting a practiced smile, before they can knock again, as prepared as I'll ever be to play the consummate host. "Merry Christmas."

Mr. and Mrs. Hargrave look up at me. They are a barrage of bags and bottles and a poinsettia so huge that I don't know where we're going to put it in our house's tiny rooms. They scurry past me with hurried cheek kisses, leaving behind Patrick's ninety-year-old grandmother, who is wearing a crewneck with a Christmas tree embroidered on it and a light-up necklace.

"Nothing gets people quite as frenzied as Christmas," Nan Hargrave says, adjusting her large, circular glasses. Patrick gets his poor eyesight from his dad's side of the family.

"Tell me about it. Come on in." I help her with her walker over the lip of the door.

"I won this at bingo," says Nan, toying with her necklace, which is meant to look like a string of lights. The colors chase each other around and around. There's a clunky battery pack at the back of her neck.

"I like it," I say.

"Glad one of us does," she huffs.

I tilt my head at her. "If you don't like it, why are you wearing it?"

"Why are *you* hosting Christmas dinner?"

I nod in understanding. *Mrs. Hargrave.* She's the reason I'm hosting Christmas dinner. Patrick was only her proxy. Making him think it was his idea all along was her goal. I know her well enough to know that.

"She insisted, and you know what she's like when she insists," Nan says. "Sat through mass this morning looking like it was Mardi Gras."

"Can't you turn it off?" I ask, trying not to laugh at the sight of this short, elderly woman with tufts of thin white hair wearing a light-up necklace through the homily. At least Christmas isn't one of the sad Christian holidays.

"Like everything else in old age, it's not working properly. The button is stuck." She sighs.

"Well, why don't you let me hang your coat, and I'll take a look at the button in a little bit."

I'm not even through hanging up Nan's coat when I hear, "Oh, my God, Bill!" Then, there is a crash.

Patrick's family has been here for two whole minutes. There can't already be a crisis.

Then, a panic shimmies through my chest. Did Hobart leave something behind last night? Are there glowing, glittering, golden orbs of magic floating in the air? I won't be able to explain that away.

When I arrive in the dining room, I don't see anything except my in-laws standing in the center of a bunch of fallen folding chairs.

"What is it? What's wrong?"

"The house." Mrs. Hargrave has a hand pressed to the center of her chest right beneath her own, non-light-up, necklace. They're pearls, of course. *Real* pearls. "It looks . . . *wonderful* in here. Did you do all of this?"

"I did," I say, because the alternative is telling her that a bunch of elves did it for us as her son and I went for a joyride in Santa's sleigh last night, which I don't think would go over particularly well even if she did take it as a joke.

"I'm amazed," she says. "Bill, take the chairs back to the car and don't bother with the other boxes."

"You got it, hun." Mr. Hargrave dutifully picks up the chairs.

Mrs. Hargrave says, "Quinn, I had no idea you had budded into such a homemaker. I came early thinking I'd give the place a facelift before the others arrived, but clearly you had that all taken care of." She pats me on the back as if she's proud of me before wandering over to the Christmas tree to admire it, leaving me to stew in my perceived shortcomings. I wish I could do this whole day on fast-forward.

I back out of the dining room in search of a bottle of wine and find that Nan Hargrave already has a lovely red uncorked and flowing into glasses.

"If I'm going to look this fun," she says, flicking the cheapy necklace again as I sidle up beside her, "I should feel this fun, too, right?"

"Right." I accept the second wineglass from her.

She clinks our glasses together. "Bottoms up, buttercup."

Only three hours until dinner, four hours until Mom calls and I can politely excuse myself to talk to her, eight hours until everyone leaves, and ten hours until Patrick and I have to make a major life-altering decision that precludes next year's Christmas from being canceled.

There's not enough Malbec in the world to combat this level of pressure.

18

TESTING THE WATERS

PATRICK

Mom has me say grace. Even though she knows Quinn and I don't go to church. She has to know, at least on some level, that it makes me uncomfortable, too. But I always try to be a good son. So I suck it up because I know this will make her happy.

Plus, she didn't ask Bradley, which kind of feels like a win for me. Since I can't tell them about my big win last night.

With our hands clasped and our heads bowed before a spread of food presumably cooked by elves, I say, "Thank you for the blessings which we are about to receive." But I'm thinking, *Aside from my wedding night, last night was the best night of my life.*

Somewhere in my comatose-like REM sleep, my mind wrapped itself around the factual existence of magic. I was tickled when I came downstairs and had it confirmed for me by the Extreme Home Makeover that happened in our absence.

Last night, when we got back, we were too bleary-eyed to notice anything in our amble up to bed. I barely shucked my jeans before flopping onto the mattress and drifting off. Quinn woke me a mere hour before our guests were set to arrive. But honestly, I probably could've slept for another twelve to thirteen hours, undisturbed. Woken up rejuvenated like a grizzly fresh from hibernation.

I look around the table at everyone I love—Mom, Dad, Nan, Quinn, Bradley, Aunt Aggie and Uncle Luke, their son James and his wife Kimiko and their kids, Chasten and Angelica. The whole gang is here to celebrate a holiday that *I made happen.*

As soon as the prayer ends, Quinn carves the ham. The sides get passed around. Angelica, who is nine and wearing a large, sparkly bow in her hair, loudly details everything Santa brought her from her wish list. "I must've been really good this year. I got a fashion show runway playset, two dolls to go with it, a Disney karaoke machine, *three* new dresses—"

"I got a dinosaur!" Chasten interjects. He's swirling his fork through his mashed potatoes. The scrape of the prongs on the fine china is grating.

"A dinosaur?" Quinn asks. His eyes flick down to me mischievously. We must have delivered these gifts last night. In the blur of the intense evening, I hadn't even realized we were in my cousin's house in New York. After a while, the routine and the rush made me so singularly focused. Quinn and I were having too much fun to worry about anything else.

Chasten nods vigorously. "You blow it up like a balloon and then you use a remote to make it walk. It scared Angelica." His smile reads as victorious. As if scaring his sister had been the mission when asking for the toy in the first place.

"It did not!"

"It did too!"

"It did not!"

"Kids," Nan says scoldingly. Though her tone is undercut by the blinking, unexpected necklace she's wearing. "There's no fighting at the dinner table."

They both zip their lips and go back to their plates.

"Yeah, and just because it's Christmas doesn't mean you get a free pass," I say before accepting my plate back from Quinn. It's now covered with two thick slices of the juiciest ham I've ever seen. "Santa's always watching. If you misbehave, you might not get anything next year. You wouldn't want that, now, would you?"

Synchronized, they shake their heads. Then we all dig in.

"Quinn, my compliments to the chef," Dad says. I try not to

be annoyed by the fact that he dispenses compliments so easily to everyone but me.

I can tell by a single flick of Quinn's eyebrow that he's conflicted about how to respond. "Oh, it was nothing," he decides on, which evokes a little chuckle from me over the truthfulness. I'm thinking back to last night when he told me he didn't like cooking.

All those nights Quinn cooked turkey chili or baked cod and sides, I thought he was doing it because he enjoyed it. If I came home while he was still cooking, I'd often hear him singing along to music or engrossed in a FaceTime conversation with Veronica. I assumed it was the way he destressed after a day in the classroom. I never sensed that it might be an added stressor.

Quinn shoots me with a look of warning over my laughter. But he might as well be reading my mind.

Since I slept late, we had no time to discuss last night nor the decision that looms large ahead of us. Even though I'm pretty certain I know which side I stand on, I still need to temperature check Quinn.

"Pat, how's work?" Mom asks, cutting her ham into equal bite-sized pieces.

Last night was not only magical and amazing, but it also offered me an escape hatch. If I can avoid the fallout of my unemployment and bring a little joy to the world in the process, I should do it. It would be selfish not to.

I clear my throat. "I'm actually fielding an exciting new career opportunity."

Quinn's head snaps in my direction. I wish I could control the heat that crops up into my cheeks. I know we have a lot to discuss. But the last thing I want to do is tell them what went down at Carver & Associates. Everything is going too well tonight. I'm not about to torch that.

"You just started at your firm not that long ago. A promotion already?" Dad asks. He sounds moderately impressed even though he's never fully supported my architectural endeavors. Before he passed, Grandad Hargrave was a lawyer. Before retirement, Dad was a lawyer. Bradley is currently a lawyer. I'm decidedly anything but.

Which is why building a home and a family with Quinn is so important to me. It's the marker of success and stability I have that Bradley doesn't. One less reason to label me "different" on the Hargrave family tree.

"It's top secret," Quinn says for me. "I barely even know any of the details."

"How mysterious," Bradley says in a lawyerly deadpan. His sandy-blond hair is slicked back with product and he's wearing a crisp, charcoal blazer. He's five years older than me, but he looks younger thanks to a multi-step skincare routine and a hundred-dollar haircut.

Mom says, after wiping her mouth on her fabric napkin, "You can't tell us anything?"

I bobble my head. "I can tell you that it would be a pivot for me."

This grabs Dad's interest. "Am I hearing that there's law school in your future? Finally reconsidering? You're not too old, you know."

"No, it's . . . it's still in the same realm that I've been working in, Dad," I say. Even if that's a stretch. A big one.

"You're so young. Don't go making any big changes," says Mom. "Carver & Associates is such a great firm. *Such* a great firm. The internet says so!"

The name of my former place of employ makes my neck hot and my hands clammy. "I know, but . . ."

"Is it a different firm? Were you poached?" Dad asks. Reading between the lines, I can tell he believes this to be the only suitable reason to leave by choice. And I'm not about to tell him it happened by force. My family has very strong opinions about work and money. Because work and money equate to success, and success allows you to keep up appearances, and appearances, in our neck of New Jersey, are everything.

"No, it's nothing like that. But it would require us to relocate for a year."

"Relocate? Not far I hope," Mom says, aghast.

The farthest away possible, I think. But Dad speaks before I can respond.

"What about the house? I suppose you expect us to come and check up on it if you take this new post?" Dad seems annoyed by this. Even though he was the one that told me that as soon as I could I should invest in real estate. He's how I got the idea for me and Quinn to take our honeymoon fund and turn it into a starter-house fund instead. An idea that soured faster than milk, considering Quinn hates this place.

I learned more about Quinn last night than I have in the last year. Have we not been talking? Or have I just not been listening?

"No, of course not. We'd work that out." I look to Quinn, who is busy staring down at his plate. Not eating. Not speaking. Maybe not even blinking.

Dad sets his fork down. "Well, son, I guess you know what's best for you." His words are unconvincing at best and sarcastic at worst.

"And I suppose it's okay if you move for a year. Yes, I suppose it's okay. As long as you're back for Christmas," Mom adds, eyes brimming with worry. As if, at any point, I was asking for their permission. They must sense that I crave it. Even if I'm too old for that.

I chuckle once more to try and lighten the mood. "That's the one day a year I *know* I'd have off."

Interrupting the moment, Quinn's phone starts ringing. Mom's gaze transfers to Quinn with irritation. She's a stickler about phones at the table. Always has been.

"Sorry, everybody," Quinn says. He's clearly a little embarrassed as he stands up from his chair. "It's my mom. She wasn't supposed to call this early. I'll just, uh, run upstairs and take this." He does a little dip and exits the room. His napkin was still on his lap when he left, so it flutters to the floor in his wake like a lilting white flag of surrender. I scoop it up and set it on his chair.

Mom exhales heavily before returning to her meal. The only sounds for a long while are the clanking of utensils and people chewing. Until Angelica pipes up.

"Did I mention I got *three* new dresses?"

"You did," Nan says. "Now hush up and eat your ham before it gets cold."

19

MOTHER, MAY I?

QUINN

I shut myself in our bedroom and answer the call.

"Hi, Mom," I say into the phone, summoning cheeriness. "Merry Christmas."

On the other end, there's loud chatter and the clinking of slot machines as coins spew out of their mouths. When Mom and Dad divorced after a shotgun wedding and twelve miserable years of "making it work," Mom moved us south to be closer to the beach and Philadelphia, where her family is originally from. She got a job working as a cocktail waitress in one of the casinos on the Atlantic City boardwalk. I spent a lot of Saturday afternoons in that casino food court, reading books and eating floppy, undercooked pizza.

Mom always said she liked the fast-paced nature of the work at the casino, but I have to wonder how true that holds when you have to work on Christmas Day. Not that she'd be here if she wasn't working. Mom loves Patrick, don't get me wrong, but aside from our wedding day, where she put on her best show, she is vehemently anti-Hargrave. She thinks they think they're better than her, when in reality, I'm pretty sure they don't think about her at all, which I guess is its own kind of slight.

"Merry Christmas, my baby. Sorry I'm calling early."

"That's okay," I say, happy to have had an excuse to leave the dining room, which was growing stuffier by the second.

What was Patrick thinking bringing up the Santa conundrum with his family? Obviously he didn't say it by name, but we haven't even discussed the matter yet. To speak about it so openly makes me think he's preemptively making the decision for us. We're supposed to be a team.

I take a cleansing breath, not wanting the anger toward Patrick to cloud my conversation with Mom.

"My break got pushed up. It's busy as anything here today," Mom says. I imagine her in that food court from my childhood, nursing a coffee and a donut. Maybe the donut's even got red and green sprinkles on it. It's a bit of Christmas spirit to get her through the shift.

"I'm sorry to hear that." I sit down at the tiny desk in the corner of our bedroom. The chair creaks like it's protesting my weight on it, as if it weren't designed for this exact purpose. This house, these things. I swear I could go mad here.

"Oh, don't be sorry." She's talking with her mouth full, but I can still make out every word. I've had practice with this. "Better to be busy than bored out of my mind. People tip better on holidays anyway. I could use the money."

I grab my planner from the corner of the desk and double-check the date I penciled Mom's visit in on. "If you need any help with gas money to get here on Thursday, Pat and I are happy to pitch in."

"Oh, damn, was that *this* Thursday?" I wish I didn't hear the rehearsed performativity in her question.

I nod even though she can't see me. "Uh-huh."

"Crap. Journee's daughter just had a baby, and I promised her I'd cover her shifts for the rest of the week while she went to New York to visit. I can't go back on that."

"Of course. I understand. Another time." It's a refrain I know by heart. Disappointment pinwheels around my heart.

"Come visit me instead! Before you go back for the second half of the school year. It's been ages since we've gone out on the town together."

The first word to come to mind when I describe Mom is *freewheeling*. Even in her midforties, Mom is still more interested in long road trips and driving too fast with the top down in a car that has had the check engine light on for months. She still loves sipping electric-colored mixed drinks from massive plastic cups with glow-in-the-dark bendy straws while some up-and-coming DJ spins a headache-inducing set. We don't have similar visions of what R&R look like.

"I don't think Patrick could get off of work for us to make that happen." It's a flimsy excuse because Patrick is now permanently off work, but she doesn't know that.

"Patrick doesn't always need to be there." Her words are clipped. I think, in her perfect world, it would still be just me and her, a ragtag team like we used to be. I don't think she's ever made peace with the fact that college, teaching, and a long-term relationship have changed me.

In my most private moments, I worry that she doesn't like who I've become, this grown-up version of me.

When I'm too tongue-tied to think up something to say to that, she sighs. "It was just an idea. I'll come up soon, I promise."

She's not coming. I add a tally to the Move to the North Pole column in my mind.

"Have you spoken to your father yet today?" Her question provokes an eye roll.

After the divorce and the move, I saw Dad one weekend a month until he moved to Nevada. I was quiet during those visits, always sticking to the outskirts of any activity. Dad was starting a new family. It was the one he'd always envisioned, where he had a brood of boys who all played and excelled at baseball—the sport of his obsession and his golden years.

The first Christmas card they sent from Nevada with all of them wearing matching sweaters despite the heat nearly broke my heart from how perfect it was. How I would never have that.

"No, I'm sure he's busy. Maybe I'll call in a few days." It's a lie. I know I won't. Depending on how the conversation with Patrick goes later, I may be moving tonight. I doubt I'll get good cell service in the North Pole.

"Okay." I hear the crinkle of a wrapper on her end. "My break's just about done. Send my love to Pat, okay? Don't eat too many cookies."

If only she knew how many I ingested last night alone.

"I'll try not to. Love you."

"Love you, too, my baby."

After we hang up, I don't go back down to dinner right away.

I exhale and lounge back in the chair, swiping through my phone. Other people's picture-perfect Christmases hog my Instagram feed. I barely post these days given that parents are apt to search their kids' teachers before a new school year. I don't need someone outraged over me wearing a tank top in public. Heaven forbid a teacher have *arms*.

I open my text thread with Veronica and type: Another stellar Christmas phone call with Shelby Muller. How's Cate Blanchett?

> **Veronica:** Still the only mother we'll ever need

> Jk, my mom is great

> But I'm sorry about yours

My parents divorced because my dad hated how quickly he had to grow up when my mom got pregnant with me, and my mom hated being a "wife" in any traditional sense. I was unplanned and (mostly) unwanted. I was hoping the Hargraves would want me, but it seems, since we got married, that they *want me* to fit the mold of perfect spouse more than they care to get to know me for the true me.

> **Veronica:** How did the ham turn out?

> **Me:** Great! But I didn't cook it.

> **Veronica:** ????????????

> **Me:** It's too hard to explain

Though, I wish I could, because I desperately need some advice right now. Veronica is the best listener I know.

> **Veronica:** Are things any better with Patrick?

> **Me:** Define "better"

> **Veronica:** Did you TALK to him?

> **Me:** Define "talk"

> **Veronica:** Sometimes you make me want to throttle you like I'm playing a pent-up housewife hungry for the Best Supporting Actress statuette

> **Me:** If I were in the Academy, I'd vote for you!

> **Veronica:** Btw, where were u last night?

> **Veronica:** Last night, my mom didn't text me when she left home like she usually does when she comes over, so I checked the little "find my friends" thing and it showed you at home, then when I was going to bed and closing out my apps, it showed you were in the middle of the Arctic???

I laugh nervously to myself, experiencing extreme heart palpitations. Veronica would never believe where I really was, so I send off the first lie I can think of.

> **Me:** Dropped my phone in the toilet last night. Tried the rice thing, but it must still be glitching! LOL

> **Veronica:** Figures LOL. Don't go breaking your phone. You're not tenured yet. You can't afford a new one.

Her text only serves to remind me of the reality of my thankless job. I'm barely keeping my head above water this year, and when my aide leaves in January, I have no idea what I'm going to do. If my performance slips too badly, I could end up classless next September. Though, maybe that wouldn't be such a bad thing.

As of late, I've been losing the resolve to continue teaching. From a group of alpha fifth graders tearing the crepe paper down off my curated bulletin boards to a select group of parents complaining to the principal that I have a photo of Patrick and me on my desk (on our wedding day! Not even kissing!) to overcrowding in our classrooms, I'm growing frequently fed up.

I can't possibly be making a difference in my students' lives because the system is so set against us teachers doing our jobs. Especially queer ones.

I think about how last night was magical. Our adventure was blissful and fun and had immediate, tangible effects. I mean, Chasten and Angelica were proof of that, sitting right in my own dining room.

If we sign on for one year as Santa and Mrs. Cl—*the Merriest Mister*—it'll be like a mini marriage vacation.

We won't be pulled away by our jobs with opposing schedules, and while I'm sure the new positions in the North Pole (I can't believe I'm even thinking about the North Pole right now!) will be stressful at times, I can't imagine we won't have our nights and weekends free. Something we can't even count on here.

The village at the North Pole had a sense of romance and wonder to it. All those couples on the Council of Priors seemed happy. Even Colleen and Nicholas, who had to be well into their eighties, seemed still madly in love.

I want that. I want the side-by-side rocking chairs that end with side-by-side burial plots.

On that beach, on our wedding day, we said "'til death do us part," and I meant that. But before our engagement, we also said we'd only stay together for as long as we were having fun, making each other better people by tag-teaming the hell out of life.

I meant *that*, too.

These days it's felt so much like we're on travelators in an airport going in two different directions. It's no fun waving at one another from opposite ends of a crowded, massive terminal.

Maybe this whole Santa thing is the spark we need to get us moving as one again.

As I tell my students, anything is worth a try in the face of adversity.

THE DECISION

PATRICK

"This was exquisite. We *have* to do it here again next year," Mom says as she hugs me goodbye. The wool of her coat scratches at my palms.

I catch Quinn's bewildered expression over my mother's right shoulder.

He was up in our room for a while on that call. I wonder what he and his mom were talking about. I hope it wasn't anything like the conversation I overheard him having with Veronica. After last night that would crush me even more.

"We'll see," I say before kissing Mom on the cheek. Even with the help of the elves, this evening was exhausting. Granted, last night I expended more energy than ever before.

My aunt, uncle, cousin, and his family all left when the kids started to crash. Now it's just my immediate family and Nan saying their goodbyes.

Dad sets a hand on my shoulder. "Call me if you want to talk out this job opportunity without being so cryptic. We gave you a good head on these shoulders. Use it."

The star of the Hargrave brood hugs me next, making me feel like an overwound clock about to shoot off its springs. "Merry Christmas. Good to see you. Be well." All my life, Bradley has outshined me. But it's not until he hugs me that I realize he's even got a couple inches on me, height-wise, giving a whole new meaning to overshadowed.

If only he'd seen me last night. If only they'd all seen me last night.

Nan hip-checks Bradley out of the way. "My turn."

"We're going to go warm up the car," Dad says. He, Mom, and Bradley step out into the cold night. "We'll pull the car up, okay, Mom?"

"Sure." Nan waves her hand at them as they go. "Thank you for a lovely Christmas, Patrick and Quinn. I probably don't have many more left in me, so it means a lot. Even if I had to wear this stupid necklace." At some point during dessert, the batteries must have died. It's lightless around her neck now, which makes it look more ridiculous. "If this ninety-year-old can gift you one thing on this special holiday, it's to remind you that life only gives you so many chances for adventure. If this new job and moving to a new place are going to bring joy and adventure, then don't listen to your parents. Do it!"

She hugs me as tight as her short, frail arms can manage, then sees herself out.

Quinn shuts and locks the door, presses his back into the wood, and sighs. "That was a lot."

The past twenty-four hours have been a lot. That much we can both wordlessly agree on.

We make our way back into the dining room to inspect the mess left behind. Quinn insisted my parents not pitch in to clean up. Probably out of pride. But now we're staring down vacuuming, laundry, and multiple runs of our barely-working dishwasher.

"Do you think the elves will come and take care of this? Because if not, I don't have the energy right now," Quinn says. He waves a hand at the wreckage of a holiday well spent.

"Me neither," I say. "Hot chocolate?"

"Yes, please."

When the last of the Swiss Miss has been used up, we settle on the couch in the living room. For a while, we stare silently into our mugs. Wisps of steam swirl up around the globs of whipped cream and tickle my nose. My mind races with a million and one ways to begin this conversation.

The ticks of the second hand on the wall clock over Quinn's head grow louder. I haven't been this nervous to talk to Quinn about something since I was about to propose.

Our relationship hangs in the balance of our next choice.

I see how hard teaching has weighed on Quinn these past months. I want to be able to turn to him and say, "If it's not bringing you joy anymore, let it go."

But we don't have the savings to do that.

And I don't have the guts.

Because if I plant the idea, and our relationship is no longer bringing him joy, who's to say he won't use the same sentiment to let me go, too?

I can turn this around. I can be the man Quinn and my family need me to be.

I must be wearing a look of consternation while I'm thinking hard because Quinn covers his mouth with his hand. "I have a whipped cream mustache, don't I?"

"No." I shake my head.

"Then, what is it?" Quinn asks.

"I'm just trying to find the words to tell you that I think we should go to the North Pole," I say finally.

"Those words were pretty clear," he says.

"Okay. So, I think it's a good idea," I say. "We had fun last night, didn't we?"

"The most fun, but we can't just leave. You heard your dad. What about the house?" Quinn asks.

"The council says they take care of that."

He bites his lip. "My class?"

"I assume they arrange for someone else to take it over."

Quinn's eyes ping downward. "That might be for the best." He doesn't expand on that. We lapse into momentary silence. "I just wonder if maybe you should go by yourself."

My hope falters. "I don't want to go by myself."

"I don't want you to go by yourself, either, but maybe that's what we both need." Quinn seems to be puzzling this out in real time. His expression shifts too quickly for me to put a name to any of his emotions. "What if we need time apart?"

"Like a separation?" I don't know why I keep asking questions I won't like the answers to. I failed at being a junior architect. I refuse to fail at being a husband, too.

Quinn visibly shivers. "*Separation* is too strong of a word."

"What other word would you use for us living a million miles apart?" I ask. I set my mug down on a coaster on the coffee table and shuffle over to Quinn on my knees. I'm not above begging. "Quinn, I know I messed up by not telling you I got fired, and I know I should've asked you before agreeing to host Christmas, and I know there are a million other injustices I should be apologizing for right now, but instead of telling you poorly, let me show you how sorry I am."

"Pat, I don't want you to be sorry," he says, setting his own mug aside. "I want things—us—to be different." His eyes scan the room. He's clearly documenting the places where, even beneath stunning, elf-done decorations, the decay of this house can be seen.

"It will be different." I grab his knees. "I'll learn how to cook so you don't have to. We'll leave this house you hate. Let's get away from all of this. Let's fall in love again."

Quinn's frazzled expression gradually cracks into a wide, toothy smile. "And you say you aren't good at words."

"Maybe I'm good at them when I have to be." I beam back at him. A compliment seems like a good sign. "It's only one year, and then we're back. One year is nothing in the scheme of a lifetime." *But it could mean everything in the lifetime of our relationship,* I think. I could pass out from the nervousness bouncing inside me. Quinn must feel how sweaty my palms are through the fabric of his slacks. "Quinn, let's do this."

Quinn's nod grows slowly bigger. "Okay."

"Okay?" I ask.

"Yeah. Okay."

We connect over a chocolate-flavored kiss that steals my breath away. I press into it, extending it. Needing to be close to him.

"Shouldn't we start packing?" he asks. Without completely realizing what I was doing, I've straddled him on the couch. I run my hands luxuriously through his curls. "We move across the world in a few short hours."

"That's a problem for twenty minutes from now." I breathe into Quinn's neck. I trail kisses up his soft skin and around his cute, winged-out earlobe. "I still haven't given you your Christmas gift yet."

Quinn melts like a marshmallow against me. "Oh, in that case, what should I unwrap first?" he whispers back. His willingness and growing excitement are straight-up shots of relief.

I'm about to kiss him once more before removing my shirt when we're interrupted by a thud on the roof, an onslaught of gold glitter raining down from the ceiling, and a scandalized elf standing at the foot of our fireplace.

"Sorry! Sorry! Sorry!" Hobart shields his eyes with his hand. He turns away with hyper speed. "I didn't mean to interrupt. We knew you made a decision so I arrived as quickly as I could."

I jostle up to standing. I clear my throat and smooth down my hair. "It's okay, Hobart. I guess we'll start getting our stuff together?" Quinn looks at me from the couch. His swollen, plum-colored lips tip into a smile as he places a pillow over his crotch.

"No need," Hobart says. "Like the council told you, everything—and I do mean *everything*—will be provided for you. All you need to bring is yourselves. The sleigh is up on the roof whenever you're ready."

"Are we ready?" I ask Quinn when he's decent enough to stand without embarrassment.

He lets out an audible exhale. "As ready as I'll ever be."

The two of us plant ourselves near the fireplace. I take one last look around the living room. *Goodbye and good riddance.* With that fizzing back in my fingertips, I take Quinn by the hand, and say to Hobart, "Let's go!"

THE NORTH POLE'S NEWEST RESIDENTS

QUINN

At the front door to a majestic chalet built into the North Pole mountainside, Hobart extracts a key from the bottomless pocket of wonder in the front of his overalls. With a flick of the wrist and a click of the lock, he lets us inside.

My mouth is agape as soon as we cross the threshold.

Patrick would be able to tell you about the type of wood that's been used, the era and style the chalet was modeled after, and which architects it was likely inspired by, but the only way I can describe this place with my limited knowledge and tired brain is absolutely *amazing*.

It's the kind of exquisite lodge that would make a perfect, scenic backdrop for a date on *The Bachelor*. Already, I'm blanketed with a sense that we can start fresh here.

The ceilings are tall, and the rooms are airy. The décor could be described as rustic chic but lavish in a way we could never afford on our own. A chandelier of antlers hangs over the sitting room where a ruby-red ornate carpet lies between geometrically interesting sofas made with luxurious upholstery.

The whole place smells like Thanksgiving: cinnamon, caramel, clove, and honey. It's like walking along the waxy surface of a pumpkin pie.

An aged, thick-trunked tree forms the chalet's centerpiece. Strand lights wrap around its bark, and a spiral staircase coils around its circumference. Steps lead to floors both above and below.

There are ginormous picture windows lining the back alongside glass doors that lead out onto tiered, wraparound decks.

Patrick isn't far behind when I push outside and stop, awestruck by the unobstructed view of the aurora borealis. Greens and purples ripple and dance across the pitch-black night sky, their sensations taking up inside my chest, undulating life into me.

And there are stars. *So many stars.*

There's even a golden telescope built into the deck boards to see them better with.

For a second, I wish my students were here so I could line them up one by one and show them the constellations. Tell them their names and watch as their eyes widen with wonder over the expansiveness of our universe.

I cut off that thought. They're not *my* students anymore.

I've chosen this. For the next calendar year, I'm not Mr. Muller. I'm the Merriest Mister.

Not quite sure what that means yet, but if this house is any indication, then it will be stellar.

Patrick ambles up behind me, wrapping me in an embrace that quiets any uncertain voices still chattering inside my head. We're here now, and it's beautiful. I lean back into his chest, which, even through the layers of our clothing, feels broader and more defined than it did before he bonded with the enchanted cloak. Maybe it's magic or maybe he's just standing taller, his shoulders slung back and down now that we've left our hardships in the garage alongside all those unpacked boxes.

Back inside the chalet, Hobart gives us the full tour, citing wondrous features and amenities before bringing us up to the third floor, where there is a huge bedroom.

"A king-sized bed in the middle of the room? This is the height of luxury," I say to Pat, running a hand along the freestanding headboard. "Or at least that's what I think I heard once on HGTV."

French doors to my left lead out onto a Juliet balcony. The en suite bathroom has a massive Jacuzzi tub with more jets than I can count in a single look. The lighting in here is soft-hued, forgiving. Perfect for masking the sleep-deprived puffiness I feel beneath my eyes.

Hobart hangs tight in the doorway. "I'll leave now so you can get ready for bed. I'm sure you're both exhausted. You'll find toiletries in the bathrooms, sleep clothes in the walk-ins, and different pillows and linens in the hallway closet if you need them. The council is meeting tomorrow morning. You're both expected to be there, but I will meet you here beforehand to escort you."

"Oh, you don't need to do that. Just leave the address. We'll figure out our own way there," Patrick says.

Hobart frowns. "No can do. I'm head elf. I'm required to escort you there. See you at seven A.M.!" He dips out.

I groan a little. "Seven A.M.? I was hoping to sleep until noon. On the twenty-seventh."

Patrick chuckles warmly. "Guess we should get ourselves to bed then."

I make my way into the left-hand walk-in closet that says MRS. C on the door. It is impeccably organized and has golden lights lining every shelf. Carrie Bradshaw would be green with envy.

Shoes are on the back wall, outerwear is on the right, and sleep clothes are on the left.

Only issue? They're all designed for the little, old, white-haired woman we all know from the greeting cards. While most of it appears one-size-fits-all, I'm uncertain what I'm supposed to do here.

"Uh, Pat?" I ask, realizing only after the fact that he can't hear me. This closet is deep, and I've ventured in farther than I thought. "Pat!" I cry when I'm near the door again. He pops his head out of his own walk-in. His hair is all mussed from the hat he was wearing earlier, winging out at the ends. He's always been his cutest when he's rumpled.

"Yeah?"

"Is your closet also full of velvet dresses, bonnets, and black patent-leather heels with decorative buckles on them?" I ask.

He furrows his brow. "No, why is your— Oh." He starts laughing when the reality registers for him.

I roll my eyes, but laugh a little, too, pushing the door open farther so he can see what I changed into—a holly-patterned nightgown that goes all the way down to my ankles with a high, frilly neckline. All I need is a lit candle on a carrier to complete the Dickensian look. "What's so funny? You're not *wildly* attracted to me in this?" I ask playfully, cocking an eyebrow and putting my hands on my hips.

"What gave you that impression? Haven't I ever told you about my interest in Victorian-era role-play?" he asks, coming out of his closet in a matching set of red flannel pajamas, fuzzy sleep socks, and holding a ridiculously long, pointed nightcap. It's a winning, cozy look for him.

"Then, Mr. Claus, it's your lucky day," I say, dropping the collar to reveal one shoulder, shimmying it a little. "There are plenty more where this came from."

"Good." He shakes his head, smiling. "Hold on. I'll grab you a pair of pajamas from my closet."

"Don't bother," I say, moving toward the bed, enjoying the sway of the loose-fitting fabric. My body is beyond tired. Socializing with your in-laws and making a move halfway across the globe can wear you out. "I kind of like it. It's got good airflow."

"Are you . . . wearing anything under that?" Patrick asks, eyes hooded.

Some of my heated attraction from the couch at our house comes roaring back. "Want to check? I'll even let you do it *twice*." I sit on the edge of the bed, hands sliding across the softest comforter imaginable.

Our sex life could use a magical resurrection.

He opens, then closes his mouth, rubbing a hand along the back of his neck. "As much fun as that sounds, I'm pretty beat now."

My heart-fire sizzles out. "Yeah, of course. Me, too." I try not to sound too disappointed, even if rejection clunks low in my stomach. I could've rallied, but better to be practical about this, I guess.

Baby steps.

Once we've brushed our teeth and washed our faces at the Jack and Jill (or, in our case, Jack and *Jack*?) sinks, we claim our usual sides of the bed and get comfortable under the covers. The mattress is the perfect firmness, and the pillows are cushy.

I'm lying down on my side when, after about ten minutes, I hear: "Quinn?"

"Yeah?"

"I'm excited we're doing this." He sounds childlike, nearly buoyant.

I smile into the darkness caused by the blackout blinds. "Me, too."

After a pause, he wiggles up behind me and spoons me, something he hasn't done in a while. His warmth is welcome as we grow accustomed to this new bed, these new roles. Maybe *we'll* be new, too.

A WARM WELCOME

PATRICK

"Rise and shine, Clauses," Hobart shouts cheerfully. A living alarm clock.

The screeching hum of the blackout blinds rising scares me into wakefulness. Hazy sunlight soaks the room all the way to the corners.

I jolt up. Swipe a hand across my crusty face.

Quinn doubles down. He hides his head beneath the pillow we'd been sharing for most of the night. "Ten more minutes," Quinn groans sleepily into the cloud-like mattress. Weekday Quinn is a master of mornings. Never snoozes his alarm. Glugs at least one cup of coffee before leaving for school. Out the door on time, always. Weekend and school holiday Quinn is a sheet creature. He lurks in the darkness of our bedroom for hours after I've started my day.

When he was student teaching and during his first year, we often lazed in bed together on Saturday and Sunday mornings. We'd kiss and cuddle and tease one another until inevitably getting up to shower together and make breakfast together and go on walks together.

Lately, there hasn't been much *together* for us.

"No can do. A busy day ahead! Up and at 'em!" Hobart has all the makings of an overly chipper sergeant. No wonder he has this job.

Quinn takes longer to get ready than I do, so I make idle small talk with Hobart downstairs in the grand foyer until Quinn appears around the corner of the floating, spiral staircase. I'm mesmerized by the look he's turned out from the disparate parts of a storybook grandma's wardrobe.

He's fashioned one of the smaller Mrs. Claus dresses into a top with a waist-cinching chunky black belt. Miraculously, he's found the one pair of slacks in the closet, and they look like they were custom-made for him. They showcase the gentle curve of his ass with each step he takes. When he reaches us, I have to look up at him, because he's wearing heels. They make his legs appear miles long. I want to rove my hands along the ridges and valleys of them.

I instantly regret skipping sex for sleep last night. A throbbing desire that we have no time to do anything about materializes low in my gut.

"Do I look okay?" Quinn asks, giving a tentative spin.

"Yeah," I utter, struck. I want to say fantastic, sexy, stunning, but Hobart jumps in with: "Yes! No time to change anyway. Out we go!"

In broad daylight, the village at the North Pole is even more picturesque than I originally concluded. It has the hallmarks of a valley town. Nestled, secluded, and yet still at one with the natural elements that surround it. The mountains appear as if they're posing for a panoramic postcard shot. There must be a height ordinance on the buildings here to maintain the stunning vista views.

Elves smile at us as we pass. Some wave. Others come up and introduce themselves like we're royalty. I grab Quinn by the hand. I'm glad when nobody looks at us funny. Maybe it's because they know how much power we hold. Or maybe it's because this is an accepting enclave closed off from the rest of the world. Prejudice has not cast its shadow across this land. Whatever the case, it's freeing.

The buildings we pass have a nineteenth-century New England style mixed with Bavarian influences right down to the half-timbered, exposed wood frames with Christmas-colored exteriors. Behind the large, fully decorated tree in the town square, there is a stone tower with a clock face in the side that chimes a carol on the hour. I know this because it's just hit seven A.M. and Hobart is pushing Quinn and me through the hordes with unwanted urgency. If given the chance, I could wander this place for days and never grow tired of gazing upon these buildings with their interesting shapes and folkloric detailing.

We end up back at the building from two nights ago. Instead of going toward the cathedral room past the portraits, we chart a course into another wing. Hobart opens the door for us to an informal dining room where a feast is taking place. The walls are linenfold paneling over which several mirrors and paintings with gilded frames hang. In the center of the room, a long walnut table is laid out with the most impressive spread of breakfast foods. It's a cornucopia overflowing with sliced fruits, croissants, scones, and various proteins.

"Welcome, welcome," Yvonne says cordially. Her hair is down in long, cascading braids. She wears a flowing crimson dress. The hem sweeps the floor as she passes.

"Finally," Ashley says, harried. She hastily butters a piece of toast and takes a crunchy bite like they weren't allowed to eat until we arrived. Her blond hair is disheveled. As if she spent the entire night tossing and turning over today. Couldn't have been me. I slept like a rock with Quinn in my arms.

"Apologies. These two take terribly long showers," Hobart announces unnecessarily to the room.

"At least they're clean," Nicholas, the white man with white hair, says. Funny that he's the oldest and the most classically Santa with the most fitting name. I'd almost call it cliché. But not to his face. He seems too stern and forbidding to find it funny.

Quinn shoots him a look. Nicholas's wife, Colleen, pipes in. "Our last Santa had—oh, how should I put it—*questionable* hygiene."

Quinn and I are escorted to our seats at the far head of the table. To my left, heavy, damask curtains are tied back on the windows, which showcase sun-drenched mountains. There's something almost too perfect about the way snow covers them with zero signs of melting. "How did he get the job?" I ask, pulling my attention away from the view. "I assume most Santas don't come to power because of a frying pan."

Laughter rumbles through the room. Samson, with the buzzed hair and the jacked body, says, "That was a first for sure."

"You two are filling a lot of firsts for our storied institution," Yvonne says. Her smile oozes acceptance. I relax, knowing that, even if they haven't said as much, we're safe to be ourselves here. "Speaking of which, Quinn, we apologize for the closet situation. Again, we were unprepared for your arrival."

Quinn smooths down his top. "Oh, it's no problem," he says while accepting a hardboiled egg in a cup from a tray passed down by Jorge.

"Of course, it's a problem," Colleen says. "Our first-ever Merriest Mister should be confident and comfortable in his wardrobe, which is why Yvonne and I would like to take you to the boutique once we're finished here."

"Oh, okay. That would be really nice," Quinn says. He punctuates this by tapping his spoon against the eggshell. He was tired on the walk over. But this seems to have perked him up. So has the rich-smelling coffee. A dark roast. His favorite.

"Don't think we forgot about you, Patrick," says Chris. I bite into a croissant. It's the exact right ratio of buttery to flaky. "You'll be with us today. We'll tour the workshop, show you where we keep the lists—"

"Wait," I say with my mouth full. "There are really Naughty and Nice lists?"

"For the most part, the songs and TV specials are strikingly accurate," says Colleen. Almost gleefully.

"Except for the Rudolph business," Ashley says. She toys with the ends of her maroon cardigan sleeves. "That was purely marketing nonsense."

"We're sure there's a lot you want to know," Emmanuella says. "Now's your chance to ask."

"And remember," says Chris, "there's no such thing as a stupid question."

"I beg to differ," Nicholas says with his whole chest. Colleen shakes her head at him.

Quinn sets down his utensils. Jumps in first. "Are you the only Santas and Mrs. Clauses there have ever been?"

"Not at all. We're the only ones who've chosen to retire here and take part in the council. There have been many, *many* others who've worked on this mission," says Colleen.

"Where are they now?" I ask.

"Living among the human population. Back in the lives they left to work here," says Yvonne. She holds her patterned, porcelain coffee cup as if she's using it to warm her hands.

"But they remember all of this? And they chose to give it up?" I ask. Slightly stupefied. We've been here less than twenty-four hours, and yet, based upon this croissant alone, I'd never want to leave.

"We don't wipe their memories or anything like that," Samson says. His plate is overflowing with protein. He pops a crispy slice of bacon into his mouth. "What would be the point? Who would believe them if they said they spent the last x number of years in the North Pole?"

"But doesn't this whole place run on belief?" Quinn asks. He's probably thinking of *Elf*.

Ashley lets out a loud, dramatic sigh. "That's another movie misconception." She's acting like we received a handbook and didn't read it.

"What she means," Colleen says, far more nicely, "is that belief in Santa does not fuel the magic here. Love does. Love among the human population, love between nations, and perhaps most importantly, the love shared between Santa and his wif— I mean, *significant other.*"

I swallow thickly. Not because of her near slipup. But because Quinn and I are wading through a rough patch. This move doesn't automatically erase that. Could we cause more chaos by being here than we already have?

"A struggle for our last Santa and Mrs. C, that's for sure," says Chris. Which begins a whole other conversation about our predecessors, their marital mishaps, and their disgraceful exit.

"The magic sure got that selection wrong," Jorge jokes.

"I'm keeping that pair of shorts Christa sewed for me at the top of my drawer just in case!" Chris says.

Yvonne playfully rolls her eyes. "I saw more of your thighs over those three days than I have in a decade!"

"Now that they've both returned to their old lives, I wish for a quick and mess-free separation," says Colleen, the only one not smiling. "Some people simply aren't meant for one another and our mission. That's nothing to laugh at."

The group appears chastened, and now it feels rude to ask any follow-up questions about the man and woman who were living in the chalet only a day or so ago.

Quinn must sense this, too, because he instead asks, "Who knows about the North Pole? Aside from you all and the other Santas."

"Everyone who needs to know," Nicholas says. He's clearly the authoritative compass of this group. He reminds me a little too much of my dad. But I'll try to look past it for the sake of my success here. "World leaders, safety organizations, toy manufacturers. For the most part, we're an open secret."

"People chalk our operation up to one of those weird, unexplainable phenomena," says Samson. He's cleaned his plate already. "Oh, there's a fast-moving shiny object soaring through the sky on Christmas Eve? I must've hit the eggnog too hard at the family party."

"Oh, there are presents under the tree for my daughter that I didn't buy for her? My husband must've gotten them, signed them 'From Santa,' and forgot to tell me," Emmanuella adds.

"It's the kind of thing people have strong inklings about but rarely discuss for fear of sounding ridiculous," Yvonne says.

"Like ghosts or UFOs," adds Ashley.

"Are those things—"

She hits me with a firm stare. "Not our circus. Not our monkeys."

I nod in understanding. Colleen cuts in, "This is all to say that we are a well-oiled, magical machine. A system of checks and balances. By no means will all responsibility fall on the two of you. We just want to get you up to speed as quickly as possible before everyone gets back to work on New Year's Day. We want you to be able to explore, relax, reset, and enjoy your new home for the next year."

I look to Quinn, who is already staring at me. Through only eye contact, we come to an immediate understanding.

If we're going to make it work here, we have to make us work too, stat!

23

A VERY MERRY MAKEOVER

QUINN

"How does this fit?" asks a kindly elf named Christa with long black hair and bubbly cheeks. She finishes adjusting a pair of red suspenders attached to fleece-lined jeans over an off-white Henley, the top two buttons undone. I've been fitted into a pair of weatherproof snow boots with little pompoms hanging off the laces. The whole ensemble is giving Lands' End but make it gay.

I pivot in the mirror. "Fits well. Comfortable but practical." I know this style. Half my days were spent covered in chalk dust or Elmer's glue, so I dressed for efficiency, not fashion. Palatability, not self-expression. A staggering shift from the fun patterns, bright colors, and genderless articles I donned in college.

When Colleen brought up this shopping trip, I didn't feel comfortable, in front of the whole table, saying that I actually felt bold and confident in the outfit I cobbled together from the old closet. It was upcycled but still cute. However, Pat and I are here to be together, not for me to rock the boat like Mrs. Hargrave suggested at Mr. Hargrave's birthday party some years ago, so I'm taking all of Christa's designs and suggestions with a nod and a gracious smile.

We've been at this boutique for over an hour now. It's a small shop with a Parisian sensibility, almost like I've stepped onto the set of a period drama. The clothes are decidedly modern, and the speakers play Ariana Grande's Christmas album at a dull roar. I'll have to get used to year-round Christmas music. Because here it's not "Christmas" music. It's just "music."

Yvonne and Colleen sit on a semicircular velvet couch behind me, chiming in with their two cents. It's all very bride-to-be in a wedding dress shop, and I don't mind it. I welcome it, even.

My own mom didn't come to my wedding tuxedo fitting, even though I asked her to, multiple times. Instead, she told me to send her pictures and she'd text her thoughts to me. At the tailor, Patrick and I had picked out matching vibrant turquoise numbers, got measured for them, and put down our deposit, only for Mom to text me hours after we'd already gotten home with: **The color washes you out too much. Try something else.**

I didn't even tell Patrick. I just slunk into our bedroom and took a depression nap.

"Let's transition into evening wear," Christa says. Her assistants scurry off with the rolling rack of clothes, swapping it out for one with more blazers, ties, and slacks.

"Will I be needing a lot of that?" I ask, picking up the complimentary mug of hot cider the designer set out for me on a tray beside the accordion mirror. I'm careful not to dribble any cider on these luxurious digs.

"Absolutely," Yvonne says. "You're stepping into a highly visible position. You are one-half of the face of this massive mission—to spread joy and cheer to the entire world. How you dress will set the tone for how our village feels about that mission for the next year."

An exhale whips out of me. "Sounds like a lot of pressure."

"It's more fun than anything else," Colleen is quick to say.

"We're thrilled that you're here," Yvonne adds. "These positions often choose people who need them most."

"Don't you mean people who need them most *choose* the positions?" I ask.

She shakes her head, smirking to herself. "It doesn't quite work like that. We're not posting on job boards or checking out LinkedIn profiles. Your circumstances may be different, but we're certain it will all work out."

I want to ask what she means, but Christa is back and ushering me behind the saloon-style doors of the changing room. On the hanging hook, her assistant has set up a deep brown suit with a lighter brown shirt beneath, the buttons of which look like bright red gumdrops. Upon closer inspection, they *are* gumdrops. "How delightful," I say to myself before licking the sugar off my finger.

Once I change and look at myself in the mirror, I've transformed into a grown gingerbread person. There are even molasses-colored spats that go over the dress shoes with gumdrop detailing. A licorice bow tie finishes the look.

"Oh, the elves will *love* you in this! Especially for when you judge the Annual Gingerbread House Competition."

"Judging a competition? What exactly will I be doing as the Merriest Mister?" I ask.

Yvonne stands and helps herself to some candied pecans from a decorative bowl. "It's pretty relaxed and open-ended for the most part. You'll be expected to be a face and a host, give speeches now and then."

I'm used to speaking in front of seven-year-olds, not a slew of adults looking to me as some beacon of holiday cheer. "Is there going to be formal training on how to do this job?"

"Don't think of it as a job. Think of it as a *calling*."

Wasn't Patrick always saying that teaching was my calling?

I believed that, too, most of the time, yet ever since September, I'd been itching to hang up the call, cut the cord, shut down the line, whatever necessary to make the emergency ringtone stop blaring every second of every day.

Despite that, I'm going to miss doing it. Parts of it, anyway.

"No training necessary," Colleen says. This eases my mind. "It's intuitive. Patrick will be brought up to speed on the Santa of it all. You'll have a daily itinerary delivered each morning over breakfast. The first half of the year will be busier than the second, but you're mostly free to explore passions, read books, whatever your heart desires."

"Wow," I say, trying not to move too much as Christa works

on pinning the hem of my pants. They need to be taken up half an inch so I don't trip. I'm more torso than legs. Though I'd prefer something flowier, I don't think it's my place to have an opinion, so I keep my mouth shut except to say thank you when appropriate.

"I'm sure it'll be a nice break from teaching," Colleen says, almost as if she had been reading my mind a second ago.

"For sure. I honestly don't think I've had a break like that since before I went away to college. Becoming a teacher was a lot of work and being a teacher came with workloads even over the summer. Frankly, I'm not sure I know how to relax anymore." My mind has an average speed of a million thoughts per minute.

"Oh, it's a quick study. Trust me," Yvonne says, paired with a bursting laugh. "Chris and I worked in high-profile real estate before Chris became Santa. I thought I'd spend my life working sixty-to-seventy-hour weeks, chasing the rush of a sale and that hefty commission, and when we first got here, the lackadaisical pace of life jarred me, but I settled in. I learned to be present for the first time in my life at forty-three."

"You're never too old for that lesson," Colleen says sagely. "Look at me. Nicholas became Claus in his sixties not long after we lost our son in a motorcycle accident."

"Oh, I'm so sorry to hear that," I say, catching her somber eyes in the mirror.

"It was many years ago now," she says before taking a big breath. "But something like that could've torn us apart. You know, ravaged our relationship with grief. Instead, it brought us closer together. Then, by chance and magic, we ended up here. Our relationship grew stronger as we adapted to our new surroundings. Bringing Christmas joy to the world helped us heal."

"For me and Chris," Yvonne says after giving Colleen's story the due respect and space it deserves, "it was about slowing down. We didn't know until we got here that Chris's blood pressure was in dangerous territory. He was one more listing away from a heart attack. This job helped us put all that high-stress nonsense behind us."

I consider both stories, and these kind women who have chosen to be vulnerable and open with me simply because I'm filling a role they once held. "Thanks for sharing that. I wonder what this will be for me and Patrick."

Part of me wants to be honest with them, tell them about the rough patch we haven't even begun sanding down yet. But what if I tell them and they cast us out? They said the last pair in these positions weren't meant to be together and weren't meant for this mission. What if they decide that about us, too?

I don't want to create unnecessary worry. I'm pretty sure Patrick and I understand each other. Being here is about being us again.

"Time will tell," Colleen says almost too-knowingly.

"For now, let's focus on how *fabulous* you look in that suit! Christa, you've absolutely outdone yourself." Yvonne snaps in appreciation.

I take stock of my reflection. Only one day in to this new, bizarre reality and my shoulders are at least an inch lower than they were on the final day of school before winter break. I stood in the staff bathroom, washing my hands, and couldn't help but notice, in the reflection of the scratched-up mirror, how dark the bags were under my eyes. I was a zombie.

Just knowing I won't be returning to lesson plans or field trips, angry parent emails or longer-than-necessary faculty meetings seems to have made all the difference in my demeanor. I'm grateful for that quick yet massive change.

THE KEYS TO THE CASTLE

PATRICK

The toy workshop is a ghost town.

"The elves won't return to work until January second, so over these next few days you'll have a ton of time to get familiar with your new workplace," says Samson as we venture along a catwalk that goes around the perimeter of the main floor. It's a candy-colored wonderland of production machines I couldn't name if I tried.

During the tour, I try to silence my inner architect who is commenting on everything. The space is huge, but still somehow cramped. The walkways are cluttered with carts and boxes.

In the present-wrapping room, ribbons are left hanging lifeless off spools for anyone to trip over. Scraps of patterned wrapping paper are piled high on tables. One wrong swing of a fan and the whole organization system would scatter to the wind.

The workflow in the workshop overall could use some serious fixing up. I already have seventeen design ideas to make this place more efficient. However, I decide now is not the time to share them with the Priors. It's my first day. Overstepping would be a bad look.

In the garage where the sleighs are kept, Jorge, a former mechanic, talks me through the ins and outs of maintenance.

Next, we enter the vaults where the Naughty and Nice lists are locked away in hard copy to be transferred to digital. They are explained, in great detail, by Chris. He even takes us into a heavily secured room—they call it North Pole Headquarters—where there's a holographic projection of the globe and a series of monitors and tablets that control it. Little red and green lights blink on and off at various intervals.

"You can look up any person from any part of the world here. We use this for Naughty and Nice disputes. We have special-mission elves go out into the human world, and we can view their feeds from here. We also use these records for vetting our next Santa," Chris says.

"Santas who don't come to the position through frying pans," jokes Samson.

"This is all a little Big Brother, no?" I ask. I'm more than a bit creeped out by the whole *he sees you when you're sleeping* song and dance.

The four of them blink back at me with apparent confusion over my reference. I tell them to ignore me and carry on.

Samson relishes detailing the production process of different toys when we enter Toy Maker Tower. As a former floor manager at a beer company, he's a self-proclaimed "how the sausage gets made" kind of guy. "As you can tell, we've got toys coming out the wazoo."

"There *are* a lot of toys in here," I say of what must be the left-over dolls and bicycles and block sets.

"No, this baby," Samson says, slapping a metallic funnel that's connected to a bunch of colorful pipes that line the ceiling, "is called a wazoo. Toys, when they're finished, come out of here."

I stifle a laugh when I realize he's serious.

It's all interesting and I'm learning a lot, while remaining in awe of how this building could combine so many levels and architectural styles and still *work*. Usually grafts have a somewhat clunky quality to them. You leave one wing, enter another, and it's like you've time-jumped into an entirely different decade. Not here. The workshop is a feat of magic. In more ways than the literal.

The final stop on my introductory tour is Santa's—*my*—office. It has the same stately, looming doors that the cathedral hall has, except when these are pushed open a more relaxed vibe greets me. There's a stone fireplace to my left, which is roaring already. Above it are the large golden initials: sc.

In front of me there are shelves and shelves of books and ledgers with weathered leather spines. To the right, there is an impressive cherry wood desk behind which a big circular window overlooks the main work floor.

This is a big upgrade from the tiny desk I had at Carver & Associates. The air in here is charged with importance. My nostrils are graced with that cinnamon-sweet scent that has followed me everywhere since I first donned the cloak.

The finger-tingle I'm still not accustomed to returns tenfold.

"This is where the magic happens," says Samson. He sits down in one of the brown leather chairs in front of the fireplace.

"By magic, he means the magic of Christmas. This is your domain," Chris says. He gives me an encouraging pat on the back.

"For the next year," Nicholas is swift to add. I can't tell if his gruffness is directed toward me or this is his natural demeanor. Seems antithetical to the glimmery magic that is the North Pole and the position he once held. "This is a trial run. Santas can quit at will, but they can also be let go at will as well, should they not be performing their duties in a way that is satisfactory to the council and to the elves."

His warning is a hard punch to the still-healing bruise of my recent firing.

Jorge leans in for a theatrical whisper. "Buuuuuuut, that has never actually happened before."

"The firing part. Not the quitting part. As you witnessed, the quitting part has happened," Samson says. He kicks his feet up on a rustic wooden coffee table. It's got rough, unfinished edges.

"As we learned on Christmas Eve, there is a first time for everything," Nicholas says, his tone harsh. He's staring out the circular window. "We can't afford any more shake-ups. This place, and our mission, are too important. Do I make myself clear?"

"Perfectly," I say. I train my expression into submission even though I hate being treated like a child or an underling. But I'm willing to prove my worth.

Jorge waves a hand. "While Nicholas is definitely right, this is also fun. It's unlike any other job you'll ever have."

"However, there is the matter of the rules and paperwork," Nicholas says. From a safe hidden behind a portrait of the first-ever Santa—not shockingly also named Nicholas—he produces a golden, glittery parchment scroll, a feather pen, and a glass well of ink. "As mentioned when we met, you will reside at the North Pole for the duration of the year, you will perform all your duties to the best of your ability including the Christmas night flight, and you will lead with love always. No exceptions."

I nod. "I understand. This seems like a lot, though, for one year."

"The legacy of a true Santa is not how long he serves, but the mark he makes while he does." Nicholas's conviction shocks the whole room to attention.

"That makes sense." I'm overwhelmed with a single thought: *I don't want to let them down.*

"Good." His dark eyes pierce through me. "Sign here."

I take the quill and ink my name onto the contract. It glows brightly for a second before the scroll snaps itself shut. Nicholas stores it away once more. It all feels a bit like Ariel giving up her voice for legs. Am I going to regret this?

"Now that the business is taken care of . . ." Jorge begins. He practically skips across the room toward a door I hadn't noticed before. "Let's get to the good stuff."

"We got you a little belated Christmas gift!" Chris exclaims. All together, they roll a large object out from the artfully concealed door.

It's a finely crafted, dark-stained oak drafting table with turn-of-the-century detailing. It has an adjustable angle mechanism. Chris brings out the matching stool. Both pieces fit in magnificently with the design aesthetic of the room, which is an important touch in my book.

"A little welcome present from us to you," says Samson, smiling. As if welcoming me to a brotherhood I didn't even know I was aching to be a part of.

"It's incredible. I don't think I've ever owned one this nice before." I run my hand along the surface and feel the pencil grooves. "Thank you."

"Moving and becoming Santa can be an adjustment, so we wanted you to be able to continue your passion for architecture here," Jorge says, stroking his black beard.

"When you're not performing your Santa duties," Nicholas says.

Samson snickers at this. He's clearly the most immature of the council, and I assume he's the youngest as well. Nicholas hits him with a disapproving scowl, and he shuts up quickly.

"On that note, we're going to leave you alone," Chris says. He corrals them all toward the door we came in from. "Explore, redecorate. The bell button on the main desk connects you to Hobart, wherever he may be, if you need him."

"By the way, go easy on Hobart," Jorge says. "He's new as well and highly skilled, but he's maybe too eager for his own good."

"Deluded by ideas of grandeur is more like it," scoffs Nicholas.

"Never mind any of that," Chris says. "Take it in. This is all yours now."

All mine now. A week ago, I was a slow-turning cog working on bathroom partitions at an architecture firm that didn't appreciate me. Days ago, I was unemployed. Currently, I'm the face of a global gift-giving and magic-bringing operation.

This is the promotion of a lifetime.

A PICTURE'S WORTH A THOUSAND WORDS

PATRICK

A MEMORY

I park my car outside Carver & Associates Architecture firm, take a few deep breaths, and then pull down the overhead mirror to check my teeth for leftover spinach from lunch and my hair for flyaways. The person staring back at me is listless. Beaten down already.

There's no chance, if I didn't get any of the last three jobs, that I'm going to get this one at one of the most cutthroat medium-sized architectural design firms in New Jersey.

"Treat this as a learning experience," I tell myself.

In the back seat, there is an itchy-looking Christmas sweater that Quinn picked out for me from an online shop. Since settling into our apartment, Quinn has asked if we can send out joint Christmas cards. He loved those glossy mailers as a kid. I thought they were a little outdated, but what the heck. If it'll make him happy.

Every fiber of my being wishes I felt as cheery as the red-and-green knit sweater suggests I am. After this, I'll drive over to the Christmas tree farm, throw it on, and pretend I'm not barreling toward professional ruin.

The firm is inside one of those cookie-cutter, modern, glass-and-steel buildings with open offices. I check in at the main desk and wait my turn in the sleek black chair, until ten minutes later, a tall dark-skinned man comes over to greet me.

He extends a hand. "Patrick? My name is Jason. You're interviewing to fill my previous position. Follow me."

He leads me down a long, imposing corridor. Heads turn up in my direction. "Any tips?"

"Don't be shy, make strong eye contact, and be prepared to say you're a team player at least five times. He loves that." Jason speaks to me like he's a confidant. I appreciate that. Most other places I've been to over the last several months, the exchanges with current employees have been fast and formal.

"I'm a team player. Got it." I smile my thanks his way. "Wait, *he*?"

Jason doesn't answer before he thrusts me through a door. In the room is Calvin Carver, the head of the operation, and no one else. The air-conditioning is on blast even though it's November. I shiver. Vacillating from cold to clammy then back again.

What is he doing here? At no point in my job hunt have I had any face-to-face time with the senior principal. I'm newly nauseated.

We exchange greetings and pleasantries before he says, "I'm going to cut to the chase. I'm impressed with you."

I blink to give myself time. Make sure I heard him correctly. "Thank you, sir."

"Drop the *sir*. Call me Mr. Carver." He leans back in his chair, and it creaks. He's got my portfolio spread out across his desk. The draft on top is a special one I've been working on for Quinn. On nights I can't sleep, I sneak out to the kitchen and sketch up our dream home. The apartment is nice for now. But I want a place for Quinn and me to stake forever in. "I've heard nothing but glowing things about you from my colleagues, and I can see why." He waves the sketch.

Pride grows in my belly. "I hope this interview proves that I live up to the hype."

And it must, because twenty minutes later, Mr. Carver offers me the firmest handshake I've ever had in my life and, much to my disbelief, the job.

By the time I find Quinn at the Christmas tree farm where we're taking our photos, I'm a piñata ready to burst. I race toward him, lift him off the ground, and spin him in a circle. My excitement is too big for my six-foot-one frame.

"I got it," I say into his hair. "I got it." The relief washes over me.

He leans back, eyes wide and smile wider. "Wow! Congrats, Pat!"

I kiss him before he can say anything else. It's a long-lasting kiss that makes the world melt away.

Until someone taps my shoulder.

"Sorry to intrude on this heartwarming scene, but I have to get home to walk my dog within the hour so if we could get this party started . . ." I turn to find a medium-height woman with curly, dark hair wearing black glasses, a matching knit hat, and an oversized hoodie that says OAKWOOD ELEMENTARY SCHOOL. A bulky camera is hanging from a thick strap that's slung around her neck.

"Patrick, this is Veronica. Veronica is a teacher at the school I'm student teaching at, and frankly, my saving grace." I give her an overly familiar hug even though I just met her because it's that time of year and I'm in such a good mood.

It's early in the holiday season, not even Thanksgiving yet, so the place is mostly empty. We go in search of the perfect spot with the best lighting to take our picture.

For the next hour, as we pose, it feels like a stone has been craned off my chest. I don't need to worry how I'm going to pay my part of the rent for the apartment I convinced Quinn to go in on with me.

Our home can be happy again.

That night, Quinn pops open a bottle of champagne he had hidden in the back of the fridge. The gesture is sweet. The bubbly is tart.

Quinn retires to the couch with his full glass to scroll through card templates on his laptop, while I sit at the kitchen table and feverishly draft again. I return to the bones of the house Calvin Carver complimented. I set out to create a magical place just for us. To grow and love and simply be.

"Come here," Quinn says from his perch on the couch. "How does it look?"

He's dropped the best photo into a template with a snowy forest scene and Santa's sleigh up in the sky in silhouette. "It looks great," I say. I lean my elbows on the back of the couch. I get a whiff of Quinn's coconut-scented shampoo. "We look really happy."

He peers back at me. "I *am* really happy."

I wrap my arms around his shoulders, kiss the crown of his head, and watch as he sends our first-ever Christmas cards off to the printer.

IT'S ALL UPHILL FROM HERE

QUINN

363 DAYS 'TIL CHRISTMAS

The chalet, like Patrick's cloak, is enchanted.

By the time we traipse downstairs—up with the sun and rested more than ever despite the hour—the coffee is brewed, the toast is made and buttered, and *The North Pole Gazette* is laid out on the table, ready to be read.

"Did Hobart do this?" Patrick asks.

"I don't think so," I say, nodding toward a cabinet to the left of the ginormous sink. It opens itself. Down float two mugs. The coffeepot up and pours itself. Somehow, the chalet even knows how we take our coffee—oat milk creamer for me, just two spoonfuls of sugar for Pat.

"I could get used to this," I say, despite the goose bumps appearing on my arms, as my plate fills itself. Patrick laughs, eyes trained on the candles spotted across the half-circle, light-wood island that hides the stovetop. "What are you doing?"

"Waiting for the candlestick to start singing." He hums the tune of "Be Our Guest" as our plates land on the table and we sit down to eat.

A whole day stretches out before us, and after a meal and a bit of exploring, I find a gear room full of skis and snowboards. There are cubbies with waterproof boots, helmets, and goggles of varying sizes and colors. Three walls have a fold-down bench.

The last wall is a painted map of the North Pole. We can go skiing right from here if we want to.

When Patrick pokes his head in, he smiles. "It's not Switzerland, but . . ." He's referencing our set-aside plans for a wintery honeymoon at the end of a swampy New Jersey summer. I couldn't be happier with how this is turning out. Without showering, we gear up and glide out.

The day is cold but not cutting, especially through our many layers of brand-new ski apparel. Intermittent flurries of snow trickle down from a light gray sky.

If I squint, between the charcoal clouds that look like eraser smudges, the shimmery edge of this pocket universe can be seen. It's probably some force field that protects the North Pole and contains its magic.

For a moment, claustrophobia weasels around in my chest—Patrick *signed* a scroll, there's no leaving here until the year is up—but then Patrick takes my gloved hand as we wait for the chairlift to stop at our location and take us the rest of the way up to the start of the slopes.

There are some early-riser elves already whizzing down the corduroy snow. They swoop by as we take our seats and latch ourselves in for the slow ascent. I grow antsy as we climb. Heights still are not my favorite, but Patrick's arm around me and this everpresent cloud of golden glitter reassures me.

I reach out and poke one of the particles. It bobs and sways as if doing a choreographed dance alongside the sprinkling of snowflakes. "Are you worried at all about what the council said about the magic during our first breakfast?" I ask, thinking back on what I almost told Colleen and Yvonne.

"Which part?" Patrick asks.

"About the magic being powered by love, especially *ours*." As I say it, it's almost like the magic responds. It moves faster, more frenzied.

"Should I be? I think our love is pretty pure." He runs his chin along my head, making my hat bunch a bit and create static against my locks.

"Pure, sure. But strong?" I knock our knees together, so my question doesn't sound as weighty as it might've otherwise. "Ever since we got engaged, I feel like our life glitched and we got stuck on fast-forward."

A November engagement, a June wedding, and by the dog days of summer we were homeowners. I barely had time to catch my breath.

"How do you mean?" Patrick wears his thinking face—eyes squinted and unblinking, chin cocked back. It's the same expression he wears when he's primed in front of his drafting table.

"I mean, I can't remember the last time we weren't planning an event or touring a house or working nonstop." I zip my lips after that last one. It sounded accusatory when I didn't mean it to be. It's not like I don't grade papers while we catch up on reality TV shows. It's not like I haven't canceled my fair share of dates because of last-minute meetings.

"You definitely don't need to be worried about that last one once we leave here." Patrick closes his eyes, tilts his head back, and lets out a low, frustrated exhale through his nose.

"Are you ready to tell me what happened?" I ask, wishing I didn't still feel hurt over him withholding this. But hurt doesn't play by my rules. It never has.

"I messed up big-time." He rips off his beanie and runs a hand through his hair. A few uncooperative strands fall back down over his face, obscuring his eyes, making him look wounded and boyish. "I took on a project outside of work for the money. Kacey needed a new cutting-edge space for her nonprofit. I accidentally made copies of Kacey's project for that meeting about bathrooms and toilet partitions. Moonlighting is, shall we say, frowned upon at Carver & Associates."

"You didn't tell me about Kacey." It comes out as redundant. I close some of the gap between us on the bench.

"I didn't want you to worry."

"Patrick," I say, voice taking on a breathless quality. My heart is ramping up like a freight train gaining speed. "I'm your husband. It's my job to worry about you."

"I know," he says. "I know. I meant needlessly worry. I thought I could keep it under wraps. We needed that extra money to turn that house you hate into some semblance of a home."

My words come back to bite me in the ass. "I don't hate it. Not exactly."

"It's okay if you do. It's not my favorite place, either. With all those loose boards and all that cracked molding and the noisy pipes," he says. It's a relief to hear him be honest about it.

I brighten. "I'm glad you think so, too. Well, not glad, I mean. But— Gah, I thought it was just me for a while." I think back to watching *Elf* alone. Just one instance in a string of broken plans that seemingly could've led to broken vows.

The divots between Patrick's eyebrows etch deeper with equal parts care and concern. "Quinn, it's never just you. That's what our rings mean. Always in this together."

I take that to heart, nodding. "Can we make a promise?"

"We already made the biggest one there is." His wedding ring glints in the filtered sunlight.

"Right." I shake my head. "I meant more of a smaller promise." I don't know why my hands grow clammy all of a sudden. It's too cold for that, and I'm too old for these kinds of nerves with my own husband.

"What kind of promise were you thinking?" he asks.

I toy with one of the toggles on my coat with a free hand, heart pitter-pattering. "A promise to really be together here. Not let anything get in the way of us."

"Of course."

"And I want to go on dates again! God, when's the last time we went on a real date? We're too young to be this boring," I say, suspiciously sounding like Mom, which, I don't love, but the sentiments are true regardless.

"I wouldn't say moving to the North Pole with a day's notice is boring, but I'm on board with dates. I would love that." Patrick's cheeks lift; they have a newfound rosiness to them. "I'm sorry if I've let my focus wander. I just want to provide for you the best I can."

I pat his knee. "I don't need you to provide for me. I just need you to be with me, okay?"

Ever since the clothing boutique, I've been thinking a lot about what Yvonne and Colleen spoke about, how the North Pole served to smooth over a potential rift on the horizon of their relationships.

While Patrick and I haven't suffered through anything as unbelievably difficult as the death of a child or a near heart attack, I could see our mountainous mortgage, the fast-tracking of our life, being akin to what Ashley shared with me over tea: how Samson was an overnight manager at a warehouse before all this, which meant they always worked opposing shifts. He was sleeping while she was working and vice versa. Two ships, and all that.

"Okay. I'm with you, Quinn," Patrick says, tugging me back to the moment.

"Good, because I'm going to need you to be *with me* as we embark down this mountain," I say, noticing our chairlift is about to arrive at the station. "It's been a hot minute since I've skied."

After the bar lifts away in front of us, Patrick helps me down with a promise. "Don't worry. I got you."

For hours, we forget about our real life, which feels more like a dream than this does. The more times I fly down the slope, wind cresting across the exposed parts of my face, the more tension jettisons away like the snow off the blades of my skis.

The poles in my hands give me power. Patrick beside me, even at this speed, gives me reassurance.

Emmanuella and Jorge appear around midday with hugs and skis of their own. Jorge asks if we want to try a bigger slope—the North Pole's version of a black diamond. I pass. This ride is already winding me. Emmanuella offers to stay behind with me.

"How's the chalet treating you?" Emmanuella asks, a hint of knowingness tinged in her voice.

"Those enchanted appliances. They're something," I say as we wait our turn.

"Right? Us Priors go back to the mortal life after we step down, but you never forget that taste of magic."

I consider this for a second. "Can you tell me more about the magic?"

Her eyes take on an otherworldly sparkle. "You've come to the right Prior. I live for the history of this place. The lore of the land is that there was once a man named Nicholas—not our Nicholas, a different one, but a similar look." She lets out a light, airy laugh. "This Nicholas was benevolent and rich and gave secret gifts to those in need. He believed in the good of humanity and his love for humanity was so strong that it manifested into abundant magical powers. He didn't know how to use those powers, though, so he went in search of someone who did. That's how he found the elves, a magical, immortal people living at the top of the world who accepted him, taught him, and believed in his mission."

"The elves have magic, too?" I ask.

"They do. It's smaller and more practical magic. The kind that makes everyday tasks easier. Not the kind that can deliver presents all over the world in a single night. They had never seen magic like Nicholas's before."

"Makes sense."

"At some point in Nicholas's long life, he fell in love with a woman. That new love in his life made the powers he possessed grow even stronger. Toward the end of his life, he knew he needed to put this immeasurable magic somewhere, so it didn't die alongside him, and his mission could continue after he was gone."

"The enchanted cloak," I say.

She nods. "It started with the cloak. But there was still magic left, so he made a house on the mountainside. But there was still magic left, so he cast a protective spell around the elves' village. But there was still magic left . . . Do you see where I'm going with this?" she asks as we inch closer to the edge of the mountain.

"I think so."

"Before he died, he went in search of a couple just like him and his beloved. A couple that had made the ultimate commitment of marriage and had a love so strong that it could power the world if need be. He moved them to the village, bonded them with the magic, and had them work alongside the elves. They wrote up by-laws and made provisions and this place has been operating ever since," she says, ending our history lesson by pulling down her ski goggles. "You and Patrick are the next chapter in a long evolution of age-old magic."

"That sounds intense."

"It is," she says with a throwaway laugh before speeding off down the mountain.

When we've had enough, we return to the chalet and strip out of our clothes. We both had a few embarrassing falls at the start, so there are maps of bluish bruises connecting like vines up our sides. We decide to soak our aching bodies in the hot tub.

In search of a swimsuit, I find my closet has been overhauled. Gone are most of the antique red velvet pieces, and in their place hang chic suits, pointy-toed boots with low, sensible heels, and a colorful assortment of shirts. There's a pair of five-inch-seam trunks in candy-apple red folded neatly on a shelf in the back.

Champagne is already uncorked and sitting on the counter when we enter the kitchen. Bubbles swim to the top of two glisten-ing flutes. We take them out back where two plush towels lie over a heated rack. Steam billows off the top of the tub, which has lights inside it that shine, pink and lovely.

Submerging, I let out a relaxed sigh. "Now this place is *really* giving *The Bachelor*."

"The coveted hot-tub date," Patrick says with a chortle.

We sit on opposite sides of the sizable tub. Water gurgles between us but we can still hear each other. Our eyes meet over the spray. "In an alternate universe, where we hadn't met at Penderton, and you're the hotshot architect chosen as the season lead and I'm just Quinn Muller, elementary school teacher from New Jersey, would I make it to the final rose ceremony?"

I surprise even myself with the question. Not that I haven't been pondering it for some months now. There was something off about the way our engagement shook out, how quickly we wed afterward, as if we were racing against a clock I couldn't see.

"Without a doubt," he says, slipping off his seat and wading through the water toward me. His wide chest is gleaming with droplets of pink-tinted water. The shimmer effect catches in his eyes, making them even more stunning. "No matter the universe, I'd pick you."

"Good answer," I say as the space diminishes between us.

"It's the only answer," he says, the tips of our noses now touching. "Because it's the truth."

If I weren't so entrapped by his eyes, I might see that, around us, it's begun to snow. Instead, I only feel the flakes as they land gently on the exposed crests of my shoulders, stick, and melt into my damp hair. Even so, those sensations are quickly usurped by Patrick kissing me, the decadent press of his lips into mine.

It's not until I pull away to steal a shaky breath that I notice, intermingled with the large, fluffy snowflakes, golden orbs skitter around as if the magic is cheering us on.

Patrick's knees bracket my hips until our chests are flush and our heartbeats are knocking back and forth on each other's sternums, like a game of tag. My hands dome around Patrick's precious and perfect face. I hold it with reverence. I kiss him with the same.

Rivulets of water sluice down the insides of my forearms. It's like we're washing away any negative emotions, any worries at all.

We make out like we did when we first met, like we're starved for each other. Patrick grinds against my lap and reminds me how desperate I am to be satiated. To be as close to him as possible.

The water ripples around us as Patrick removes his arms from around my neck. "Shall I grab the towels?"

"No," I say firmly. Aware that my voice is not the only firm thing between us. "No time. I need you. I need you so badly and I need you now."

"Take me, Quinn," he says, his arms returning to my neck, his mouth returning to my ear. *"Have me."*

THE RIGHT WORDS

PATRICK

By New Year's Eve, we've exploited every luxury that the chalet has to offer.

We've soaked in the hot tub every evening while watching the northern lights. We've read novels side by side in the well-stocked library. We've stayed up until the wee hours of the morning in our cozy bed talking about regrets, dreams, and everything in between.

In the mornings, we take steaming mugs of coffee and freshly baked cinnamon buns out onto the front deck, sit in separate rocking chairs with warm blankets draped over our legs, and wait for the village to wake up. One by one, lights in the cabins and cottages flick on. Elves emerge from their front doors with greetings for their neighbors. Children sitting in a row on sleds are tugged toward the town square. The clock tower chimes, and a carol plays. Its jingly notes reach all the way up here.

Six days. We got six days of uninterrupted time to celebrate us. Secluded up here in our chalet, we've made love by the fire, reacquainted ourselves with the other's favorite snacks, and, in our screening room, binge-watched all the TV we've been missing out on.

Tonight, we make our first official appearance as Santa and the Merriest Mister at the village's New Year countdown.

The North Pole doesn't have a flashy ball drop. Instead, the elves take the entire day to rest before congregating in the town center beneath the stone clock where the year's Santa gives a rousing speech right before the stroke of midnight.

It's exactly the kind of low-key night I need after nearly a full week of eating delicious food, choreographing ridiculous ice-skating routines to throwback jams at our private ice-skating rink, and writing a speech that will introduce me to the North Pole population as not Patrick Hargrave, but as Santa Patrick.

"Would you read over my speech?" I ask Quinn nervously. I pass him a gorgeous red leather-bound journal with the golden sc insignia stamped on the front. Over the past several days, I've feverishly jotted down notes in there. I think I've strung them together into coherent sentences, but Quinn will be a better judge of that.

Nicholas's words the other day have stuck with me: "The legacy of a true Santa is not how long he serves, but the mark he makes while he does." Those are the words I plan to live by for the next year.

"Figured this was something Hobart would do for you," Quinn notes. He flips through the pages. There are a lot of them. I maybe went a little overboard. I hope he's able to help me patch together the disjointed parts.

I've always been overly attentive to details. I see buildings for their unique parts and not as one monolithic entity. I had a mentor in my architecture program who impressed this on me.

"Every building has a story," he would say. "Every room is a chapter."

That's why I always dreamed that one day when I had the clout and the finances, I'd open Chapters Architecture. Our slogan would be, "Let us help you tell your story."

But obviously, if I couldn't even hack it at someone else's firm, how can I ever go out on my own?

"Oh, Hobart offered," I say. I close my eyes for a second. Start to rock gently. The rhythmic back-and-forth motion soothes me.

Helps me forget about home because this majestic place is "home" for the near future. "Then when I turned down his offer, he insisted. He even tried to suggest I should get you to write it for me. But I really wanted to do this myself. It's their first impression of me as a leader. At Carver & Associates, Calvin gave this big speech at the top of every big project, and you could tell his assistant, Selina, wrote it. We all received enough emails from her but signed by him to know. But nobody said anything. Those empty platitudes felt emptier knowing he hadn't even done the work to write them himself. He was probably off golfing or wining and dining his mistress."

"I had no idea your boss was such a sleaze," Quinn says with a grimace. Probably remembering office parties where he played the consummate spouse. He always entertained my coworkers with cute stories about his students.

I pick up my mug again. "It wasn't even a big firm, yet I felt small there, Quinn." The warmth of the ceramic in my hands serves to keep me grounded. Not let me fall too far into the negative emotions I battled on the daily while working there. Jason was my only ally, but he was further up the ladder than I was. No way was I going to drag him down into the depths with me when I went.

"I'm sorry to hear that." Quinn has his feet on the seat of the chair and his shins angled toward me. He rests his head on his blanket-covered knees and asks, "Why didn't you say anything?"

"What was I supposed to say? The job I've dreamed of having, that I went against my dad to pursue is grinding me down to dust?" I ask. I shrink even from the memory. "I spent five years of intense study to earn my BArch degree. Those six to seven months after I graduated were a slog. Just bad interview after bad interview."

"You were always so positive." Quinn's converged eyebrows project his confusion. "I never figured that was a front."

I bet he never figured that I spent my days, while he was student teaching, playing video games and eating microwave mac and cheese and dithering, either. I should've been networking or adding to my portfolio. But what are you to do when inspiration is a butterfly that's outsmarting your net?

Now I'm not as scared to peel back the layers. Let Quinn see the truth of me. He hasn't run screaming into the mountains to get away from me yet.

"I had to be positive to get through it. I was raised to be." I stand and cross to the railing. For some reason, putting some distance between us makes this all easier to say. "I clung to the idea that it was going to be everything I imagined it to be. Every day, I kept thinking it would get better. It'll be better tomorrow. It'll be better when I'm promoted. It'll be better when I'm partner. It was never better. By the time I realized it wasn't going to get better, I'd gotten us married and sucked into a humongous mortgage."

"It takes two to do both of those things," Quinn says. I appreciate him not letting me bear this weight alone. Even if I was the primary instigator.

"That's true." I press the heels of my hands into my eyes.

Quinn's arms wrap around my torso. So comforting I could cry. But I won't. That's peeling the layers back too far for my liking.

"I wish you'd told me." Quinn's whisper sends a chill through me.

"I didn't have the words until now," I say.

He nods into the meat of my shoulder. "I'm glad you were able to share them with me. Plus, I'm glad you were able to share this with me." He wags the notebook in the air in front of my face. "How about we grab those snowshoes and poles we saw in the gear room, pack a picnic, and hike up one of the trails to the viewpoint? I'll read this there."

I swivel my body around so we're chest to chest. "That sounds perfect." I kiss Quinn because not only are his suggestions perfect, but so is he.

TAKING IN THE VIEW

QUINN

While Patrick is changing his clothes and grabbing the snow-shoes, I pack our picnic. Two medium-sized thermoses of hot cider, two canteens of water, one large thermos of vegetable soup, some bread wrapped up, and some cookies to boot. I slip Patrick's notebook in a front waterproof pocket of my backpack for protection. From a drawer, I nab a red pen for official editing purposes. I only wish I had my scratch-and-sniff stickers with the smiley faces on them to add some positive reinforcement to his work, in a fun way.

The last item I grab is the map of the grounds Hobart left us a few days ago. He explained that every amenity in the chalet was designed by a previous Santa. One Santa was a competitive swimmer, hence the heated Olympic-sized swimming pool. Another Santa loved to hike, so he had trails carved out, marked, and maintained throughout his season, all leading to the best views of the North Pole.

When Patrick comes back in his red flannel, khaki jacket, and tan boots, he looks rugged. I swoon. My husband has always been handsome, but he's even more so now that he was so vulnerable with me out on the porch. I pass him one of the packed bags, and we head out.

Snowshoeing properly requires a kick-step technique. I enjoy the satisfying crunch of the cleated deck that's bound to my boots as it presses into the snow. The crisp sound of spearing my pole in front of me to maintain my balance adds to the harmonious song.

It takes a half hour to reach our destination, but once we're there, the view is too spectacular to begrudge the sweat beading beneath my knit hat.

The village, from this vantage point, looks even more like a miniature, and a light, sporadic flurry has started giving it the appearance of a snow globe come to life.

We lay out a blanket in the snow and unpack our provisions. Patrick goes straight for the soup. I grab a piece of bread, his notebook, and my pen.

I nestle inside Patrick's words. He always says he's better at drawing, and in the years I've loved him, I know that to be true, but his mind is far more beautiful than he gives it credit for. Sentences jump out at me like: *Christmas has always had a special place in my heart, so I hope you'll welcome me into yours while we work together.*

My red pen hovers over the sentence. From someone else's mouth, it could be cheesy, but coming from Patrick, his sincerity will bleed from the statement. He's earnest to a fault. I bite back a smile, eyes flicking up and over to Patrick, who is pretending not to watch my every move while he leisurely eats the soup.

"I read slower when you're staring at me." It's mostly a joke, but I have always been sort of incapacitated by Patrick's steely blue eyes. Their intensity is one of the first things I noticed about him when we met.

He shrugs, peers into the thermos of soup. "Read as slow as you want. We've got all the time in the world."

I love that. All the time in the world. In New Jersey, it always feels like the clock is conspiring against me. Not enough minutes in the school day to finish all my lessons. Not enough hours in the evening to spend quality time with Patrick. Here, time is our ally.

I go back to reading. He goes back to his soup.

I make light grammar and line edits. I suggest some reordering of paragraphs, and I adopt his voice to add some transitional language that will tie it all together with a neat bow. "It's really great," I say, passing the notebook back.

"Are you sure?" he asks.

"I wouldn't lie to you." I realize that sounds bad given what came before this, but if he flinches, I don't catch it. Besides, he didn't exactly lie. He withheld the truth. Knowing what I know now, they're not as similar as I assumed.

One page at a time, he digests my notes. "Will you miss it? Teaching?" The question surprises me.

"Like a toothache." It's not entirely true, so I don't know why I said it, or specifically said it like that.

"Has it really been that bad?" The notebook is closed now. There's no dodging the conversation. His tone is too serious and his conviction too strong.

"No. Not exactly." I reach for a cookie even though I haven't had my lunch. "I'll miss my students a lot and my classroom. I'll miss the organization of my days. I won't miss the administrator observations or the microaggressions."

"Microaggressions?" The werewolf of Patrick's protectiveness rips up to the surface.

"No need to get excited. It's nothing," I say, not fully buying it myself but wanting his alpha mode to go back into remission. "Right before winter break, they asked me to take down the photo of us on our wedding day, so I did."

"What? That's not nothing." He closes the soup and repositions onto his knees. "We got engaged in front of your students. Nobody batted an eyelash then."

"Yeah, different year, different students, different parents. Besides, those are the drama kids. The parents who enroll their kids in the arts know what's up." I don't need confirmation to know that the parent or parents who complained were the same ones who commented on my Pride flag at back-to-school night, the ones who regarded me with iciness during parent-teacher conferences, as if my queerness or diverse book choices were the reason their child was reading below the state standard level.

I try to do right by everyone who walks through the door of my classroom, no matter their age or their intellect, and yet, I don't feel that being reciprocated, especially by adults who should know better.

Patrick's nostrils flare. "You should've texted me when it happened."

"You were at work," I say, then regret it because I know now that he wasn't, but that's not the point at present. "Never mind. It wasn't a big deal. I took it down. I didn't want you to feel the need to—I don't know—defend the sanctity of our union or something. It wasn't that deep."

He drops off his knees with a plop. "It sounds pretty deep to me."

I've clearly offended him, so I reach out to touch his shoulder. "Pat, I'm sorry. I would've told you, it's just—" *I didn't know how to bring it up without catastrophizing the whole thing and breaking down in tears from the stress and the grind,* I think, but instead say, "I just don't need more battles to fight in my life right now."

He moves away from my touch. "You took it down. Doesn't sound like you fought the battle at all."

I hate that he's picking this argument right now. Even more, I hate that he's mostly right. Mrs. Birch has a photo of her and her husband hung up in the music room. Nobody says anything to her. Mine was in a frame on my desk, facing me. But I don't press the subject because the simple fact is that: "I'm not a fight-the-power kind of person," I say.

"Positive change is worth the fight," Patrick says simply. "Will you promise me you'll at least consider putting it back up when we get back?"

"Maybe."

"Quinn, your students need a good example of unconditional love because you know if their parents have a problem with a *picture,* the love they're getting at home is anything but."

"Seriously never say you're bad with words again." I shove his shoulder, amazed at how perceptive he is. How a change of scenery has already unlocked this poet inside of him. "Tonight's going to be amazing. You're going to crush your speech. Let's focus on that for now, okay?" He nods, tentatively, tapping his gloved fingers on the spine of his notebook. "Have a gingersnap. They're delicious."

Patrick accepts the cookie with a smile.

We stay out for another few hours, enjoying the view and the fresh air. Our conversation is more periodic, but lighter in tone and flirtier in nature. Patrick draws in his notebook. I crack open the paperback I tucked into my bag—a collection of Christmas-themed short stories by literary greats. It's nice to be reading something for pleasure for once. I miss absorbing words and worlds for the sheer joy of the experience.

I break out the cider thermos in the late afternoon. Patrick surprises me by producing a bottle of bourbon to make hot toddies.

"To take the edge off my public-speaking nerves," Patrick says, as if we need a reason to day drink on New Year's Eve.

"Whatever you say, Mr. Saint Nick."

The bourbon does the trick to warm us and draw us close. So close, in fact, that we're snuggling on our picnic blanket with gloved hands roaming all over. Our cold, gingery lips come together. It's pulse-spiking and surreal.

"I take back the saint part," I whisper headily. "You kiss like a sinner."

He gives me a wolfish grin. "I know another thing that would take the edge off my public-speaking nerves."

Without hesitation, we climb all over each other right there on the blanket overlooking the town.

THE GREAT WORK BEGINS

QUINN

"Sorry about the letterhead," Emmanuella says when she hands the first Merriest Mister itinerary to me on that first Monday of the New Year. In the upper left, there's a pleasant, wispy script that reads: *From the desk of Mrs. Claus*. "We are going to get new stationery printed for you."

"There's no need to waste perfectly good paper like that," I say, refilling my coffee cup and reading through the to-do lists, which are broken down by day.

Emmanuella shrugs, almost too acceptingly. "If you insist."

Most days have vague agendas like *spread Christmas cheer to villagers* or more concrete items like *approve acts for Elf Extravaganza*, while Sunday has a big circle around it with the words OPENING DAY written across it. I ask the council what this means.

"The Merriest Mister and the new Santa have been invited to be the celebrity team captains at the first game of the Sunday Night Snowball Fight season," says Emmanuella, as if those words aren't the most ridiculous words ever spoken in any human language.

Scratch that. The most ridiculous words ever spoken in any human language are, "I'm the Merriest Mister, and I live at the North Pole now." What Emmanuella said is a close second.

I nearly do a spit-take with my coffee. "I'm sorry. You want us to do what now?"

The last sport I played (against my will, I might add) was the Oakwood Elementary charity dodgeball game. We used the spongey balls meant for children in gym classes. The whole event was mostly for students and parents to get a good laugh out of their teachers making utter fools of themselves.

If I do this, I'll be making an utter fool out of myself on an even larger scale without intent. Patrick's New Year's Eve speech went well, so I know the village supports us, but I basically stood behind him the whole time and smiled, dolled up as arm candy. This is way more out-there than that.

"It's a hoot!" Samson says, throwing me an encouraging smile. I can tell he's an avid fan.

"Snowball fighting is the North Pole's most special sporting event," says Colleen, showing off her Team Evergreen scarf. I wouldn't have suspected fandom from her of all the council members. "This is the elves' way of welcoming you both. It's a tradition of theirs. They do this battle of the se—"

Colleen meets my eyes and abruptly ends her sentence. Battle of the sexes was what she was about to say, but obviously my gender throws a wrench into that outdated idea and language.

"I'm not sure about this," I say, panic rising in my throat.

"Don't worry," Patrick says to me. "I'll go easy on you."

If only he knew that's not what I'm worried about.

"Couldn't Patrick throw the first pitch alone?" I ask.

"He could," says Chris. "But the elves would likely take offense to that. They'd think you don't want to participate." He flicks a wary glance toward his fellow council members.

"I could still participate! I could just do a speech or something?" I can't control the upward pitching of my voice.

There's a round of shaken heads and eye rolls.

The council tries to talk it up, telling me how exciting it will be.

Emmanuella even tells me that she did it when she was the missus, that it was completely low-pressure.

Still, I'm going to make a mockery of myself.

351 DAYS 'TIL CHRISTMAS

My dread has only magnified.

Patrick and I take a horse-drawn carriage to the Tundra Dome, a massive, covered event arena on the outskirts of the village that looks like an igloo on steroids. It rivals Yankee Stadium, a place my father dragged me to as a child when he still had hopes and an interest in me.

As the white, majestic horses come to a halt, I want to make a million apologies about why I have to back out. Finding a replacement shouldn't be too hard. Thousands of elves descend upon the venue. The smell of fried concession-stand food wafts out through the propped-open gates. The excuses get stuck in my throat.

Hobart leads Patrick and me into a special entrance that takes us under the stadium. Above us, the excited throng roars and stomps its eager feet.

"Patrick, you'll be with Team Evergreen here on the left," Hobart says, pointing toward a locker-room door. Inside, the team is chanting. "Quinn, Team Poinsettia for you."

Before we go our separate ways, Patrick extends a hand to me. Not to hold, but to shake. "May the best man win." There's a cockiness in his voice that lets me know he thinks *he's* the best man.

I want to say that I'll show him, but I don't want to eat my words in front of an entire arena.

I enter the other locker room, where I'm greeted by sporty, jaunty elves who are all geared up and ready to go. There's one locker set aside for me. Inside, there's a jersey, a puffer jacket, and boots. I experience the same unpleasant jitters that plague me on the first day of school every year when a new crop of students enters my classroom.

As I try on a few different pairs of gloves laid out for me on a waist-height table, I consider that a clean slate is one of the major reasons I decided to come out here. I think about what Nan Hargrave told us to do, chase adventure.

Because of that wise, wonderful old woman, I spin my attitude around one-eighty. With my hat on my head and my long scarf wrapped around my neck, I join the rest of the team in a warm-up before throwing the door open and announcing that I'm ready for action.

Up on the main level, we wait inside a tunnel. The vibrations of the rowdy crowd pour into my chest. "People must really love this sport, huh?"

Hobart is there next to me, and he nods. "We don't have soccer, football, basketball, baseball, or tennis, but we do have this." It's clear he's not one of the superfans himself yet he appreciates the spectacle of it all.

Ten minutes later, a jovial-sounding announcer's voice rings out. "Welcome one and all to the start of a very special season of Snowball Fighting. As a treat, our teams will be captained by our new Santa Patrick and our first-ever Merriest Mister."

I break out into a jog, veering to meet the announcer at the center of the snow-packed field. Patrick comes at us from the opposite direction, waving.

The crowd is even bigger than I imagined. No seat in the arena is empty as far as I can tell. Some wave pennant flags. Others have their entire faces painted their team's colors.

"Patrick and Quinn, thanks for coming out to help us celebrate another mighty season!" the announcer says. He tells us they're going to do a coin toss to see which of us will throw first.

"Heads," Patrick shouts as the oversized, golden coin goes spiraling into the air.

It lands on tails, which means Team Poinsettia gets the first go. Patrick looks peeved, which shouldn't please me, but it does.

My team leads me over to a pyramid of prepacked snowballs. Four referees in candy cane–striped uniforms surround the perimeter of the playing field. There's a clearly delineated boundary between our two sides, and I know, as per the rules, not to cross it or risk a penalty.

Cognizant of two-thousand-plus pairs of eyes on me, I take a moment to choose the best snowball in the bunch. I toss it back and forth between my hands getting a sense of its weight, its dynamics.

You've done this before, I remind myself. *Well, not* this *but something similar. It's a skill like riding a bike.*

"Merriest Mister, are you all set to start us off?" the announcer asks, and I nod. "Terrific! Let's count him in, everyone."

I roll out my shoulder, take my aim, and at the end of their countdown, a whistle blows. I close my eyes and hurl the snowball as hard and fast as I can, trying to overwrite a painful memory from my childhood that scared me away from sports entirely.

Crunch. Silence.

I'm afraid to open my eyes because I've heard churchgoers quieter than this mega arena.

I've screwed it all up.

But then, out of the silence come triumphant cheers.

When I finally brave a peek, one of the Team Evergreen elves is walking dejectedly to the sideline. I don't have time to relish my success because the announcer shouts, "Let the Snowball Fight season commence!"

Another whistle sounds, and the game breaks out in earnest.

I channel all my frustrations from the past into this game.

This is for Principal Masterson making me take down my wedding photo, I think before hurling a snowball over the line at a speedy elf who is taunting my teammates.

This is for expecting me to play stay-at-home spouse, I think before targeting, and missing, Patrick.

This is for worrying about how others judge the way you dress, I think of my own annoying inhibitions. It works in getting another elf out.

The more fuel I add to my internal fire—miscommunications and failures abound—the better I play.

It doesn't matter if the throws don't hit on the other side because the act of throwing the snowballs relieves me of some of the burden of these silly grievances, and without that burden, I become a light-on-my-feet snowball fighting machine.

The best man is definitely going to win, I try telepathically sending to Patrick. *Because the best man is* me.

30

THERE'S NO CRYING IN SNOWBALL

PATRICK

Quinn and Team Poinsettia are clobbering us. They pick off my teammates one by one without breaking a sweat.

Who is this guy? I think of Quinn. I narrowly dodge a lumpy snowball hurled at my torso. I would be more impressed if I weren't so winded and afraid of losing. Quinn's got a speed and grace I don't think I've ever seen from him.

Smartly, only half his team is playing offense. They're running up to the line and attacking. The other half is building snow mounds. They use them as places to hide and catch their breath. I had not considered this strategy. I wonder if Quinn is the one who came up with it. He is brilliant. I just didn't know that brilliance extended to sports.

I run for our snowball supply. My team's morale is low. Half of them are already out. They stand around kicking snow on the sidelines. They're barely even cheering. They've forecasted our loss.

I summon my second wind by packing a tight snowball and javelin-tossing it across the center line. It strikes an elf. She lands on her butt and slides several inches back. Score!

The game goes on like that for thirty more minutes. The crowd's enthusiasm never wanes for even a second. Quinn and I remain in contention as our teammates meet their fates.

Even after so long together, I'm unable to anticipate Quinn's moves on the field. When I go left, he goes right. It frustrates me. I know he's not trying to embarrass me. But he kind of is. I'm the new Santa around here. The big man. A loss could be a blemish on my reputation. Hargraves don't stand for things like that.

In a Hail Mary move, I charge forward despite knowing I'm a large, moving target. I have to do this. Now or never. I take aim at Quinn's final teammate. I nail him right in the shoulder as he attempts to swerve.

The large clock over our heads switches from the upticking timer to a ten-second countdown that zeroes out before either Quinn or I can get a good throw in at the other.

"Showdown!" the announcer shouts. The stands go wild as I try to muster a third wind.

Quinn and I retreat to our sides. Two of the referees run out to the middle and place two perfectly round snowballs within reaching-distance. And then, using brushes, they dust away the centerline.

There are no more sides. The whole field is fair game.

There's the faintest hint of a smile on Quinn's lips. He licks them like he's tasting victory.

I shake my head. He has no idea I've got him right where I want him.

Only, my cockiness might end up being my downfall. Because when the whistle sounds, I'm slow to react. Quinn has his snowball already. And now I'm rushing to find cover.

I don't know how it happens. All I know is that I make a mad rush for my last and only weapon and end up splattered in ice, snow, and the bitter nip of shame.

A pair of peppermint martinis are delivered to our VIP suite after the dust has settled. The funneled, chilled glasses have chocolate coating around the rims, which are sprinkled with crushed candy cane bits. Hobart sets our tray down and dips out.

Quinn and I clink our glasses together. "Quite the game," Quinn says. "I hadn't imagined such a jolly people being so aggressive out on the field."

The acrobatic ways these elves could dodge throws and jump over barricades were both impressive and mind-boggling. I make a noncommittal grunt in agreement.

I keep my eyes on the field. I don't mean to be short with Quinn. But my fuse for failure is burnt out after getting fired and nearly chewed out by my family over Christmas dinner.

Quinn must sense this. "Please don't tell me you're mad that my team won."

"I'm not mad," I say. I hate that the heat blossoming on my neck is probably leaching onto my cheeks and betraying my words.

"Angry? Frustrated? Annoyed? All three? Come on, I do this all the time with my students. I'm good at helping them identify which emotion they're experiencing," he says.

"I'm not a second grader," I snap. Even though I know that's not what he meant. I'm sore and tense all over.

"I know you're not, so don't act like one." Quinn takes a big swill of his martini.

He's right. I'm being a baby. A big, immature baby. "I'm sorry." My shame magnifies. Good thing what happens in the North Pole stays in the North Pole. My dad and my brother would love to rag on me about this.

"Don't be sorry. Just tell me what's going on," Quinn says. "We live in the Arctic, I'm not letting you *ice* me out anymore."

I can't resist a corny joke. "You know my family, Quinn. You know losers are basically not allowed a seat at the table."

Quinn sets his martini down to deliver this. "One loss does not make you a loser."

"Two losses."

"What?"

"I lost my job, remember?" I hang my head.

Quinn lets out an understanding noise. "Losing something that isn't serving you is a win."

My chest contracts with a new kind of panic. He isn't talking about us, is he? Since arriving, we've been much more connected. "Sometimes," I say. So he doesn't think that's a hard-and-fast rule.

"Patrick, you are a talented architect. When we leave here, you will be able to start over," Quinn says with confidence building behind his words. "You have a great portfolio, Jason will give you a glowing reference, and you're going to crush Kacey's project."

"Shit," I mutter. "I really need to figure out how I'm going to finish that while I'm here."

"You really do, but let's not bother with that right now." Quinn reaches for my hand. "Right now, let's just sit back, enjoy the second game, and get more of these martinis because they're delicious." He tips his glass upside down to show that he's already finished. I haven't even started.

I finally take a sip. "Wow, they really are delicious." I go to down more of it.

"Okay, slow your roll, Santa. Losing would be the least of your worries if you get blackout drunk," Quinn says with a light laugh. "Besides, I want you to remember how I kicked your ass."

I roll my eyes, despite enjoying this interesting cocksure side of him. "By the way, where the hell did all of that come from?"

Quinn's face flames the color of the Team Poinsettia puffer coats. "What do you mean?" he asks in a way that suggests he knows exactly what I mean. He sighs heavily before launching into it. "Remember when I told you my dad coached a Little League baseball team when I was a kid?"

I nod. Even though I'm uncertain where he's going with this. "Yeah, you told me he was pretty obsessive about it and that you never wanted any part of it."

"That wasn't entirely the truth," Quinn says. "The first year he coached he had signed up because he wanted me to play. He had been a star high school athlete, and he had aspirations for me."

A flash of the Christmas card we got from Mr. Muller and his second wife, Sharon, plus their kids appears in my mind. Both of his boys are wearing baseball jerseys and holding gloves. I even remember there being something in his handwritten note, included in the envelope, about his oldest son getting a starting position on his travel team. I didn't pay much attention at the time. He's not a part of our lives, but clearly, he's still looming over Quinn.

"And you couldn't live up to those aspirations?" I ask.

He shakes his head. "No, I was actually amazing." He snorts reproachfully into his empty cocktail glass.

I chuckle at this. "You're kidding."

"I wish I was." He sets his glass down with a clink. "Even at eleven, I had clearly inherited my dad's talent. It was a low-stakes, recreational league but we were crushing the competition every weekend, and I was the star player."

I can't wrap my head around this. It's so antithetical to the unathletic guy Quinn's always projected himself to be. "Wait, the first time you brought me over to your mom's place, she had that old baseball card–style magnet on her fridge of you in a batting helmet. I didn't say anything, but I saw you take it down and stick it in a drawer so I wouldn't see it. I assumed you were embarrassed."

He says, "I was, just not for the reasons you probably assumed. I was the star player that helped take us all the way to the championship, which is laughably small potatoes thinking about it now, but it was big then, especially to my dad who was a first-year coach and always bragging about how well we were doing to our neighbors. The night before the final game, I got up to use the bathroom and heard my parents arguing. Their bedroom door was open a crack." His gaze wanders away dolorously as referees and snowball rollers prep the field for the second game.

"What were they arguing about?" I ask.

"Everything and nothing. That's how it always went," he says. It's as if he's watching the scene from his childhood played out on one of the JumboTrons hovering above us. "But my dad shut down the argument by saying, 'You're going to wake Quinn. He's got a big game tomorrow. It's very important. To both of us. He needs to be rested. We need to win. Winning is going to make him into a man.' My dad was always saying stuff like that to my mom, 'More veggies will make him into a man' or 'Babying him less will make him into a man.' Then, I heard him start collecting stuff, which made me worried he was packing a bag to leave us, but then I realized it was just stuff to take down and sleep on the couch. I ran back to my bedroom, heart absolutely racing, one, from almost being caught eavesdropping and two, from the anxiety of maybe not winning. And guess what?"

"You lost?"

He nods glumly. "It was all my fault. I think they call it the yips. If you can even get the yips that young. I fumbled a catch in the outfield that would've kept our lead, which wouldn't have normally mattered because my superpower was my throwing arm. I could've gotten the runner out. Only something short-circuited. I didn't let go on the follow through. The ball made it maybe a foot in front of me before it hit the grass and started to roll. The kid on third base wasn't sure whether to leave his position and run for it or stay, so the kid on the other team got a home run and got the kid who was sitting on second all the way home. My dad was pissed for a long time."

I lean forward in my cushy chair. "I'm sorry. That's ridiculous. It was one bad throw." I have met Mr. Muller only a handful of times. One of those times was our wedding day where we barely exchanged eight words total, one of them being "hi" and another a brief "congratulations."

"It wasn't just one throw, though. It followed me into the next season. It got so bad that I quit after the second game of the second year and refused to try another sport." His shoulders slump as if he's encumbered by this experience all over again. "Because of what he said, I got this idea in my head that I'd never be a man because men in my family were supposed to be athletic. Well, athletic or smart—preferably both—but since I fumbled the bag on the sports part, I threw myself into books."

"There's no one way to be a man," I say. Though I feel hypocritical saying it. Moments ago, I was pouting over losing a silly sports match.

"Sure, right, but that's not something I could internalize at twelve," he says. He shakes his head. "Then, my dad served my mom papers not that long after and I felt like it was all my fault. I wasn't talented or smart enough; I wasn't enough of a man to make him stay."

"Quinn."

He holds up a hand. "I know. I don't believe that anymore, especially after that." With his right hand, he gestures out to the field. The players are beginning to take their positions once more. "That game felt like it exorcised me of something."

"I can't believe," I say, "that I didn't know *any* of that."

Quinn shrugs. "It never came up and if not for today, I'm not sure I ever would've talked about it."

I grab my drink and finish it off. "I'm glad you did, my secret all-star."

He lets out a little snort-laugh. "Me, too."

31

AN ENGAGEMENT TO REMEMBER

QUINN

A MEMORY

Sorry, can't make it. Held up at work. Patrick's text thrusts a disappointed sigh out of me.

I'm standing behind a concessions window handing out cups of water and hot chocolate to grabby, sweaty students in ice skates and winter coats.

Across the way, on the other side of the rink, the school choir is singing, accompanied by Mrs. Birch on a keyboard plugged into an amplifier that is more static than sound, but we're making do. It's not a wealthy school district by any means so we're scrappy, and that often entails teachers taking on multiple duties beyond the classroom.

Case in point, I am now the drama club's co-advisor. As such, I helped put together this fundraiser for the spring musical, *Frozen Jr.*, which is off to a pretty solid start despite Patrick's absence.

That's okay. See you at home. Though I'm worried I won't see him. Since he began at Carver & Associates last year, if I arrive home any time after eight P.M., he's either locked into his work or conked out in our bed. It's silly maybe, but some nights I find myself missing him, even when he's inches away on the opposite side of the bed.

I give my uneasiness away alongside mini marshmallows in another cup of cocoa. "Thanks for lending a hand tonight," I say to Veronica, needing a change of topic.

"Oh, it's no biggie." She offers a cookie to a passing kid. "I would've been here anyway." Her head rocks back like a bug has flown in front of her face.

I'm about to ask what she means by that and what that reaction was for when a girl from my class, Katie, comes over holding a pair of ice skates that look to be about my size. "Mr. Muller, you're needed out on the rink."

I kindly maintain that I can't leave my post, but Veronica assures me she can hold down the fort.

Minutes later, confused, I skate out onto the rink on Bambi-legs. Under the sound of my heart in my ears, the opening notes of "Love Is an Open Door" ring out, then when the chorus kicks in, the doors to the rink thud open.

Patrick, surprising me, skates out onto the rink, cheeks pink and eyes bright, green scarf flapping in the breeze behind him. Effortlessly, he slides down onto one knee, stopping an inch from me. He plants himself, and then in front of a majority of Oakwood Elementary School, he pops the biggest question there is.

"Mr. Muller, will you marry me?" Patrick's blue eyes sweetly bore into mine. Veronica, off to the side, is filming this spectacle on her phone, surely so we can share the happy moment with our families after the fact.

I'm speechless. We didn't discuss this. I mean, in the abstract we have "one day when we're married" conversations like every long-term couple does, but those plans always feel far-off, something we can aspire to. I never imagined I'd be staring down the barrel of marriage so young.

Is that how I think of marriage—a loaded barrel, a threat?

Conflict crisscrosses inside me, pummeling elation into the recesses of my heart. The one emotion that can't be beaten back, though, is my love.

My love for Patrick is undeniable.

I love our life together. I love the closeness we share in our tiny, messy apartment. I love his lopsided smile and his collection of unstylish sweater vests that somehow look good on him regardless of the occasion. I love his willingness to take on challenges headfirst.

But do I love Patrick enough to be the husband he deserves?

Scratch that.

Can I be a husband, period?

"What do you say?" Patrick asks, his voice a gentle hook reeling me out of my mind and back into the present. Optimism shimmers across his expression.

The rink is awash with anticipation for an answer. I don't want to disappoint them, myself, or most importantly, Patrick, so I give one.

I hold out my right hand to him, beaming for everyone to see. "Yes, yes. A million times yes."

32

TIME FOR A CHANGE

PATRICK

From my desk in the office above the workshop, which I've come to love, I'm humming along to the soundtrack of cheery tunes the elves play while they work.

At Carver & Associates, there was a no-earbuds policy, so I had to work to the drone of office chatter. Chairs rolling. Papers shuffling. Keyboards clacking. Back in my office at the house in New Jersey, which could barely fit my drafting table let alone a fireplace and whole sitting area like this one, I worked in silence. The quieter the room, the better I could focus.

Here, I don't know if it's the lack of pressure or the freedom from financial instability, but I can dial in to the music. I let the jangly notes of "Sleigh Ride" infect my body and lift my spirits. No wonder Santa is always depicted as jolly in commercials and cartoons.

From my fingers down to my tapping toes, I *feel* jolly.

Especially because things with Quinn have been going spectacularly. Our revamped love life has inspired me to start working on a special project. On one level of my desk, I have the original blueprints of the workshop main floor unrolled and pinned down flat. On the drafting table, I have initial sketches for the redesigned workshop I'd like to build. They're very much a work in progress. But they're getting there.

Over the last couple months, as I worked as an overseer and

the manager of toy production, I'd make notes about how to boost efficiency, worker happiness, and optimize the space here. My creative brain kicked into high gear.

I'm once again reminded of the sketches for the hub for Kacey's nonprofit. I disappeared from New Jersey overnight. I don't want her to think I've ghosted her or forgot about our plans. The work she is doing is important. Now more than ever, really.

I wonder if I can send an elf back to our house to grab them. I can finish it up here and then get someone back in New Jersey to see them through down there. I know it's a tall order.

I'm about to leave myself a note on the topic when Hobart materializes in my office, as he usually does, without knocking.

"Can I get you anything?" Today he wears a pair of puffy green pants, a thermal long-sleeve shirt, and his usual pointy hat. There are bells tethered to his shoes. Every step he takes is a mini concert.

Head elf might as well be code for personal assistant. He has made my magical life immeasurably easier over the last month. And it's not like any of my current duties are rocket science as is. Which leaves me plenty of brain space to focus on Quinn and architecture, my two true passions. "No, I'm all good, but can I get your eyes on something?" I shuffle around some papers.

Once he's peering over my right shoulder, he says, "What exactly am I looking at?"

"That, but better." I jab my thumb toward the window behind me.

Hobart looks out the window at the work floor that's bustling with whistling workers. "What's wrong with how it is now?"

"There's nothing inherently wrong with the way it is now, but as I've been observing, the flow of the space is cramped and isolating. I understand this is a workshop operation, but it all feels a little too humdrum. I want to let in more natural light while mixing workspaces between departments. No more locking the designers away up in Toy Maker Tower and the builders solely in the factory. I want to integrate design and production to make our workshop more inclusive and social."

"I like the idea."

A belly-laugh (an entirely Santa-like belly-laugh, to be exact) bursts out of me. That's been happening more and more. The longer I'm here, the more Santa-like I become. Quinn even pointed out that I've started to grow light, soft facial stubble when not wearing the cloak. A major perk in my book.

Ever since moving here and opening up to Quinn about my shitty work environment, I've been thinking a lot about what elements of Carver & Associates served me least. Everything from my desk placement to my ability to speak in meetings to my ideas not being taken seriously all served to shrink me professionally. I was made to believe I was a minor unit in a big machine. I served only to make the most senior members look good. I want to do the exact opposite here. A win for one is a win for all.

"I obviously need to get approval from the council before I enact any of this." I check the ornate cuckoo clock mounted to the wall across the room. In ten minutes, it'll chime the hour and a wooden Santa figurine will pop out of the doors and do a little jig. It scared me the first few times, but now, the silliness is a small spark of joy. This time, it will signal a lunch break.

"True. You should share it with them and explain your vision once you're finished. Most of them will be enthused to have someone with your experience willing to reinvigorate our mission. Others will be more resistant." Hobart's eyes pointedly scan to the other side of the room.

"You mean Nicholas."

He continues to avoid my gaze. "You're welcome to make your own conclusions. If you don't need anything else before lunch, I'll take my break now."

My office door is a magician's trick box. One being leaves and another appears. This time, it's Quinn. His arms are weighed down by two heavy-looking brown paper bags. They hang by twine handles. "I brought lunch."

I stand to brush my pants free of eraser shavings. "What's on the menu?"

"Meat pies!" *Pop* go the lids off two mini pastries. Utensils get separated. "Which I helped make! Don't be too surprised when I tell you that I had a lot of fun baking these. Kitchen work can be peaceful when your mind isn't elsewhere."

"And there's magic involved," I point out.

He rolls his eyes at me and takes a bite.

For the past couple of months, Quinn's been spending his time meeting the elves and learning about their trades. A true Mister of, by, and for the people. Except those people aren't people at all; they're elves. Complex, passionate, immortal, and awesome elves.

"I feel very Meghan Markle," Quinn mused one night. We were splitting a Hawaiian pizza from the enchanted oven in the least tropical place on the planet.

Resting in the chair beside the fire and across from Quinn, I pick a pie and poke around with my fork. "What's the meat in these meat pies? I'm assuming it's not ham."

Quinn scrunches up his mouth before bobbling his head. "I'm actually not sure. I didn't ask."

"You're a regular Mrs. Lovett."

Quinn's singing Sondheim in a bad cockney accent when Hobart pokes his head back into the office again. "Sorry to interrupt," he says, obligingly. His attitude toward us has thawed significantly since that first ultra-stressful night we met. His real personality has unmasked itself.

"What brings you back, Bart?"

"I came to say that I was thinking more about your plans for a redesign."

"Plans for a redesign?" Quinn asks, confused.

"I was keeping them under lock and key until they were finished, but I guess the cat's out of the bag." I gesture him over to my drafting table, lunch untouched. My stomach gurgles. Not from the lack of food but from showing this to Quinn.

We assume our usual positions with me on my stool and Quinn looking over my shoulder. I don't glance up at him. I simply intuit his reaction by how his body clings ever closer. As he takes in the product of my creative, mathematical mind.

"Far cry from bathroom partitions, huh?" I joke because he hasn't said a word yet.

After a breath, Quinn says, "It's inspired." He jostles my shoulder encouragingly. Pride overrides my worry. Every new drawing is a chance. Every new project is a risk. I already took a major one by coming out here. Can I take another by putting this plan into action?

Hobart clears his throat. "I know you said they're not finished yet, but I think you should show them to the council this week. Tomorrow, actually, if possible. The sooner the better! While we're still in our slow season, we can allocate the resources and elf power to make it happen with minimal disruption to our toy timeline if the council approves."

The back of my neck is suddenly slick with sweat. "I—" My mouth is both overrun with saliva and yet dry as a desert.

"Do you love your design?" Quinn asks with needed gentleness.

"I do."

"Do you believe this design will make a difference?"

I hesitate, but ultimately nod. "I do."

Quinn rubs the width of my back. "Then, Mr. Claus"—he crouches down so he's level with my ear—"I think we've got a presentation for the council to put together."

My chin rebounds. "You want to help?"

"Of course," he says, like this should've been obvious. He plants a kiss on my cheek.

I think about all those nights I locked myself away in my office in the house. Embarrassed that I didn't finish my work at the office. Worried I was one slipup away from foreclosure. One broken date away from divorce.

Maybe I should've leaned on Quinn a little more. Maybe relationships aren't always a perfect 50–50 split. Sometimes they're 70–30 or 60–40. You have to trust that the other person is ready to pick up the slack, and you have to be willing to do the same when the inevitable time comes.

Hobart looks excited out of his mind to be involved in such a massive undertaking. "I'm here to help, too! Whatever you gentlemen need, I'm your elf!"

I let loose a loud exhale as I inspect my work. "There's still a lot to get done. If we're going to do this tomorrow, we might need to pull an all-nighter."

"Who needs sleep anyway?" Quinn asks.

"Not me!" Hobart says, nearly jumping out of his boots. "But I will need food! I'm heading into town to grab us another round of caribou pies!" He's out the door in a flash.

Quinn and I look at one another with surprised disgust.

"Caribou? *Really?*" I warily glance over at the table where we've left the remnants of our first, and definitely last, North Pole meat pies. "How am I ever going to look the reindeer in the eyes again?"

We share a rueful, uncomfortable laugh and then get down to work.

Night falls like curtains on a stage. One at a time, hour by hour, I switch on the lamps around the room. I light the fire. I stifle a yawn.

No matter how late it gets, we continue to work. I'm too in the zone to stop. I'm nursing an espresso while Quinn collates some data. He's sitting cross-legged on the area rug, using the coffee table as his workspace. The tip of his pink tongue pokes out the left corner of his mouth. His nostrils flare. His focus flags. Until his eyes land on one of my sketches. Suddenly, he's taking a small break by picking up a pencil and replicating my work.

I don't say anything. I don't even think I breathe. I just observe.

He's so consumed by his tangent that he doesn't react when I get up, round my desk, and stand behind him. "Don't worry so much about if your lines are straight," I say. He snaps out of his daze. "Confident strokes that overlap are more important than perfectly straight lines. Sketches are ideas, not finished products."

"What are these?" he asks of the small, hyphen-like markings on my drawing.

"Directional hash marks. They're for texture. They show a surface like a roof." I use the eraser end of my pencil to point at lighter lines that I've slashed through the boxy sides of the workshop. "These are construction lines. They give depth, dimension. Sketching is all about layering."

He tries for himself, but his hand is too heavy. I squat down behind him. Lightly, I wrap my calloused hand around Quinn's fist, which is holding the pencil. I guide him in feathering the page. Goose bumps chase each other up the outside of my arms. "You try now," I whisper. Like I'm letting go of the handlebars on someone's first bicycle.

Quinn's mouth droops in frustration when he doesn't get it right. "God, my students could do better. Why am I so bad at this?"

"You're not bad at it," I say quickly. "You just need practice. And patience."

"Not my strong suit," he admits.

"That's not true. You teach second graders. Your whole career is an exercise in patience."

"Very true. I guess I just use up my limited well of it on my students." He shrugs. His eyes have glazed. "And the administration."

"Save some for yourself."

"Huh?"

"You always give one hundred and ten percent of yourself," I say. "It's okay to sometimes just give one hundred or ninety-five percent. You're allowed to save some for yourself." I plant a kiss on the crown of his head before returning to work.

33

THERE'S SNOW BUSINESS
LIKE SHOW BUSINESS

QUINN

256 DAYS 'TIL CHRISTMAS

On my way to the theater in town, I pass the elves working hard on the workshop redesign. My satchel bounces at my side as I wave to the friendly faces. They whistle while they work, a happy tune that underscores the click of my boots on the cobblestone pathways that has become synonymous with freedom.

Up ahead, Patrick is decked out in red, holding a clipboard and pointing authoritatively into the distance. Even from far away, even without hearing him, I know he's giving an impassioned speech, his hands moving frenetically. They paint the picture in his mind for the others. From the way the elves and council members around him nod and smile, donning hard hats and tool belts, it's obvious his vision is well received.

Patrick was right. All I needed to do was reserve a percentage of my energy for myself, so I wasn't depleting myself for the sake of others. For the last month, I have been dusting off more books in the library for pleasure, learning to drive the town trolley, and exploring curiosities beyond my wildest imaginings.

Today, however, I'm tied up in preparations for the Elf Extravaganza. It's a North Pole tradition where many of the elves turn out to showcase their talents in a cabaret unlike anything Broadway could compete with.

Like Colleen and Yvonne had said, learning how to relax after being hyperactive for so long has been a blessing. I approach to-day with open eyes and ample excitement.

In front of me, there is a glorious marquee circumvented by unlit bulbs. Its signage reads: AUDITIONS TODAY.

I push into the theater. The lobby is a lush, gilded oasis dropped in from another time. To my right is a bar. To my left is a coatroom. Just ahead are multiple sets of doors leading into the theater. Around me, hopeful elves warm up their voices and stretch out their limbs.

As the Merriest Mister, I'm charged with vetting and selecting the acts for the upcoming bill.

Inside, I find Christa, who is heading up costuming and tech, and Ashley, who is billed as my co-director. In the months we've been here, Ashley's been the most spacey and distant, not warming to me and Patrick. I'm unsure why.

I take my seat at the table in the center of the house. A massive chandelier presides over the auditorium. Above that, a classical mural of the North Pole is painted in immaculate detail. If I squint, there are outlines of figures that look like Patrick and me. A year-long legacy prematurely preserved in paint.

"Nice fit," says Christa, eyeing me up. I've got on one of her designs—a red sherpa sweater with white trim and tapered black joggers tucked into bulky boots.

Ashley skips all pleasantries. "Let's get started."

The elves and acts range in age, size, and skill. Some of them, like the Voices of Hope children's choir and the Great Squallini magician, are well-rehearsed. Others like the dog trainer act—which makes my heart jump into my throat at the memory of the near rottweiler attack last Christmas—could use some work.

After hours of taking notes and making yes, no, and maybe piles, we've seen everyone there is to see. Before we make any final deliberations, Christa suggests a break to stretch our legs, grab snacks, and reconvene.

In the hallway near the restrooms, I almost stumble over a child sitting on the floor with a crumpled-up piece of paper in their fist. Underneath a full face of makeup, they appear upset. My teacher instincts swim up to the surface.

"Hey there," I say, keeping my distance but crouching down to the elf child's level. "Is everything all right?" The elf looks up. Their shoulders are rounded forward in protection. "It's okay. I'm Quinn." I reach out a hand.

"I know. The Merriest Mister. Hi." The elf shakes my hand with such little enthusiasm.

"You are . . . ?"

"Mick," they say. "Mick Flurry."

I doubt this elf has ever heard of McDonald's and its staple ice cream concoction, so I don't make the obvious joke. I swallow my laugh and give them a friendly smile. "It's nice to meet you, Mick. Were you here for the auditions? I didn't see you inside."

They continue toying with the crumpled-up piece of paper. "I was but I changed my mind."

"Why's that?"

"I'm not good enough."

"Not good enough. Who says?" They shrug. "What's that you have there?"

They unravel the ball a bit. "Just—nothing. It's nothing."

"Doesn't look like nothing. Can I see?" I ask, holding out a hand.

I keep my gaze as warm as possible. Their color-changing eyes go from ice blue to soft pink, almost as if they're a mood ring. "Sure. I guess."

Careful not to rip the page, I undo the ball. It has a thick quality, and the words are dashed out on it using an inky quill. Blotches of black make it hard to decipher all the words, but the heading is unmistakable: *North Pole North Star* by Blizzard.

"Who's Blizzard?" I ask knowingly.

"Uh, me," they say. "It's my numb-de-plum."

This laugh I can't choke back. "I think you mean nom de plume. Your pen name."

"Sure. That." They wilt like a flower as they angle away from me. I shouldn't have laughed.

I sit back on my haunches and read the entire poem. "This is really good. Can I ask how old you are?"

"Eight." The same age as my former students. I must be out of practice, only now remembering how kids this age possess an easily offended seriousness. This poem is Mick's inner world.

"I'm sorry I chuckled before. It wasn't you or your work. Rhymes always get a laugh out of me," I say to defuse the awkwardness. "This is a really impressive poem, Mick. Were you going to read it for us?"

They nod. "I thought about it, but then I heard all those great singers and saw all those amazing tricks and I decided to forget about it." Of course, their presence in this hallway belies that.

"How come?"

"Because a poem can't compete." Their words splat like saggy water balloons. Unwarranted defeat spills between us.

"It's not a competition, Mick. Besides, comparison is the killer of good art, and this"—I shake their paper in the air—"is good art. You know why?"

"Why?"

"Because it's authentic. I think you should share it."

They let out a deep breath. "I've never shared one of my poems before."

"There's a first time for everything. Look at me, I'm the first ever Merriest Mister."

"I don't think I can," they say, accepting the paper back from me, riffling through a bag to their left.

I don't want to press too hard and scare them off, so I say, "I like your outfit." They wear rainbow boots, sparkly tights, a tulle tutu, and a top hat.

"Thanks. I picked it out myself. Whenever I draw Blizzard, this is what they look like."

"Dressing as Blizzard makes you feel confident?"

Their eyes widen, clearly happy somebody understands them. "Yeah."

"I have an idea. What if Mick doesn't audition, but Blizzard does?"

Their eyebrows, which have a line of jewels stuck above them, crinkle. "What do you mean?"

"I mean this is Blizzard's poem, right? Blizzard should be the one to share it. It probably wouldn't be as scary if Blizzard got up on that stage," I say.

Comprehension ripples through their features. "That's true."

"What do you say? Does Blizzard want to give it a try?" I ask.

"Blizzard hasn't practiced," they protest.

"We'll do it quick. Read it out loud. Right now. You and me. How about that?" I ask, getting excited by the prospect of helping this child find their confidence.

They nod, slowly standing. I mirror them. "Okay. But can you—" They keep their gaze cast down. "Can you turn around?"

"Of course."

Mick reads the poem once with me facing the far wall, which is signed by hundreds of elves who've performed here in the past. Mick's voice is shaky but they make it to the end. When they finish, I ask if I can turn halfway. They agree, and read it again. Finally, on the third try, I'm facing them. They don't look up much, and they don't meet my gaze, but their words are clear and their stance is strong.

"Quinn, are you out—" It's Ashley come looking for me. She stands in her oversized sweater inspecting the scene with evident confusion. "We're ready to start casting."

"We can't yet," I say. "We have one more audition to see."

Ashley must understand. "Oh, okay. I didn't see Mic—"

"This isn't Mick," I'm quick to say. "This is Blizzard. And Blizzard is going to read us an original poem. Isn't that right?"

Mick beams, adjusts their top hat, and says in full voice, "Right," before following us inside the theater.

FROM WORKSHOP TO WERK-SHOP

PATRICK

It takes a village has never been truer to me than it is today.

After months of intense planning, the full workshop is re-opening.

I look out upon the collected crowd for the ribbon-cutting ceremony to usher in a whole new era at the North Pole. I take in the faces of the many, many elves who made my vision possible. Their belief in me causes pride to swell in my chest.

By the time I finished the sketches, the redesign shaped up to be a massive undertaking. An all-hands-on-deck operation. While the chalet may be magical, the workshop required hard, manual labor.

Since it was early in the season, toy production hadn't revved into full gear quite yet. We're still gathering wish lists from around the world and testing prototypes. As such, we were able to collect a legion of elves who were willing and ready to roll up their sleeves and get to work.

New walls. New windows. Strategic paint jobs. Division relocations. Even new technology! All in the name of Christmas and a simple yet important mission.

There's a chunky, velvety strand of red ribbon behind me. It's pulled taut across the threshold to the workshop. I nervously toy with the bow on it with one hand while I hold a pair of comically large scissors in the other. Quinn and the council approach from around the side. They join me up on the steps.

I've been here all morning doing last-minute walk-throughs. I needed to make sure everything was perfect. With Quinn by my side, now it is.

"How do you feel?" Quinn asks after a hello kiss.

"I feel like my blood is hot chocolate and my bones are marshmallows," I say. My eyes stay glued to the crowd. Everyone is clutching steaming paper cups of hot chocolate to keep warm, so my mind is stuck on it. My heart smacks on the walls of my rib cage faster than ever before.

I'm afraid they won't like it. And if they don't like it, they'll turn on me. And if they turn on me, the council sends me back to New Jersey with my tail between my legs.

"Hey," Quinn whispers, swiping his hand along my upper back. Even through the several layers I'm wearing, the touch is soothing. Even before North Pole magic, Quinn's palms possessed a calming spell meant especially for me. "Everyone is going to love what you've done. Trust yourself."

I want to trust myself. But out of the corner of my eye I spot Nicholas whispering to Colleen. His eyes are laser beams of apathy. It's obvious he believes all this hubbub is a waste of time and resources.

It's ridiculous how much I want to impress this man who has barely said more than two dozen words to me since I landed here four and a half months ago.

"What if they hate it?" I ask.

I'm thrust back to my elementary school classroom. Spencer Haven's beady eyes stare at me over that stack of dream homes I made for him.

Spencer then morphs into Mr. Carver *tsk*-ing at me. Little droplets of spit fly out from between his thin, dry lips.

Mr. Carver becomes Dad. He's praising Bradley without even acknowledging my presence. *In my own damn head.*

My self-doubt lingers over this event like a Macy's Thanksgiving Day Parade balloon. I wish a strong gust would roll through the valley and blow it to hell.

Quinn's second touch brings me back to earth. "Pat, every elf I've talked to who worked on the remodel has said how amazing it's going to be, and every elf who didn't work on it is shaking in their boots to see it. You did good work, and I'm not just saying that because I'm your husband. I'm saying that because I'm your biggest fan."

I close my eyes and take a deep breath. If Quinn believes in me, I can, too. "Thanks. You're right. I did good work."

Quinn steps up to the podium first. He calls the crowd to attention through a microphone. His words echo off every nearby building. Shopkeepers poke their heads out of doors. Children rush over from the direction of the schoolhouse with teachers close behind. Nobody wants to miss a single second of what I hope is a momentous occasion.

Our work was a never-ending montage of sawdust, wooden planks, and perseverance.

Even if people hate it. Even if Nicholas despises it or the elves get mad. I have a sense of accomplishment by seeing it through to completion. That's a solid consolation prize if everything goes south here in the North Pole.

"And now, a few words from the big man himself, an ingenious architect and my husband, your beloved Santa Patrick!" Quinn starts a slow clap for me that rolls out through the crowd.

As I stand at the podium, prickling tears pester me once more. I clear my throat to compose myself. "Thank you all for coming out today. Ever since I was a child, I've been obsessed with buildings. Their shapes, their functions, their ability to tell a story both inside and out. When I arrived here, I learned how rich and beautiful the story of the North Pole is. I also learned how far that story goes back. Stories evolve over time, which is why, after a lot of research, I wanted to bring a modern sensibility to this storied workplace. Without further ado, I give you the brand-new North Pole Toy Workshop."

I angle myself so the poised cameras can catch me cutting our way into a new tomorrow with cold, metal scissors.

Nobody waits for the stairs to clear. The crowd of elves rush inside. Members of the council, who lent their hands and time to the project, are ready to take the public on tours.

For the next several hours, I lead my own tour groups as well. I get a rush of excitement every time a detail or a change evokes an ooh or an ahh from the listeners. They love the expansiveness and the various light controls that allow workers to switch the brightness, tone, and saturation of their personal workspaces. We've implemented collaboration rooms with fidget toys and table games, so our designers and our makers don't feel like two separate teams. Community calendars are displayed everywhere possible to promote socialization.

"Using color psychology," I explain as we head around the catwalk above, "we've made the production and brainstorming areas red since that color is conducive to physical labor, which needs a more elevated heart rate. It's also good for getting the creative juices flowing. Greens were reserved for outdoor and relaxation spaces that promote balance and health. Your happiness was paramount to my designs."

I get a great response to the glossy snack bars stocked with candies and healthier options like granola mixes. We conclude the tour in our renovated, temperature-controlled atrium complete with rippling water features, plenty of thriving greenery, and ample places to sit.

Nicholas, who had been hovering at the back of the group this whole time, sports the faintest of smiles. Unlike his wife, he did not pitch in, so this is his first time seeing the new space. He lingers when the group dissipates, which leaves me with a resounding uneasiness.

"I wanted to hear about the changes from the horse's mouth," Nicholas says gruffly.

"In this case, I'm the horse?" I wish my voice wasn't so shaky.

He nods like that isn't a little insulting. "I have to say . . ." I brace for the crushing weight of his disapproval. For a replay of my firing from Carver & Associates. "I'm impressed."

"If you just give it a chance, I think—" My words roll out automatically. Then, I replay what he said in my head. And I nearly flop onto the ground from surprise. "Oh, sorry. I wasn't expecting that."

. Nicholas laughs. It's a booming thing. I don't think I've ever heard this man give off more than a grunt or a groan. "I know I project toughness, but in fairness, as the oldest member of the council and the person with the most experience, I have to. The last guy in your position nearly crashed our entire operation. Forgive me for my bluntness and coldness. Blame my generation or my age or my sentimentality, but at some point, I got stuck in my ways. Not all shake-ups are bad. I see that now."

Those words stick with me after he offers his congratulations. He even invites me and Quinn by for dinner in a few weeks before he goes to find Colleen.

Not all shake-ups are bad.

While getting fired from Carver & Associates seemed like the end of the world, maybe it was one of those good shake-ups. I needed it to forge a new beginning. For my career. For me and Quinn.

I can't help but think that the North Pole is the home Quinn and I have been chasing after ever since we met. Santa and the Merriest Mister might be the roles we were born to play.

"What was that all about?" Quinn asks. His eyes are trained on Nicholas, who is sampling from the snack station beside his wife. Quinn sounds about ready to go to battle for me and my designs. Mr. I-Don't-Fight-the-Power might be growing a set of claws out here.

"I think he apologized. Or, close to it anyway." I'm still stupefied.

Quinn's jaw drops. "Nicholas? Did he get a brain transplant? Every morning over breakfast, the eggs are too runny, or the toast is too dry, or the jam is too sweet. He didn't have any critiques?"

"None," I say. I'm still not sure there wasn't a backhanded remark embedded in what he said to me. I run it back again in my head and don't find one. I shrug with my palms up. "I think he really approves."

"Wow." Quinn shakes his head slowly. "Look at you. Your designs turn even your greatest critics into fans. I'm glad you were able to make this happen, and so quickly, too! You barely lost any necessary production days. You'll be up and running again at full speed by Monday."

"Speaking of, let's go up to my office," I say.

When we arrive, Quinn purrs, "What are we here for, Mr. Claus?" He's draped himself in the doorway like a starlet in a black-and-white movie.

I huff out a laugh. "While I wish it was for what you're thinking, I wanted to check this." I push a button and out pops a mechanism that looks like the wheelhouse of a ship. There along the dashboard of it are three meters: Love-o-Meter (which tracks the love among the human population), Nice-o-Meter (which gives a relative overview of how good people are being), and lastly, the Happiness-o-Meter (which monitors the quality of life in the village). On the third, the needle has moved exponentially closer to the big red heart on the right side.

"Where was it before?" Quinn asks, stepping in close beside me. He smells like the homemade, organic peppermint soap he keeps stocked in the shower at the chalet.

I point somewhere a little past the halfway mark. My finger shakes with pleasure. "We're really making a positive difference here," I utter. The tingle I now identify as purpose gathers force in my fingertips.

It prompts me to reach out for Quinn's waist, pull his pelvis flush to mine, and kiss him with all the heady passion that's been swirling inside me. "I'm so lucky to love you," I say. "Thank you for coming on this adventure with me."

Quinn blinks at me. His face reddens as he smiles. "Any adventure with you is an adventure worth taking."

35

STAGE FRIGHT-OR-FLIGHT

QUINN

208 DAYS 'TIL CHRISTMAS

Electricity surges through the backstage for the Elf Extravaganza. I'm helping with any final touches before joining Patrick out in the audience.

I'm stuffed into the tailored tuxedo Christa made for me. It doesn't matter that it was cut to my exact proportions or that the finest maroon fabrics were used, I'm still a sausage inside a casing. Mashed-up bits masquerading as something I was never meant to be.

"We're missing an act." Christa's voice crackles in my headset.

Finding an MIA elf was not on my bingo card for tonight.

"Who is it?" Another voice chirps in my ears. It's Ashley this time. She sounds frustrated.

I don't hear Christa's answer because one of the wardrobe assistants rolls a mostly empty rack of costumes through the wings and across my path. There's a pair of leggings and an unmistakable top hat unclaimed.

I'm off like a rocket in search of Mick.

Ashley was hesitant to cast Mick, worried the nerves might get to them too much. I fought for Mick. I promised that I'd work with them on their poems, help them get performance ready. In the last two months, Mick has displayed an unmatched confidence. Bravado that was sure to earn them *bravos* from the patiently waiting audience.

Stage fright is nothing new. I've seen it infect dozens of kids at Oakwood Elementary. That anticipatory vibration that could turn sinister if not tended to. However, back home, by the time the curtain rose, shy kids turned into superstars and mouthy kids learned valuable lessons about being cooperative in the chorus. Now as I run around the backstage helplessly asking after Mick, mere minutes to showtime, I'm not sure I can save this one.

The Voices of Hope choir takes the stage for the opening number—a rousing rendition of "Carol of the Bells"—and I realize there's one last stone left unturned. The basement door is unlocked. It's a slate-gray subterranean space that feels out of place in the North Pole, but I suppose even magical villages need storage.

Mick brought me down here one day because they confessed this is where they found the tutu and top hat originally. They were looking for a place to practice before the audition, found the basement, got lost in all the old props and costumes, and decided to don a few pieces.

Among the painted moons and rusty tap shoes, a figure is frantically digging through a plastic box. "Mick, everything okay? It's showtime."

"I can't go on," they say, hands still burrowing around. *Clink, clank, swish.*

"What are you looking for?" I ask, drawing closer.

"A pin. A pin. I—" They hold up their tutu. It's torn in half. The colorful swaths of tulle spiral down to the floor, looking more like a magician's never-ending scarf than a skirt.

I nod. "Okay. Well, there are plenty of other options up in the costume shop—"

"No," they cut in. "The tutu. I need the tutu."

I had feared that. Not only does Mick find confidence in the tutu, but they find comfort in it, too. They can be the character of Blizzard. Perhaps, even above that, the character of Blizzard isn't a character at all, but a truer version of Mick. At eight, identity starts to form. It's a lifelong journey, sure, and Mick being an elf, that journey will last into infinity given their immortality. Regardless, it's beautiful to witness someone so young know themselves so well.

I'm as determined as ever to make this work. "Follow me."

We race to the costume shop. I put my sewing skills to the test, racing to claim a machine, wind a bobbin, and stitch the unmatched pieces of tulle. I nick myself only once before the machine bends to my will.

Ashley pings into my headset. "Quinn, what's going on? You promised Mick would be ready. Where are they? They're on deck."

"They'll be there," I chime back. "Trust me."

I knot off the stitch, holding up my work. It's a little lopsided, but it will do. "Better?" Mick nods.

I take Mick by the hand, and we barrel for the wings.

"What if I forget my poems onstage?" Mick asks, worry still hot on our heels.

"That's the beauty of original poems. Nobody knows them. You can always make something up," I say.

"What if my mind goes blank?"

"It won't."

"But what if it does?"

We curve into the darkness of the backstage area where the other acts mill about, antsy to get out there. I check us in with the stage manager, who sends a message to Ashley. I kneel in front of Mick and look them right in the eyes. "It's okay. Whatever happens out there, happens. We've polished your poems. You've practiced. You're ready. Performance is meant to be fleeting. Do you know what *fleeting* means?"

Mick shakes their head, eyes as wide as pancakes.

"It means temporary. It means even if you mess up, it's not the end of the world. It's one moment in time and another moment will always come right after it. Take a deep breath and do your best," I say.

Once I send Mick onto the stage, it's a bit like I'm sending a piece of me out there, too. The lights pick up on the glitter dabbed on Blizzard the Poet's cheeks, the subtle sparkle embedded in the fabric of the tutu. The words shine just as brightly, spoken with clarity. I couldn't be prouder.

After congratulating Mick on a job well done and sending them back to the greenroom to hang with the rest of the acts before the big finale, I start toward the audience and then make a pit stop in the costume shop.

While I was sewing, I noticed this jumpsuit on one of the mannequins. It was a Christa design, and it looked to be about my size. It has a deep V neckline, a gathered waistline, and long, flowing legs. Delicately, I undress myself before undressing the mannequin.

The lights are low in the house when I finally make it out to my seat. Patrick's box is pivoted toward the stage, where heavy, red curtains hang down. Golden fringe tickles the boards below as it sways. The cast must be moving behind it, prepping for the next act.

Patrick sits alone, thumbing through the program. It's not until I clear my throat that he looks up. His cheeks lift one at a time. "You're here. And you changed."

"I did," I say, trying to combat the self-consciousness that always comes with being perceived, even by my husband. "It was hot back there." Though there's no reason I should have to qualify how I present myself. Except maybe to Christa, who will probably want to know who stole her creation.

"You look great," Patrick says, standing to allow me to pass and get to my seat. He kisses me on the cheek. His big, calloused hand slips down the silky fabric from my shoulder and lands in the crook of my lower back. Desire rolls through me. "And Mick was— Wow. Really something. They were lucky to have you."

I smile and nod, but ultimately say, "I think it was the other way around."

The smile doesn't slip from my face for the rest of the show, which goes off without another hitch.

"What do you plan on working on next?" Patrick asks during our slow amble back to the chairlift after it's all over. The streets are filled with elves still buzzing about the show, but Patrick and I stick to the sidewalks, to each other. I don't want the bubble of our perfect night together to pop too soon.

I shrug. "Enjoying the freedom of not having my days planned down to the second?" Working with Mick has shown me that I was never married to the academic aspect of being a teacher. Maybe I only ever wanted to help young people, be a mentor. The connection is the part that I love. "I have a lot of options."

"Seems like the elves really like having you around," Patrick says. "Every time you're out and about, the happiness meter in my office spikes."

"That's nice to hear," I say, feeling a blush rush up my neck and across my cheeks.

He guides me closer to him, so we fall into perfect step, and he leans in to whisper: "*My* happiness meter spikes when you're around, too." His voice is feather-light and his breath ghosts over my ear.

The blush from a second ago becomes a scorch. I laugh at his dirty joke, shove him playfully away.

As we approach the town center where the gargantuan tree glistens against the evening sky, a faint song floats on the wind. It echoes against the buildings. The snow flurries slow to a nearly choreographed flutter. Flakes catch on Patrick's long, blond eyelashes as his pupils dilate.

"Do you hear what I hear?" Patrick asks, eyebrows bouncing. Everything is a Christmas pun around here. I've grown to love it even if it's corny.

Straining, I faintly make out one of our favorite songs to joke-sing together. "Baby, it's cold outside," I say.

"I know it is. Why do you think I'm all bundled up?" he jokes, performing an overblown shiver.

I shake my head, biting back a smile. "What a dork."

"Yeah, but I'm *your* dork," he says. He whisks me into the square where some musicians are playing outside of an overflowing pub called Hand over Hearth. The cast and crew from the Elf Extravaganza are raising frothy, chilled pint glasses in celebration while some of them harmonize along to the lead singers that are dueting the holiday classic for all to hear.

Plenty of elves have taken to the street and are holding each other close. The indigo evening overhead is swished with green and has the distinct aesthetics of a Thomas Kinkade painting. My breath gets swept away as Patrick sweeps me into a dance hold.

I fall into the steps easily, even after so little practice. "Go easy on me," I say. "I don't think we've danced together since our wedding night." In our first apartment, after particularly stressful days at work, in the cramped living room, we'd move the coffee table and the couch out of the way, and we'd put on a rowdy playlist to dance our cares away.

Close by, Ashley and Samson are dancing to the song as well. He twirls her under his muscular arm.

Ashley notices me and without missing a step says, "Quinn, sorry about my attitude earlier. The Elf Extravaganza is my one big task a year and it means a lot to me. You really came through. Thanks."

"No sweat. It was fun," I say before she twirls away, leaving me with a hope that I've finally garnered her favor.

"We're coming up on our anniversary. Can you believe it's almost been one year of marriage?" Patrick says, continuing to lead us in a step-touch.

"Time flies," I say. Though, it doesn't quite fly here. It ripples. Every day is more expansive than a simple *X* on a paper calendar.

"We'll have to do something special," he says, sounding serious.

I blink back at him, a million love bugs tickling my heart. "I'd love that," I say before swinging him out, rolling him in, dipping him low, and kissing him hard on the mouth.

36

TYING THE KNOT

PATRICK

A MEMORY

This is supposed to be the happiest day of my life. So why does it feel like I'll be happier when it's over?

I'm sweating buckets in this tuxedo. The sun is unforgiving. Beating down on the back of my neck. Keeping me reaching for the hankie in my pocket. Blotting every inch of exposed skin.

The ocean waves crash melodically on the sandy shore in the distance. Part of me is tempted to shuck my clothes, jump the railing, and dive into the surf.

The old saying goes: Rain on a wedding day is good luck. What does stifling summer humidity portend?

We should've gone with shorts instead of trousers. Airier fabrics. A different day. A different season . . .

I wish the weather would break already. Gray clouds dome over buildings in the distance. Like they're waiting to make a fashionably late entrance. Shout "I object!" with thunder and lightning right after the vows.

Bradley taps me on the shoulder. In his hand is his monogrammed hankie. Much nicer than my own. "Here," he says.

I only take it because the sweat is getting in my eyes. And my own is drenched. We should've thought this through before booking an outdoor ceremony. Though, I suppose we didn't do much of the thinking ourselves. Between our demanding jobs, most of the planning fell to Mom. Which is probably what she wanted anyway.

"At least we know you don't have cold feet," Bradley jokes. I mean, I think it's a joke. I can never tell with him. He speaks like Wednesday Addams. "Mom looks happy at least."

There she is. Front row on the left. Pivoted around in her chair to look back at us and smile. She's in a flowing white gown. ("There's no bride!" she'd said when she'd shown me what she planned to wear.) A handheld fan buzzes, blows her cropped, recently dyed hair. I'm tempted to ask her to pass it back to me.

"She does," I say. Hoping that will squash this conversation while we wait for Quinn and Veronica.

"Thanks for asking me to be best man," he says. Voice maintaining its even keel but dropping slightly in volume. I would turn to look at him more fully. But I'm honestly scared of what his eyes might tell me.

I didn't ask him anything. The title and his positioning beside me during the ceremony are entirely Mom's doing. He didn't throw me a bachelor party. He didn't write a speech, as far as I know. This is perfunctory. For the pictures. I don't even think Mom knows there's tension between us. Then, I make the boneheaded move of meeting his gaze and, weirdly, I'm not sure he knows, either.

A gusty wind blows in, carrying the scent of brine on it. It causes the gauzy, decorative fabric and string lights to rattle against their posts and test their fastenings. Women, including Mom, grab for their sun hats so they don't blow away. Right as Quinn and Veronica appear.

Quinn's forehead is shiny. His shoulders are rounded. His eyes are squinted. Veronica leads him by the arm over to the aisle inlet. We're going to walk down together. To the tune of a song from the eighties whose title I can't even remember. Maybe I wasn't even told. My mind is anywhere but here.

"Ready?" Quinn asks.

He tugs at his collar. I wonder if he's having reservations, too.

It's not that I don't love Quinn. Or don't want to get married to

Quinn. It's that . . . Well, I look out on this place. A beach, because it's not a church. Tuxedos both, because there's no bride. It feels unlike us. Too soon, too fast, too scary.

I want to turn to Quinn. Make these thoughts known. Grab his hand and run with him back toward the safety of yesterday.

But the song—*is it Aerosmith? I think it's Aerosmith*—comes on, and it's too late.

The congregation stands. Bradley and Veronica walk ahead. It's happening.

Later that night, in the rose-laden newlywed suite, we're alone for the first time in forty-eight hours. And, of course, we're naked.

Quinn's heavy head finds purchase on my chest. Our legs intertwine. Knotted tightly together. A symbol of the other knot we tied today. With vows and rings exchanged, we are man and man. Made for each other. We've done it now, and even if the day flew by in a blur, I'll honor that forever.

"I promise I'm going to make every day of our lives as magical as possible." My words go unheard, though. Because not even two seconds later Quinn lets out a soft, wheezy snore. He's dozed off on top of me. I stay as still as possible and let him sleep peacefully as the night ends and our marriage begins.

LOVE AND MOLASSES

QUINN

As of today, Patrick and I have been married for one year.

A full revolution.

Though, in earnest, it feels like a million tiny revolutions. My head grows woozy when I consider all the spinning we've done. We've held up a million revolving plates of responsibility, while orbiting one another so as not to collide.

The North Pole has, if you were looking at our life through the lens of a camera, refocused the frame. Stillness, unimaginable back in New Jersey, has cushioned around us.

I'm standing in my closet, debating what to wear to the Annual Gingerbread House Competition. But it's what's happening after the competition that I'm most excited about.

I didn't see Patrick before he left for the workshop today, which is a good thing because I was afraid that he might read the surprise I have in store for him written all over my face. Weeks of planning would've been wasted had I spoiled it.

On the hook on the back of my closet door hangs the brown suit with the gumdrop buttons. I still want to wear it, but something about it doesn't sit right anymore. A voice in my head screams that it's the pleated, fitted pants. Fashionable but somehow wrong. At least that's how they felt on my body when I tried them on in front of the full-length mirror a few minutes ago. I let out a sigh of frustration.

I'm reminded of Mick and how their unique style was applauded by the audience at the Elf Extravaganza. How Patrick's eyes lit up when he saw me in Christa's jumpsuit. I get an idea.

In the back corner of the closet, the elves left behind an antique vanity with a pouf in front of it. Over the last several weeks, I've spent many mornings sitting here, doing my hair or applying moisturizer, and my hands always itch to rummage around in the jewelry boxes I found on one of our first days here.

A sneakiness invades my body as I give in to the temptation. While the North Pole has begun to feel like home, the chalet still feels temporary. I'm comfortable here, but nothing about this space is uniquely mine.

Which is why, as I open the square, red velvet box with the difficult hinges, I feel like a thief enacting a heist. Inside, there is the world's most beautiful pearl necklace. *Real* pearls that bring *real* tears to my eyes.

I clasp them around my neck. In the reflection of the mirror, I like what I see.

Without taking them off, I go riffling through the few femme pieces of clothing the elves missed when they came to overhaul the closet. There are, of course, the sleep dresses that I asked to keep because I've grown fond of wearing them, but there's also a series of classic Mrs. Claus looks that I think they wanted to preserve without knowing where to store them, obviously for whoever takes over my position next year.

I'm reminded, once more, that this position and this place are both short-term. That's what Patrick and I agreed upon when we left New Jersey. The council made clear that we had no obligation to them beyond this Christmas.

While our first year of marriage may have been rocky, our experiences here at the North Pole have been anything but. Perhaps what Colleen and Yvonne had said at the original wardrobe fitting was true. Our marriage needed this life vacation to reset itself, so we can take what we've learned here, pack it in our suitcases, and bring it home with us.

Thinking back on that original fitting has me walking toward the front of the closet again with a knee-length red skirt in hand. The vibrant color matches the hue of the gumdrop buttons on the shirt, and the white accent around the bottom hem complements the white frosting details on the jacket.

Tossing the pants to the side, I outfit myself in this new combination, adding in a pair of thick brown tights beneath the skirt. I step into the bedroom to see myself in the full-length mirror.

Again, I like what I see.

I like it because I see *me*.

The elves here have been accepting of me and Patrick since day one. There's no reason I should edit my self-expression for the sake of palatability.

I embraced my masculinity out on the field at the Tundra Dome. I'll embrace my femininity for this gingerbread event. Both of those traits live inside of me, and both, just like our wedding anniversary, deserve to be celebrated.

Before I leave the chalet, I find sparkly nail polish in the bathroom and give myself a marvelous manicure to match.

THE GINGERBREAD BALL

PATRICK

At first glance of Quinn at the gingerbread competition, I'm bowled over by how stunning he looks. Confidence reverberates with every step he takes.

His sparkly red nails dazzle in the light as he inspects a mega gingerbread house modeled after the redesigned workshop.

While I can't wait to see that specific entry up close, I can't tear my eyes away from Quinn. When we first met, back in college, he dressed like this. In bold colors and with a camp sensibility. Over the years, though, that impulse slowly seeped out of his closet. Out of him.

Or so I thought.

Maybe he was repressing those impulses.

For whom, though?

For his job? For *me*?

I couldn't live with that last one. Especially since he looks goddamn enticing. Sexy and adorable and good enough to eat.

I mean, literally. He's a walking gingerbread cookie judging gingerbread cookies.

My stomach rumbles. Though that could be more nerves than sexual hunger.

"We're all set for you!" Hobart says. He comes up behind me and scares me half to death. I've been crouching in a doorframe. "Sorry, didn't mean to interrupt your spying."

"Oh, I—" I stop myself. There's no sense denying it. "It's okay."

"The display is all set on the rolling cart, and I know my lines. I practiced all night," he says.

Over the past months, I've been tied up with the workshop redesign. I'm sure, to some degree, Quinn assumes I won't remember our anniversary. Which is something failing-architect Patrick might've done. It's not something Santa Patrick would ever dream of.

I've been working on a separate project for weeks. I'm ready to surprise the pants—er, um, *skirt*—off him.

Before Quinn announces the winner of the contest, Hobart bursts through the doors as planned. "We have a last-minute submission."

The elves in the room gasp, even though most of them have been prepped about what is going to happen.

I scratch at my hands. The last time I made a grand gesture like this one I was proposing. In a way, this feels like a proposal of a different sort.

Hobart clears a path through the crowd. I pop up behind a cart with a gilded handle. I roll it forward toward Quinn, who does a double take. His skirt waves with the motion.

"Quinn," I say, once I'm at the center of the room beneath a blazing spotlight. "Happy anniversary!"

I gesture at my creation. It took weeks. Using gingerbread, icing, and a little ingenuity, I built a replica of the dream home I envisioned for Quinn and me before we settled on our place in New Jersey. I couldn't make that architectural wonder a reality there. But with the right combination of cookies and candies, I could make this.

Immediately, Quinn's eyes are swimming with unshed tears. His hand sits at the base of his throat. "Pat, it's beautiful."

"It's incredible!" comes a shout from the crowd.

"Elaborate!"

"Too good for an amateur competition!" Everyone laughs at that one.

"Don't worry," I say to the crowd. "This isn't an official entry. It's a gift." I did, perhaps, get too into it. But ever since the completion of the workshop, I've had all this mismanaged energy coursing through me. This gingerbread model is just the tip of the iceberg. Since year one is the paper anniversary, I plan on giving Quinn the blueprints. I'm going to submit them to our special building elf task force.

I'm going to get our dream home built. Here. In the North Pole. A small (okay, *huge*) gesture to introduce the idea of us staying on as Santa and the Merriest Mister beyond this single year. Professionally, I've never felt more rewarded. Romantically, we've never been more united. Going home at the end of this year no longer feels right to me.

Because everything I could ever want is right here.

Quinn leans in closer to take in all the details. His smile nearly expands off the edges of his face. "I love it," he says when he returns to my side. "I love *you*. This is such a special surprise." He kisses me. "Good thing I have a surprise for you, too."

I cock my head. "You do?"

He nods excitedly. A procession of elves follows us out of the competition room and down the hall of the main building.

Those enigmatic, luxurious doors that hid the council behind them on that first night are propped open. Beyond, you can see the room has been transformed for a ball. Tables are scattered about. Trays of food are lining the far walls. Candles are lit, and a string quartet is playing music. The air sizzles with anticipation.

"You did all this?" I ask. My throat grows thick.

"Some," he says humbly. "Hobart and the elves all pitched in, too."

Hobart pokes his head around. "The village really loves you both. We wanted to do this to show you how much we appreciate your work and your spirits. Congratulations on your anniversary."

"After you," Quinn says so I'm the first to enter.

An elf in a bespoke tuxedo comes by with a tray of champagne flutes. We each take one. And then another. We end up drinking until we're appropriately buzzed and dance until our feet are pleasantly sore.

The council members come by and wish us light and love for the years ahead. We thank them, one by one, with hugs. Even Nicholas, wearing a classic suit and reindeer-shaped cuff links, opens his arms to us. Surprisingly, he softens in my embrace.

"What's the secret to a lasting, happy marriage?" Quinn asks right as he intercepts an hors d'oeuvre from a passing platter.

Emmanuella and Jorge share a quizzical look. She whispers to him. He laughs then says, "Knowing when to speak your mind—"

"And when to shut up," Emmanuella interrupts by slapping him playfully in the stomach. We all laugh.

Quinn pivots his attention to Yvonne, who grabs Chris from a side conversation with one of the elves. "Oh, that's a good one," he says. He's gazing deep into Yvonne's starry eyes. She speaks for the pair: "The secret is to slow down and enjoy the small things."

"I still remember a joke Yvonne told me on our first date, but I don't remember the name of the couple we made our last vacation property sale to and that wasn't even all that long ago." Chris shrugs. "I think that says a lot about what's important."

"I love that. What about you two?"

Ashley seems surprised Quinn would want her advice. "Oh, I don't know. Good communication? Is that too cliché?"

"Not at all, babe," Samson says. He wraps an arm around Ashley's waist. She wears a drapey, Grecian-style green dress. His hand disappears into the folds of the fabric. "I agree. Good communication. And good sex never hurts, either." Ashley rolls her eyes, but even I can tell it's a loving eye roll.

"Last but not least." Quinn sidles up beside Colleen. She's wearing a floral perfume that reminds me of one Nan Hargrave would wear or might've worn in my childhood. A slight pang of missing my family hits me.

"Trust and faith have served us well in our many years,"

Colleen says, reaching out for Nicholas's hand. "What would you say, hun?"

"I'd say understanding." We all nod before we realize he's not finished. He clears his throat into a cocktail napkin. "Even on our worst days, even during the lowest lows, if you can find it in yourself to see things from her—erm, *his*—perspective, you'll be a-okay."

"Damn, this got real sappy real fast," Samson says, letting all the air out of the moment.

"He's right," Colleen says. She claps her hands together. "Who wants to dance some more?"

39

FADE TO BLACK

PATRICK

The ballroom empties slowly. Like with all good parties, nobody wants it to end.

How do I tell my husband that I don't want *any* of this to end any time soon?

"Tell me more about this outfit," I say. Because I'm unable to express anything else in this perfect moment.

"Of course," Quinn says. He moves his face closer to my ear. His voice drops an octave. "But I'll tell you when we get home, up in our bedroom. I'll tell you about each individual piece as you take it off of me."

My head buzzes. My heart rate spikes. I have never performed an exit with such gusto and expediency in my life.

"Should we really be leaving a party thrown in our honor without saying goodbye and thank you to everyone who helped put it together?" Quinn asks. I'm rushing to grab our coats from the back of a nearby chair.

"Yes," I huff out. My mind is single-tracking for the sake of what's to come. "Yes, we *really* should."

Before either of us knows it, we're back at the chalet. Breathless from the trip. Growing more so by the second.

As soon as the door clicks shut behind us, I scarcely get a word out because Quinn's insatiably kissing me. I can barely keep up with the high supply he's demanding. But I'm loving every second of trying as we stumble up the staircase. As we start to shed our layers.

"The gumdrops on my jacket are edible," Quinn purrs. Without hesitation, I remove my mouth from his neck. Rip one of his buttons off with my teeth. The grainy, gummy candy is ecstasy on my tongue.

"Mm-hmm." My lips pucker at the sweetness.

"The frosting detailing is edible, too." He's not even finished speaking. I'm already licking it off. Every ribbon of it. Every intricate design. It's probably unsanitary. But I don't care one bit. I'm ravenous right now.

"The skirt was left over from when we arrived," Quinn says as he undoes the zipper. Lets it fall to the floor. Leaves himself in only the thin tights that show off his delicate calves and irresistible thighs. "Like the sleep dresses, I love the flow and the freedom I feel when I wear it."

"I love *you*," I growl before diving in for another gumdrop.

"The pearls are hand-me-downs, too. A previous Mrs. Claus probably wore these to dinners and galas galore. They make me feel old-world powerful and classy. Like I'm the president's wife." He lifts his chin to show them off.

"They remind me of those fake ones you used to wear when we started dating. They drew so much attention to your beautiful, long neck." I brush my hand gently from his collarbone all the way up to his striking jawline. My fingers halt in the indent just below his ear. Quinn's eyes have gone soft and dreamy with the memory. The heat between us rises. "I loved taking those pearls in my mouth while I was in—"

He presses his pointer finger to my lips. Derails my sentence. "Don't tell me. Show me." It's a command that I'm more than happy to follow.

I scoop him up in my arms like I did on the night of our wedding. I whooshed him over the threshold of the honeymoon suite at the decadent beachside inn we were renting for the weekend.

There we were greeted by a king bed covered in red rose petals; every flat surface was speckled with lit tea candles.

Before that night, I had had sex. But I don't think I'd ever made love. With rings on our fingers, I suddenly understood the difference between the phrases.

Sex is about release.

Making love is about holding on.

Quinn koala-bears to my front. Kisses up and down the outside of my throat. I push our way into the bedroom, where a fire is already roaring.

I lay Quinn down on the king bed. I slip over him horizontally. I connect our lips again. My hands sink into the white fur-like texture of the throw blanket beneath us that both tickles and delights me.

"This is *perfect*," Quinn whispers. He runs his tongue across the hot shell of my ear. A gasp escapes me as he shucks the last of his clothing.

Bathed in the flickering orange glow of the fire, naked Quinn is a Gehry-designed building at sunset. Ribbons of muscle and flesh fused together into something sculpturally breathtaking. You can't help but lean back and admire it.

"What?" Quinn asks. I've remained motionless above him for too long.

"It's just," I say. All that practice with words, and they're still escaping me. "You're . . . *you*."

He must know that by *you* I mean beautiful, vivacious, tempting, sexy-beyond-belief. Because he pulls me into a deep, meaningful kiss that nearly knocks the wind out of me.

The proximity to the fire makes our skin slick and salty to the taste.

Love leaches out of every touch we share. Time taffy-stretches out in all directions as we become a mess of mouths and limbs. Of *I love you*s exchanged. They're tagged onto the ends of moans that are even more delicious than the gumdrops I devoured on the stairs.

I wish I could capture this flawless moment. Stick it inside a snow globe. Come back to it when we're old and gray and senile and I need to be reminded that we were once young and hot, wild and passionate.

But even with the magic of the North Pole, I know that's not possible. So, I settle for staying as present as possible while we celebrate our year of love while making infinitely more of it until dawn breaks over the North Pole.

183 DAYS 'TIL CHRISTMAS

I barely register that it's early morning. I'm sitting up in bed. Wide awake.

I'm replaying last night in my head. Quinn sleeps peacefully beside me. He's got the sheet, the comforter, and the blanket all bunched up around him. My bare legs are exposed. But I don't mind the chill that cuts across me. He looks too cozy and cute to care.

The scent of last night hangs heavy in the air. Sweat, cinnamon, *us*.

I know there's no going back to sleep for me. Just as I know now that there's no going back to New Jersey for me, either. This is where I want to settle.

Needing coffee, I try to get up gingerly so I don't disturb Quinn. But the traitorous mattress undulates. He lets out a groggy little moan. "What time is it?"

"Too early to matter," I say. "Go back to sleep."

"Okay." He rolls over toward me. His eyes are still closed. "Last night was amazing."

"It was." I smile at him even though he doesn't know that. I'm admiring the way his features are all half-sleep scrunched. So adorable.

"I wish we could stay here forever and ever and ever." His whisper trails off.

Hope sparks fresh inside me. "Maybe we can."

"Wouldn't that be nice?" he murmurs dreamily.

"So nice," I say to Quinn, who has dozed off again already. "So, so nice."

40

REINDEER ARE BETTER THAN PEOPLE

PATRICK

160 DAYS 'TIL CHRISTMAS

I do my best thinking under the vast sky out at the stables. It's the one place I can go where Hobart won't immediately pull me into a meeting. Or tell me I need to complete a task. Or alert me that some part of my redesign has caused confusion among the elves and I need to sort it out as soon as possible.

I'm not complaining. It's the kind of chaos I've always craved. Because I'm in control. Finally, a job and a mission I can get behind.

I fill my lungs with chilly, crisp air. The shock to my system is welcome. It reminds me how at home I am here. How the cold is my friend and the reindeer are my confidants.

Vixen, the most playful of the reindeer team, uses her scratchy tongue to take an apple out of the palm of my hand. She's careful not to spear me with her long, imposing antlers, which jut out from her flat, sandy-colored face. She lets out a big huff of gratitude before wandering out into the snow-packed pasture to be with her friends. The other reindeer are playing and running and shooting up into the sky in preparation for our first test flight, which is only a month or so away.

Since we arrived, Chris has given me a crash course on companionship with these three-and-a-half-foot flying wonders. I went around petting, feeding, and bathing each of our two-fifty-to-four-hundred-pound friends. This was the beginning of our bond that will be put to the test on Christmas Eve.

"It's important that the trust is strong to sustain the magic needed for an all-night flight," Chris had said. I helped him haul barrels of hay into their stalls and fill their feeding basins with alfalfa. "Your relationship with them matters immensely. They are sensitive creatures."

Quinn is a sensitive creature as well. As toy production ramps up and Christmas creeps closer, my time away from the chalet grows longer. Responsibility grips at me around every corner. But I make it my second mission to ensure he knows how important he is to me. That I'll never go back to my old, avoidant ways again.

Prancer and Dasher play-fight some distance away, while Blitzen trots over. He sniffs at my legs. "Wondering if I have any more apples, huh?" His nostrils flare. His breath is not the freshest. "You're in luck." I produce a tasty treat for him, which he accepts without restraint.

While he munches, I pet his hide and talk aloud. "What would you think about us staying in the North Pole? Quinn seemed taken by the gingerbread house. That was just a gesture. The real labor of love is building the damn thing."

We broke ground shortly after our anniversary. Yellow cranes dug up frozen ground. Elves in neon vests and hard hats scurried around with tools in hand. For the second time, one of my designs is coming to life in the North Pole.

I should be elated. But the process has been a little slow for my liking. I want it finished and the interior decorated before I unveil it to Quinn. On a special night. In a special way.

Blitzen grunts as if telling me to proceed. "Before we got here, I talked Quinn into buying this ancient two-story house because, well, we got married. Married people don't rent. They own. That's what my dad said. We toured so many duds. We also toured some amazing homes that looked just like my sketches. But we couldn't afford them. I think we made the best decision with the options we had." I sigh. "But, between you and me, Quinn told me he hates the place."

Blitzen does a full body shake like he's surprised.

"Truth be told, I was pretty miserable there, too."

Blitzen's head turns. His colorful, serene eyes wander up toward me. He's probably looking for another apple, which in fairness he deserves for listening to me babble like this. "You're right. Maybe I'm overthinking. I want us to stay happy. Be like we were at the beginning. The rush of newness and young love and conversations that lasted until morning. We've found that again here. And if we go back, the real world might cause us to lose it all."

"Lose what?"

My heart jumps into my throat. Thank God it's only Hobart. He's standing a few feet away holding a clipboard. He's in a big white coat that makes him look like a walking, breathing snowman.

"Oh, nothing," I say. "Please don't tell Quinn about any of the stuff I said. I was just blabbering."

"Understood," Hobart says. He gives me a straight-faced salute. "Speaking of Quinn, here's that second list of elves who helped on the workshop redesign you wanted. Certainly, some of them will also be available to join the force for your new house."

I thank him and inspect the list before registering the furrowed set of his eyebrows. "Is something the matter?"

"Not exactly," he says. "I just thought I should let you know that while happiness is up among the workforce, productivity is down. We're operating less efficiently than we were this time last year, which means we're slightly behind our target toy goals."

"'Slightly' doesn't seem so bad," I say. "Plus, if happiness is up, that means everyone is doing *better* work even if they're not doing it as fast. That's a positive, isn't it?"

"That's true." Hobart doesn't sound entirely convinced.

"Should I be worried?" I ask.

He shakes his head vigorously. "As Santa Chris usually says, worrying is a waste of time. I just wanted you to know! It's my job to make sure you know everything that goes on in the North Pole. That's all."

I take his words to heart. I need to hold my own in both arenas of my life: professional and personal. That means excelling at being Santa while also excelling at being Quinn's husband. Having this house is a physical reminder to him that I'm willing to put in the work to make sure our marriage lasts a good, long time. I'm quite literally pouring us a newer, stronger foundation to build our life on.

"Then, I still think we should continue with the house," I say, leveling my voice to sound confident. "Let's chalk these numbers up to expected strains during a transitional period. Quinn and me living closer to the village will boost happiness even more. Maybe if our workforce is even happier, they'll kick into high gear. I'm believing in that."

Hobart takes down some notes. "Right-o, then. I'll let these elves know of their new posts for the next month." He thanks me before heading out.

There's a questioning glint in Blitzen's right eye, which is trained on me. "What? You think I'm making the wrong choice? Quinn deserves a beautiful home. *I* deserve a beautiful home." Blitzen's gaze grows even sharper. "I know the chalet is beautiful, but it's beautiful in the way pictures in *Architectural Digest* are beautiful. Aesthetically pleasing yet completely removed."

Blitzen trots closer. "You're quite the listener, huh? I know Quinn. I know he wants cozy and personal. Maybe I can send some elves back to Jersey in the sleigh to grab our pictures and clocks and some of our furniture. Oh, that reminds me, I need Hobart to go back and get my designs for Kacey's nonprofit. I can't believe I keep letting that slip my mind."

Blitzen bumps my side with his nose.

"I know!"

Bump again.

"I'm making a note."

Blitzen bumps me a third time and my paper and pencil land facedown in the snow. "Now look what you've done." Then, I realize he's after the burlap satchel slung around my torso. "Oh, you just want a third apple, don't you? Fine. I've whined enough at you. Here's a Granny Smith for your troubles."

Blitzen lets out an overzealous noise before racing off with his treat.

"Gosh, is this what I'm going to be like when I have kids?" I ask myself before shaking my head and clomping off the field.

PHONE HOME

QUINN

There are no seasons in the North Pole, so I'm surprised I even realize that the calendar in the kitchen has flipped itself magically to a fresh page.

August. It arrived so quickly.

I pour myself a cup of cocoa while looking out the window at the unchanged landscape. Everything is always glistening with snow—from the mountaintops to the thatched roofs. I'm startled to find that, for the first time, I'm more indifferent to than amazed by it.

Back in New Jersey, I'd be tactfully sidestepping prep for September while lapping up the last delicious drops of summer. The weather would be warm and somewhat humid, but I don't think I'd mind the stickiness. Trudging through soupy air while working up a sweat is a sensation I didn't know I could miss, yet here I am, missing it.

I sip my cocoa and find that even this I wish I could swap out for a sweet, refreshing Aperol spritz.

Veronica and I would usually be, right about now, packing for a quick, last-minute trip to Seaside, where we'd stay at the cheapest motel with the highest rating and work on our tans before the madness of another school year inched back into our lives after Labor Day.

Interestingly, I'm missing the seasons and New Jersey, but I'm not missing teaching. This experience has been a crash course in balance. Oakwood Elementary left me wrung out. As the calendar becomes a ticker toward our inevitable departure from the North Pole, I contemplate what a career looks like beyond the snow and the magic.

I do something I haven't done in months. I text Veronica.

I've avoided contacting anyone from home out of pure how-do-I-explain-this panic. I left the state, dropped out of their lives. Hobart and the council assured us they've tied up any loose ends that might lead to inquiry, but with four and a half months left in our yearlong sabbatical, I'm needing this connection back to the real world, a reminder of my roots. I imagine this is what celebrities must feel like after getting used to fame and fortune and access.

It's only after I send the message that I realize she could be sleeping or working or the service could be spotty. I don't have a handle on the time difference. Antsy, I slip on my coat and boots and trek into town for a distraction.

When I get tired of walking, I hop aboard the trolley that clangs and dings. Stuck inside my head, I barely notice as the trolley car ventures toward the outskirts of town in the opposite direction from the Tundra Dome.

"Last stop," the conductor announces and I get out in front of what looks like a school building. Through the sizable front windows, a masculine-presenting instructor is framed at the front of the classroom giving a lesson, using a pointer. A bunch of elf children sit at desks nodding, as comically large pencils *scritch-scratch* back and forth.

A pang goes through my chest. It starts small but grows unignorable.

Out here, pulling my coat tighter against me to keep out the cold, looking in on a skewed version of my old life, I meditate on whether I'd be okay never stepping back into that role again. Is there another *calling* out there for me?

Behind me, there's a café. I make my way inside the small cabin-like building, where the chairs have swirly backs and the coffees have fancy names. The music playing creates a gentle ambience in dissonance with the hiss of the espresso machine.

I plant myself near the window to eat a muffin, sip a matcha, and elf watch. I used to do this a lot back home. Though it was much easier when I was a teacher among humans and not a human among elves. I stick out too much. Everyone tips their hats at me as they pass. The baristas make sure my mug is never empty.

I'm starting to miss doing tasks for myself. The enchanted chalet is wonderful and the elves are superstars, but leisure comes at a price, too.

I'm the only person who could find trouble with paradise.

My attention is captured by a gaggle of elves in hard hats bursting through the door, a mishmash of booming voices. I didn't know there were any construction projects happening in the village. I wonder where they're working. I'm tucked into a corner far enough away to eavesdrop.

"I don't think we're on track to finish in time," says one elf, jostling for a position to see the menu board better.

Another helps himself to the black coffee in the self-serve canister. "It's for Santa Patrick. Let's take a shorter break and get back to it."

A brunette elf toys with the safety goggles hanging around her neck. "I agree. Santa Patrick is the best so we need to try our best. No excuses."

I glow hearing this. But it only stokes my wonder about what they're working on. My hands grow clammy with intrigue.

The first elf lets out a big sigh. "You're right. Let's get our coffees to go, huh, folks?"

I'm about to stop them and ask for clarification when my phone lights up on the table with a booming ring. All the elves turn around. Red-faced, I avert my eyes and answer the call without thinking.

Veronica's face takes up the screen. With her hair pulled back, her eyes are unobstructed, full-up with incredulity. In the distance, a seagull squawks. She must be at the beach, on the trip I'm not there for. My stomach plunks with FOMO.

"Where the hell have you been?!" Veronica shouts. Her words bounce around the café, making me even more embarrassed. I slip in tiny, wireless earbuds, thank the baristas for their service, and step outside.

My eyes scan the streets, searching for the gaggle of elf laborers, but they've already disappeared.

"Hello?" Veronica's voice chimes bright and frantic in my ears. "Earth to Quinn. You ghost me, you text me, I call you, and now you're frozen? Literally? Wait, what are those snowcapped mountains in the background? Why are you all bundled up? Where the hell are you?"

This barrage of questions is exactly the reason I was avoiding everyone back home. I can tell the truth, but she probably won't believe me. However, I started this conversation, so I guess I have to try to make her.

"Remember when I told you I dropped my phone in the toilet and that's why your Find My Friends app pinged me in the Arctic?"

"Yes," she says, squinting at me with apparent confusion.

"That was a lie. That's where I've been for the last eight months. At the North Pole."

"On some sort of expedition?"

My eyeline is fixed ahead at where I'm walking, not down at the phone. She's probably getting a whole lot of double-chin and giving me a whole lot of scrunched-face confusion. "Not exactly. We are sort of, kind of working here . . ."

"You mean on a ship?" she asks.

"No."

She clears her throat, practically demanding my undivided

attention. I stop to sit on a cleared-off bench. "There's no civilization there, Quinn. It's moving ice! The only way that would be possible is if magic existed."

Summoning all my conviction into a single stare, I look right into the lens of my iPhone camera.

"Quinn, we spend half our days as second-grade teachers telling our students that unicorns and fairies and ogres aren't real. Don't tell me that magic is real because if magic is real and you were living and working in the North Pole, then that means—"

I continue to stare.

She shakes her head vehemently. "No, nuh-uh. I would sooner believe you were out there as geologists, oceanographers, meteorologists, cartographers, or atmospheric physicists than I would believe you were"—her voice drops to a whisper—"*Santa*."

"Well, *I'm* not Santa," I say. I'm far enough on the outskirts of town that only a few elves pass by. None of them slow down or stop. They all smile or wave and then carry on their way. Thank God. I've got a frazzled friend screaming at me through the phone, "Quinn Muller, what do you mean?"

I have no words with which to answer that question, so I flip to the rear-facing camera and show her the North Pole.

She cycles whip-fast through the many stages of disbelief, including denial and bartering and fragmented logic. She half convinces herself I've converted to acting and I'm on the set of a movie in Canada somewhere. "Are you the gay Lacey Chabert?"

Eventually, I've had enough of her nonsensical babbling, so I head straight for the reindeer stables. A bunch of her questions garble together in my ears, intermingled with sporadic static.

Once I reach the fence, I turn the camera to face me. "I'm going to show you something incredible, but for the sake of my very sensitive eardrums, please keep your reaction to a minimum. Remember, you're in a public place."

"Whatever. As you wish. Show me."

Timing it perfectly, I flip back to the rear-facing camera right as Vixen shoots off into the sky, does a few laps with golden orbs trailing behind her, and then lands gracefully back on her hooves. On the screen, Veronica's jaw hangs open. At least she's quie—

"Holy shit!" I'm shaking from the sheer volume such a short woman has produced. Shock rattles every one of my nerve endings awake. "Okay. I'm sorry. That was a lot. I'm packing up my stuff. I'm going back to the motel. I'm going to call you again, and so help me, if you don't pick up, I will find a way there. Boat, plane, I don't care. You're going to tell me how the hell this happened and *why* you didn't tell me sooner."

After I promise to pick up, she ends the call.

I'm about to start back to the chalet when, across the field, Patrick appears. The fading sun dips behind him, turning him into a silhouette outlined by slashes of sherbet light. Beside him, one of the reindeer nuzzles in, tilting its head up as if they're conversing.

I call out to Patrick, but he doesn't hear me, so I hop the fence and crunch my way across the field. Bits of his conversation float on the air. "Almost ready," he says. "The finishing touches are—" A reindeer sneezes beside me. I'm about to say "bless you" when I hear, "I just really hope Quinn likes it."

"Likes what?" I ask.

Patrick Hargrave turns with the speed and precision of a professional figure skater. "What? Oh, hi. Quinn. Hi."

"Hi to you, too," I say. "Hope I like what?"

"Yeah." He fishes into his satchel for an apple for Blitzen. Patrick loves these reindeer so much that he spoils them. I bet Chris wouldn't approve of Patrick messing with their diet so much. They're an elite sleigh-guiding team that needs athletic discipline. Last thing we want is any of them becoming too lethargic to sustain the all-night flight. "The, um, new bells and whistles Jorge has implemented on the sleigh."

"Oh, cool. What sort of features?"

"Bells . . . and whistles."

"Oh, you meant literally."

Patrick nods. "They're to deter flocks of nocturnal birds from crossing our flight path."

"Got it."

"What are you doing out here?" he asks, as if he wishes I were anywhere else.

"I was just taking a stroll. I'm on my way back to the chalet to talk with Veronica."

"Veronica?" Patrick wears a new shade of surprise. "I didn't realize you'd talked to anyone back home since we got here."

"I haven't," I say, uncertainly. "This was the first time. Honestly, this is the longest Veronica and I have gone without talking since we met, and since all the Merriest Mister duties have slowed down as Christmas preparation ramps up, I've really started to miss her. A video call is the least I can offer after eight months of silence. Is that a problem?"

"No, of course not." Though, he sounds as uncertain as I feel about his downward-sliding expression.

I decide not to push it because maybe he's thinking about how he wouldn't have someone like Veronica to call if he wanted to. I wouldn't peg Patrick as antisocial, but when he started at Carver & Associates, he fell out of touch with all our college friends. He tends to stick to himself.

"Will you be home for dinner?" I ask.

"Yeah," he says with a smile. I nod, moving closer to give him a kiss before heading back. "Wait, no. I won't. I have a few urgent tasks to attend to tonight. I'll be late."

"Have Hobart bring you something to eat, okay? Don't forget." I think back to my running thoughts only an hour ago, about how if I leave teaching, I may still never find a *calling*, but in our time here, Patrick morphed into a more self-assured man. The

Santa role suits him. He's taken his passion for architecture and his natural affinity for leadership and fashioned it into a winning combination.

Next year, in New Jersey, back in our house, I hope he finds a job that lets him shine as much as this one does.

A HOUSE IS NOT A HOME

PATRICK

A MEMORY

Our Realtor could sell insect repellent to an army of ants.

Keegan Sommers of Nearby Neighborhood Real Estate treats every property like it's a villa in Versailles. Gesturing grandly and using flowery roundabout speak like, "And here we have one of the many luxurious amenities of the property, a first-floor half-bath perfect for entertaining guests complete with vanity mirror over a porcelain sink and a working commode."

Quinn asks in a low voice, "Is he suggesting indoor plumbing is an *amenity*?"

I shush him. Mostly because this man stands between us and homeownership. Which is an important step in getting my parents to regard me as the success I desperately want to be. I got the job. I got the husband. All I need is the house.

"Seems like a fixer-upper," Quinn says. This time directly to Keegan, so I stifle my shush.

Keegan, without balking, says, "The fun is in the fixing. That's how you turn someone else's *house* into your *home*."

But as we stand in the soupy August air on a crumbling back porch looking out at a backyard overrun with tall stalks of grass and weeds flowering over other weeds, my stomach drops another notch. If we didn't have a strict budget, maybe this wouldn't be so torturous. If I wasn't an architect, maybe I wouldn't be thinking, "I'd have done it this way or that" in every room we walk into. And it's not like we're sitting on the funds needed to flip a place. We make enough for the basest repairs at best.

"Isn't this stunning?" Keegan asks. He plants himself between me and Quinn. Not that that's hard to do. Quinn's left a full foot of space between us as we stare blankly into the expanse. "This is a great way to do your part in going green. Maintaining a manicured rear lawn is an environmental nightmare. Look at how you can celebrate biodiversity with all these natural wonders right on your own property."

When he's not looking, I roll my eyes. But as he goes on about the acreage and the many possibilities for home gardening, I find myself starting to agree with him. And then when we go back inside, I convince Quinn to take another lap, alone with me.

"This could be a home office," I say to Quinn on the far side of the upstairs. In what's considered the "den" but is really more of a walk-in closet without the shelving. "Can't you imagine us getting ready for work here?" We're standing at the sink in the bathroom just off the main bedroom. It's roomy enough for us both, sitting beside a tub that's decidedly not claw-foot like I dreamed up for us but at least isn't a walk-in shower. "You could soak in here and read on Friday nights. Wouldn't that be nice?"

I borrow Keegan's inflections as if I'm the one about to make a commission and not a massive capital investment.

"I don't know, Pat," he says, wringing his hands. "This all seems so—I just think we shouldn't rush this."

"Of course. But you know how the market is. Houses get snatched up like that. What if the place we're meant to be in is for sale now like this one and we let it pass us by?"

"But what about your design? Building our own house?"

"That's"—I wave my hands in the air—"for the future. This is now. A starter house."

Quinn's mouth reminds me of a guppy. I half imagine little bubbles of unsaid thoughts pouring out and popping at the surface of his tank.

I hold out my hands for Quinn to take. "I know you had your heart set on a honeymoon skiing in Switzerland, but right now, I'm glad we have that money because I think this could be the house for us. It's got two floors like you wanted. There's room in the main bedroom for a desk of your own. Plus, a dining room for when we host holidays."

"When do we ever host holidays?" he asks, skeptical.

"Never, because we can't in the apartment, but here we can. Here we can do anything. We can deck the halls completely," I say. Knowing I sound like some animated character but meaning it still.

Despite my cheesiness, his nod grows faster. I lead us back downstairs and into the kitchen. His eyes flick to the fridge.

It's an old, yellowing thing with brown handles but it buzzes with enough life to keep kicking. "Here, we'll use magnets to hang all the Christmas cards from family and friends and our new neighbors, and over there"—I point to a space in the family room beside the fireplace—"we'll put up a full-sized Christmas tree. No more miniature, plastic ones. We'll go to the nearby farm and cut down a ten-footer."

"The ceilings are eight and a half feet," Keegan interrupts.

"We'll go to the farm and cut down an eight-footer." I beam at Quinn. Growing weirdly excited about a future I just now decided for us. "What do you say?"

43

THE WALLS CLOSE IN

QUINN

Mick intercepts me on my way to the workshop in mid-September. The day is fading fast. The school-aged elves pile out of a steepled building, books tucked under their arms. Mick, however, has a knapsack slung over one shoulder and their hands are hidden behind their back.

"What have you got there?" I ask.

"I made something," they say, feet shuffling. "My parents helped me. It's a first draft. I was waiting until it was ready to show you. I got it printed, bound, and . . . look." Mick produces a collection of papers held together by stark blue spiral binding. The title page reads: A FLURRY OF POEMS BY BLIZZARD.

I beam as I hold the flimsy book they've handed me. A familiar feeling coils up inside my chest. It's the same one I'd get when a struggling student aced an exam or a shy student delivered a stellar book report to the class. I flip to the first page and the dedication reads: *For the first-ever Merriest Mister. Thanks a bunch!* "This is incredible. What do you plan to do with them?"

Elation dances over Mick's features. "After the Elf Extravaganza, a bunch of people came up to me asking where they could read my other poems. I typed up the ones I performed and polished up some others and made this. Once I feel like it's perfect, I'm going to print a bazillion and do a reading at Hand over Hearth and pass these out."

"That's amazing! When are you planning it for?"

"Oh, my mom says not until January, at least." They shrug. "Gotta make it through Christmas before. But I hope you'll come!"

My enthusiasm dims. "I—I won't be here anymore. This was a one-year post. I go back to the human world after Christmas."

Mick nods glumly. "Oh. Okay. Yeah. That makes sense. I get it."

"You're going to do great things, Mick Flurry," I say, harnessing the remnants of my excitement over Mick's flourishing craft. Aside from turning out looks and judging gingerbread competitions, I'm glad I made a small difference here in one young person's life.

"Hey, Mick! You coming to the cocoa bar with us?" yells an elf with pigtails wearing a fire engine–red dress and clogs across the plaza.

"Be right there! See ya around." Mick flashes me the biggest smile before racing off to join their friends.

I tuck Mick's collection into my bag and continue toward the workshop, ready to wind down this chapter of my life. This magical detour has brought me fantastical memories to last a lifetime. I'm motivated to see how I can utilize everything I've cultivated here back home.

Patrick and Jorge are in the garage, where I get a firsthand tour of those bells and whistles Patrick was going on about out in the reindeer pasture. There are whole percussion and woodwind sections strapped to the flying beast, like we'll be conducting a symphony for the skies.

I get buckled in while Jorge discusses the other improvements made by the elves over the last year.

He might as well be speaking the way adults do in old Peanuts cartoons because I don't understand half of what he's saying. Patrick, on the other hand, is nodding vigorously, white beard bouncing.

For most of the year, Patrick didn't need to wear the cloak. Since this is his first test flight in preparation for his second Christmas, they need to replicate as many variables as possible to avoid any hiccups.

The reindeer are harnessed and ready to go.

I am, too. Ready to complete this practice run and be one day closer to returning home.

Honestly, I'm not even sure why Patrick wanted me to come on this practice run. I made the present delivery rounds last year out of necessity. This year, it feels like the council would want Patrick to go alone, as is custom. But I guess me being the first Merriest Mister has thrown custom out the window.

Patrick calls each reindeer by name, and we zoom out of the garage and into the air.

Unlike on Christmas Eve, we don't have far to go. It's a puddle-jumper flight. We're ascending longer than we're in the air. We circle until we come upon a replica of a suburban neighborhood on the outskirts of the village, which eerily reminds me of both *Monsters, Inc.* (a staple on movie days in my classroom) and *The Stepford Wives* (a movie Mom loves). The combination of simulation training mixed with movie-set Americana artifice is enough to give me the heebie-jeebies.

I shake them away as best I can, helping Patrick as much as I did last year.

In the first house, a holographic adult putters around in the kitchen for a midnight snack. I hang close to Patrick so the cloak's circle of protection includes me as we hide in a coat closet until the coast is clear.

The second house doesn't have a chimney, so Patrick pulls the magical emergency chimney from the sleigh. It's a four-by-four cube that attaches to the roof, expands to his width, and shoots us waterslide-style inside. I set out the gifts while Patrick samples the peppermint Oreos.

It's not until we're coming up on the third house, which is set apart from the rest and much closer to the village, that electric wonder strikes me with full force. My attention piques as I pitch forward in my seat and grab for the binoculars fixed to the dash-board.

From above, I get a bird's-eye view of a stone-exterior farm-house with a snow-speckled roof, which is undeniably English-inspired—a tidbit I most definitely picked up from one of Patrick's prized coffee table books. A porch wraps itself in an L shape around the front of the house. The rockers from the chalet, or replicas of them, sway in the gentle breeze.

I've seen this place before in blueprints and 3D digital render-ings and as a gingerbread creation. But this is a whole other level of jaw-dropping.

The sleigh slows to a stop atop the dream house. *Our* dream house.

Patrick doesn't act surprised by this place. Instead, he word-lessly slips down the chimney with a mischievous smirk partially hidden by his overgrown beard.

I follow him down into the place he envisioned for us. There's exposed stone throughout. The furniture choices could be summed up as quirky—none of the upholstery matches. There's a striped sitting chair, a floral couch, and a polka-dotted ottoman all keep-ing company in the same cleanly cluttered room.

I recognize this clutter as *our* clutter, from our first apart-ment. The organized chaos I grew to love. Our books, our picture frames, some of our New Jersey life has been moved here.

Patrick is tiptoeing toward a tremendous Christmas tree, lit proudly in the living room of my dreams, when I stop him with my voice. "Did you do all this?" I ask, both overwhelmed and per-plexed.

The mischievous smirk makes way for a full-blown smile. "I did."

"Why?" I ask. Then, I'm hit with the fear that I sound ungrate-ful. This is a stunning display of his love, that's for certain. My heart doesn't know whether to glow or go dark.

"For us," he says, outstretching his hands to me.

I take them, even though uncertainty has inched up into my throat like it did during that first tour of our house in New Jersey. "For us? For three and a half months?" It seems like a waste of resources. I've seen the progress reports Hobart delivers over breakfast. Toy production is way down.

"I was hoping for forever," he says, staring deep into my eyes.

The uncertainty in my throat gets usurped by panic that blocks my airways like dry bits of cookie. "Wh-huh?" I croak. "But we're leaving. In January. After Christmas." Each fragment overlaps with the last until I take a deep breath.

"What if we didn't?" he asks. My nerves get shocked into a state of paralysis. "You said the morning after our anniversary that you wished we could stay here forever and ever, so I built our forever and ever home here to make that happen."

I look everywhere but at Patrick. That doesn't prove helpful. I'm noting all the care and craftiness he and the elves poured into this place, into getting it right. Yet I know in my heart this is all wrong. "Figuratively. I meant that figuratively, Pat."

His expression drops. "I may have Santa magic, Quinn, but I still can't read your mind."

"I'm sorry. This is all coming out wrong. We agreed to one year. That's it. We have families and friends and lives and jobs to go back to." I bite my tongue hard. I shouldn't have said that last part. It's such a force of habit.

Patrick barely flinches this time, which I suppose is a good thing. "Why do you want to go back to that school where they treat you like a workhorse and our marriage like it's an abomination?"

"I don't," I say, surprising myself. It's the first time I've voiced this. The words taste equal parts bitter and delicious. They ring clearly, announcing their truth. "I think maybe I want to work in a nonprofit that specializes in mentorship for queer youth. Something tangible and connection based. No more teaching toward a test or ripping my hair out with district mandates or trying to siphon my attention in thirty different directions."

"You can have that here. Look at all you did for Blizzard," Patrick says.

"I helped one elf inside a perfect utopia," I begin, flabbergasted we're having this conversation when he's supposed to be practicing for Christmas-present delivery. Hobart should be rushing out to stop this. "I can't stop thinking of all the queer kids, like Tyler, who we delivered the unicorn pillow to last year, who need support and guidance and a soft place to land when the people in their lives meet their identities with roughness and disapproval. The mission of the North Pole is to make the world a better place, but I can't do that when I'm stuck here, cut off from the world. I have so much more to accomplish back home. Don't you feel that way, too?"

He shakes his head, causing my stomach to free-fall. "I have so much more to accomplish here. I belong here."

"It's only been eight and a half months."

"I knew you for less time when I realized I belonged with you."

His sweet words hit me in a sour spot, square in my upset stomach. He's right. I've seen his evolution. Far be it from me to negate his truth. "Pat, are you really okay with giving up our life?"

"This can be our life now," he says. He does what he did that day we toured the New Jersey house: he stretches out his arms, spins, physicalizes the expansiveness of what this could be for us. "We're so in love here."

"That's true, but I've been treating this like a vacation," I tell him. "It's easy to be in love on vacation." Just like it was easy to be in love in college, I want to add but don't.

"It doesn't feel like a vacation for me, Quinn. This is work. Maybe even my purpose."

The determination in his blue eyes scares me. I've never seen him this set on shaking up his life, and by extension mine, before.

I'm at a complete loss for words when a child's voice rings out behind me.

"Santa Claus? Is that really you?" The mousy sound comes

from a holographic girl in Christmas pajamas behind me. Clearly the elves have not yet shut down the simulation.

"Yep, kid," I say, stepping out of Patrick's golden circle of protection. "That's really him." Because it is. I can't believe I hadn't wrapped my head around it sooner, but when I stare over my shoulder at Patrick, my husband, the storybook man standing there is unmistakable. I don't know what to do with that information, but I know I can't remain here fizzling out any longer.

Feeling like the harried, frazzled Santa we met on Christmas Eve last year, without a goodbye, I walk through the hologram, through the foyer, and right out the front door into the vacuous night with no sense of direction and a wounded heart.

(IM)PRACTICAL MAGIC

PATRICK

We end up back where we started.

Quinn's sleeping down the hall. I'm awake in the middle of the night. Worrying about what my game plan is now.

Even our move across the globe and abundant magic couldn't repair us. I'm saddled with a fear that there isn't any hope left.

I stayed to finish the simulation because I couldn't risk losing my husband and the Santa position in the same night.

The fact that I had to finish it in a lovingly crafted dream home that Quinn turned his nose up at and then stormed out of was the biggest lump of coal in the stocking of my night. My whole year, if I'm being honest.

On my trudge back to the chalet, I removed the cloak and stuffed it into my satchel. Back in my real body, I could breathe again. At least enough to face the music of my miscalculations. However, Quinn wasn't awake to talk. He was tucked away in a room in the far wing. Tossing and turning or dreaming? The closed, locked door won't allow me to know.

The déjà vu of it all is too strong to stomach.

In the main bedroom now, I remain sleepless. The darkness is too bright. The silence is too loud. My heart is a malfunctioning wind-up toy, fritzing one second and failing the next.

I replay Quinn's and my argument over again. I can't believe we said all of that in front of the elves. I thought walking with my head hung low and my box of belongings out of Carver & Associates was rough. But our public showdown was a whole new level of brutal.

My spiraling thoughts are interrupted by a whirring I haven't heard in the chalet before. A shaft of cold air blows straight onto my face. I reach over to turn the light on. It's only then that I notice I'm positioned right under the air vent.

There's a thermostat in the hallway. I need only a quick glance to confirm the air-conditioning has kicked on. Drowsily, I clamber downstairs. The sun is cresting on the horizon, but the light hasn't touched enough of the village to show me what I sense but can't quite see.

Storming through the kitchen, the chalet anticipates my thoughts. Lights turn on, preceding each one of my frantic steps. At the picture windows, I splay my hands on the glass. The snow is melting.

"I don't think that's supposed to happen," I mutter to myself. I'm already throwing on boots, a coat, and a hat. When I step outside, I'm knee-deep in gray, disgusting slush. It has to be at least seventy degrees and muggy.

The cinnamon scent that usually hangs in the air is replaced with an unpleasant odor. Fumes mixed with rotting sewage. I plug my nose.

It takes one long, single lap around the property to absorb the magnitude of this. The ice-skating rink has turned into a pond. The gazebo, unreachable without a bridge or a jet pack of some sort, is askew and slowly sinking.

In the front yard, the sharp and shrill cries of the reindeer echo. I resist the impulse to run to them. Instead, I grab the binoculars from their perch on the porch. Each reindeer tries to rev up and fly, only to flop back down to the ground, landing in a crumpled ball.

On the hour, the clock tower chimes as usual. Only it doesn't play a Christmas carol. It's ... "Monster Mash." I groan at the obnoxious melody.

What in the world is happening?

As if it couldn't get worse, a heavy downpour rolls in. Lightning strikes in the distance. Thunder rattles the ground. I rush inside, where a wide-eyed, pajama-clad Quinn has appeared by the door. "What's going on?" He sounds scared. I want to hold him. Tell him it's okay. But I know it's not okay. And I know he doesn't want me to hold him. Which is worse?

A ping lights up on the house communication system. It's Hobart. "Not to alarm you, but we need you in the village right away."

Before long, we're standing in the cathedral hall. The Priors form a tribunal before us. We stand nervously with Hobart to our right like he's our criminal defense lawyer and we're awaiting sentencing. The air is thick with impatience. My brow is sweaty.

"It's happening again," Nicholas says with an unmatched fury. It strikes me in the chest like the sharp end of a sword. Until I notice he's wearing completely uncharacteristic board shorts with a tropical pattern on them. How can something sound so bad and look so funny?

"Now, hun," Colleen says. In a yellow sundress, she's the only one who doesn't appear disgruntled by the heat.

"What's happening again?" Quinn asks, shucking his coat.

Chris speaks evenly. "As we mentioned when you arrived, the magic of the North Pole runs on love. Namely, the love between the two of you." My heart takes off in a frantic gallop. It's like we've inadvertently walked into a high-stakes couples' counseling session. "If the balance gets thrown off ..."

My skin grows tight and clammy. I thought we were doing the world a service by coming here. I thought we were doing *us* a service.

"The previous Santa and Mrs. Claus were deeply in love when

the magic chose them, but their love buckled under the pressure of their roles," says Yvonne.

"Which is why you were able to knock Santa out last Christmas Eve. Their love was weak, so the magic was, too," Samson adds. "When the magic is weak, it acts out. At least, that's what we think. It hadn't happened before in any of our times here."

"Of course now it's happened twice. Back-to-back. We can't catch a break," Ashley bemoans, biting at her nails.

I want to reach out and hold Quinn's hand, but I couldn't if I tried. I'm frozen in place. And Quinn's standing so far away. Like we're repelling magnets.

"What can you do?" I ask. Fear piggybacks onto me.

"We can't do anything," says Nicholas forebodingly. "Only the two of you can."

"We'll do it. We'll do anything. Right, Quinn?" He gives me his profile. He bites his bottom lip. Tears gather in the corners of his gemstone eyes as he nods. He's scared, and I feel useless.

Chris stands to deliver this next part. "The last Santa refused, so thank you both for being willing. We know you both understand the importance of our mission. This won't be easy, but it is necessary. Once again, you're faced with a choice. The fate of Christmas will hang in the balance. Option one, you two both rescind your positions and leave the North Pole together. Christmas is canceled. Option two, you invoke a marriage separation and Quinn departs to appease the magic."

The top of my throat towers high with reservations that I can't spear my voice through.

It's Quinn who speaks. "Will that work? If we separate, and I leave?"

"We can't say for sure. All we can say is that we presented the last couple with the same choice. Instead of following our guidance, they decided to stay here while trying to mend things between them. It didn't work, and it caused chaos," says Emmanuella.

"The snowballs in the Tundra Dome turned to Nerf balls and

the ribbons in the wrapping room turned to snakes. It was random and unstoppable. No matter how hard the previous missus, Nessa, tried, things just got worse and worse until her husband quit, and she left," says Jorge.

"From the start, we knew this was a risk. We should've expected this given how you two came into your positions," says Nicholas. "It's on us as much as it is on the two of you. We shouldn't have pushed you into this. True love is a scarce resource. The magic made do with what you were able to give, but now it's out of sorts again."

Colleen clasps her hands together in front of her chest. "We know this is an impossible ask. We believe if we remove the element altogether, we may be able to reset the magic."

"Like unplugging it and plugging it back in," says Samson. Everyone shoots him an annoyed look. It sounds too simple to work.

Quinn nods. Clearly not sharing my thought. "I'll go."

The blockage in my throat clears enough for me to choke out, "No. We'll go. Together."

He turns to me fully. His head shake is a somber toll. "I can't let you do that."

"I can't let you leave." Once again, we're having an important conversation in inadequate quarters. I wish the council could dematerialize for a second. I need Quinn alone. I need Quinn to know how desperately I need him. How consumingly I love him.

His watery eyes lock on mine. "You have to. I had time to think about what you said last night. You were right. You do belong here. I don't know where I belong. I don't want to be the shadow behind the mythical man. I've never been happy inside a mold, and frankly I can't live with being the reason Christmas is canceled."

"Quinn." It comes out garbled.

A single tear tracks down his cheek. Almost in slow motion. That tear is going to haunt me forever. "Maybe the space will be good for us." Two big steps and then he's holding me. Kissing me. I can taste goodbye on his lips.

He turns and lets Hobart escort him out of the room.

"One last thing, Quinn," Nicholas says, standing and striding toward him. "We'll need your ring."

I could disintegrate into the floor. Float away as dust. I don't want to witness this.

"My ring?" Quinn ekes out. "What for?"

"The magical bond. When Patrick donned the cloak and signed the scroll, the magic fused to your union. We can't let you leave with it," Nicholas says. "It's precautionary. You understand?"

Quinn wrestles the ring off his finger. He looks dully at the empty space where the ring has sat for the last year before slapping the band down into Nicholas's open palm. Nicholas could be holding a grenade given the pace with which my heart is racing. I want to chuck it into the ether. Save our relationship from the inevitable explosion.

"Thank you," Nicholas says.

"Good luck," Quinn says. His stormy eyes meet mine one last time before the doors glide closed behind him. Sealing our fate for the sake of Christmas.

HOME, BITTERSWEET HOME

QUINN

Hobart parks the sidecar on the roof of the New Jersey house, helps me down through the chimney, and makes sure I'm safe and settled inside.

At least that's what I think he's doing. We haven't spoken the whole ride. What's there to say? Everything about this is impossibly awful.

Except, I'm surprised to find, as I move through the living room, that the walls of this house no longer seek to smother. They breathe steadily with freedom.

I shuck off my boots, fling off my coat, and go directly to the kitchen for a glass of water. The pipes gurgle before the finicky faucet spits anything out, but when it finally does, the water is cold and crisp and exactly what I need to combat the altitude- and speed-induced headache I got from the trip.

Thankfully, the council had been telling the truth when they said they'd keep our house in order while we were away. It's probably cleaner than it was before we left, which is a relief.

"I'm sorry about all of this," Hobart says. It was pin-drop silent only a second ago, so his voice makes me jump. His mood-ring eyes have gone glassy and bright blue.

"Hobart, no. I'm the one who should be apologizing. I'm sure this is not what you imagined when you dreamed of being head elf."

"None of this is what I imagined," Hobart says, almost meditatively. "I don't think it's what I wanted, either. I related a lot to what you said back there in front of the council about molds and not knowing where you belong."

I've never heard Hobart sound this introspective. "How so?"

"I think head elf isn't for me. I wanted a position that allowed me to engage more with the human population. I wanted to go out and make connections. But unfortunately, everyone said I'm not built to be a special missions elf. You know, the ones who get to go to the mortal realm to remind people of the innate goodness and love all around them? I thought that being head elf, working closely with the new humans and helping them acclimate, would be the next best thing," he says wistfully. "Don't mistake me. I've loved working closely with Santa Patrick. He's wonderful and creative and kind. None of which I need to tell you of all people."

"It's still nice to hear," I say. I become acutely aware of my naked ring finger, which still has a weight to it. The ghost of a promise lost. Any minute, I half expect Patrick to round the corner in search of a post-trip snack. "Why can't you be a special missions elf?"

"Because special missions elves are spontaneous and thrill-seeking agents of disguise who can fit seamlessly into the human world with little to no notice. I'm order and stress and too green for my own good sometimes," he says with a shrug.

"That's very self-aware. That's a strength in and of itself."

"I suppose. I've been on the path to head elf too long. I've hit my peak. It's too late to deviate," he says.

I think about teaching, how coming back here is a chance to carve a new way for myself. "You're immortal. I don't think it's ever too late to deviate. Trust your gut."

His head seesaws. Emotions flicker fast across his face. "I'll consider it. Is there anything I can do or get you before I go?"

My first instinct is to have him tell Patrick I love him when he returns, but I know that might only make a hard situation even harder, so I tell him no.

THE MERRIEST MISTERS 249

Before he disappears back up the chimney, he says, "I know in my heart that you and Santa Patrick will work it out. The kind of love you both share always prevails."

And then, I'm alone.

Is my heart racing from excitement or fear? I'm not even sure it matters.

This is brand-new to me. In my life, there were the family years, the years of just me and Mom, the three years of roommates in college, and then Patrick and I moved in together. It's strange to think that never, in my twenty-six years of existence, have I been completely independent.

I continue to ponder this as I tread the rickety steps (alone), brush my teeth (alone), and crawl into bed (alone).

I cocoon myself in the blankets, build a fortress of pillows around me to protect from whatever monsters might be lurking in this house, and let the fateful moment where the magic turned against us rocket back to me.

I still can't comprehend how Patrick decided I would want to stay in the North Pole beyond our agreed-upon year.

That's how Patrick works, I guess. He decides, and then he sticks to it.

For a long while, I felt lucky that a decisive man had decided on me. It proved I was worthy.

My dad could leave, my mom could wish me different, but Patrick Hargrave could love me. And, at the time, that would fix everything.

I know now, in this bed that's too big for one person, that that's not true.

Going along with the wants of others has only left me empty and incomplete.

Still, in my heart of hearts, I also know the scattered pieces of my relationship are not unsalvageable. I just don't have the vision or the energy to put them back together again. Not yet.

So for now, I hold Patrick's pillow tight in my arms, and I sleep.

98 DAYS 'TIL CHRISTMAS

There's no fresh pot of coffee waiting for me in the morning. I can't plop an egg in an unheated pan and expect an omelet. I can't even expect the fridge to be full. I swing open the door, and I'm greeted by nothing except a burnt-out light.

I wait for the annoyance to race out of me. Instead, there's an invigoration to change it, to make myself useful after so many months of forced leisure.

On a notepad from a junk drawer, I write a to-do list:

- *Grocery shopping*
- *Hardware store—fridge lightbulb*
- *Call Mom*

All I need now are my keys, which aren't to be found in any of the usual places. I check the banana hook by the coffee pods, my backpack in the hall closet, and even the pockets of coats I vaguely remember wearing before leaving for the North Pole. I settle, finally, on taking Patrick's car instead.

This proves a fool's errand when I slip into the driver's seat and his scent wafts up from the upholstery. Not his Santa scent. No, this is the ocean breeze body wash and spicy deodorant combination I miss more than anything. I buckle my seat belt and pull it tight to snap my body out of its odor-induced stupor.

That only works until I reach the stop sign at the end of our block, turn on the radio, and the Hozier song we had our first dance to crackles from the old speakers. I get lost in the memory of it until there's a shout from outside the car. A kindly neighbor walking her goldendoodle is waving excitedly at me from beside a fire hydrant. "Quinn," she shouts. I roll down my window. "It's wonderful to see you're back!"

"It's wonderful to be back," I say, remaining sparing with the details of my absence. The interaction helps me reset back to the human world. By the time she's pulling a plastic baggie from her pocket to pick up after her dog, I'm lighter.

The to-do list takes me a good chunk of the afternoon. I didn't mark down which kind of lightbulb I needed, which meant I had to get the store employee to look up the make and model of my ancient refrigerator, so I didn't accidentally buy the wrong one. The grocery store has shuffled sections around since I was here last, so I text Veronica about my frustration (I'm back. Without Patrick. Long story. Where the hell are the avocados?!) and then spend a good fifteen minutes hunting for said avocados.

When I finally make it back home, marginally accomplished, I'm met with another woman and another dog. This time, they're taking up residence on my front step.

"V?" I call, getting out of my car. Luca, her eight-year-old black Lab, is curled up by her feet, strapped into his harness.

"I've come to see you," she says, obviously having sensed I would need her based on my chaotic text about the missing single-seeded berries.

Overwhelmed by the sight of her and relieved to have a friend like her, I leave my bags and race to her, enveloping her in a hug so long and hard I'm afraid I might crush her.

"Thank you," I whisper-cry into her curly hair.

"I missed you," she says, squeezing me tighter. That squeeze presses an emotional button hidden inside my torso. The water-works I've held back since last night come on with a vengeance. Hiccupping, choking cries. I've never felt uglier or messier, but like a true best friend, she doesn't care. "Come on, let's get you inside. I brought tissues. Plenty of them."

WHAT A MESS WE'VE MADE

PATRICK

The wazoo is out of whack.

Over two weeks gone; the magic is still pissed.

I'm crouching in the workshop as elves scatter about on hands and knees like rats being chased by a broom in a restaurant kitchen. The wazoo is shooting finished toys out at odd angles. Action figures become projectiles fired off across the room. Everyone's ducking for cover. Including me.

I race to turn the machine off, but like that old copier at Carver & Associates, it mocks me with its defiance. Several wires pulled and a few swear words later, we corral it into off-mode.

"We're okay, everyone," I announce. "Take a break while we, uh, try to assess the damage." The main floor is overrun with dislodged toy parts. No matter how many fans I rolled in here, I can't quite mitigate the smell of rotten eggs that has permeated the North Pole since that first unruly thunderstorm dispersed.

Everyone clears out to the atrium for snacks, coffee, and to talk about me. How bad a job I'm doing. My legacy is going to be remembered as the first Santa to ever cancel Christmas because he couldn't get his shit together.

Jorge and Samson come to assist me. We turn cranks and pull levers, and we get the wazoo back to work, albeit slower than it was before. This would be an okay sign if it weren't about to decrease production even more. And if production decreases even more, we're not going to make our quota for this week. And if we don't make this quota for the week, we're going to be racing against the clock for Christmas.

I'm in a perpetual state of stress, sweat, and acute heartbreak. This would all be much easier to manage if heart shards weren't trying to carve their way out of me. Exorcise my hurt. Every. Damn. Step. I. Take.

At the end of a dreadful workday, I slog home, begrudging our separation. Because seeing Quinn's smile when I swing open the door would at least brighten my dour mood.

The regrets are at their loudest tonight as I wander the dream house (which is more like a nightmare house now) alone. I shuffle about through the impeccably decorated rooms. Aimless and over-whelmed.

Sometime after three A.M., I stagger through the picturesque village toward the toy workshop. At first, I think I'll get some work done on the Naughty and Nice lists, then I spot the North Pole Headquarters control room with its Big Brother screens and its access to the core memories of every human on Earth. This sparks an idea.

I can't see Quinn. But I can still *see* Quinn.

After I'm through the secure archways, which creep me out no matter how many times I've been in here, I'm startled by the shape of a man flopped over in a chair. A memory of a family projects onto the enormous screen. It's shown through the eyes of a father, singing as his son blows out the candles on a Fudgie the Whale birthday cake. The woman with the close-cut hair beside him is familiar to me, though I know her as a much older woman.

Nicholas notices me noticing him. He uses a hankie to swiftly blot at his eyes. "Didn't hear you sneak up on me." He's struggling to regain his composure.

"I'm sorry." The apology is weak but the best I can come up with in my present state.

"Don't ever be sorry for existing," he says. "That's what my father used to tell me. That's what I told my son before he passed. That's what I'm telling you now."

"Solid advice." My eyes flit back toward the screen. "Is that your son?"

"It is. I come here some nights to reminisce. We all need that when we lose sight of what's important." There's a loaded silence. "I'm guessing that's why you're here as well."

I nod, head chock-full of loaded, clattering dice. "Does reminiscing help?"

His nod is far surer than my own. "It helps to remind me that there's so much love in the world, even in the face of adversity."

"Does that still hold when *you're* the cause of the adversity?" I ask. The crushing weight of my emotions doubles.

He stands and grabs my shoulder. I lift my chin and our gazes connect. He's staring at me with the assured intensity I've always longed for from my father. "Santas come and go here, but you? You embody the spirit. That spirit has worked miracles before."

"A miracle is a lot to deliver."

"Miracles come in all shapes and sizes, son." The moniker carves its way into my sternum. Takes my heart and cradles it. "Remind yourself of that. Remind Quinn of that."

"How?" I ask, voice as paper thin as the straws I'm grasping at.

"Here." He presses me down into the chair he just got up from and types in *Patrick Hargrave*. Up pop hundreds of thousands of my memories featuring hundreds of different people in thousands of different locations. Some forgotten. Some still stored in my own memory bank for safekeeping. All containing sensations and experiences that made me who I am today. That turned Quinn and me into the couple we are.

My shaky hand taps the first one that calls out to me. It's when Quinn and I first met.

"I still have hope, Patrick." He's facing the door now. Hand on the sensor. Words barely above a scrape. "Hold on to yours, too."

PLAYING DRESS-UP

QUINN

"Nickel tones or gold and brass tones?" I ask Veronica as we stand in an empty, industrial aisle of the local hardware store deciding on a new centerset faucet for the downstairs bathroom.

For the last month, I've worked in a fugue state.

After a night of wine and pizza and recounting everything for Veronica, she went off to school and I surprised myself by turning my pent-up attention toward the house. I changed into an old college T-shirt, ripped-up denim overalls, and a pair of workout sneakers that have seen better days. My relationship may be in shambles, but the house doesn't need to be.

In the garage, I catalogued the towers of untouched moving boxes. I unpacked lamps I thought we'd lost in the move and books I received as gifts for birthdays or Christmases or from my students. I found permanent places for them inside the house. The more personal effects I set out, the more the place came to life.

Wedding presents we never made use of—a juice press and a purely aspirational hand-crank pasta machine—got unboxed and placed in the kitchen cabinets. I jotted down in a notebook where I've put everything, so nothing is missing when I'm ready to use it.

One day, my hands got coated in an obscene amount of dirt and dust, so I went into the bathroom, turned the hot water handle, and was not even shocked or annoyed when it fell off. I had another project for my idle mind and hands.

"The gold and brass tones will go better with the bath mats you ordered last week," Veronica says, effortlessly pragmatic.

I settle on a royal style, placing it in our cart alongside a wrench and a drop bucket. On our way to the checkout, we pass the Halloween decorations. I nearly clock an oncoming cart. Stopping short, I glance up and find Kacey Ortega, our old college friend, with a basket full of jack-o'-lanterns, ghouls, and boxes of orange lights.

"Quinn, it's been forever. Where have you been hiding?" She circles around her cart to embrace me. I eye Veronica over Kacey's shoulder, unsure how to respond.

"Oh, here and there," I say noncommittally. To segue, I introduce Veronica. I can't help but notice her gaze as it takes in Kacey fully. She is objectively beautiful with long, flowing black hair and golden skin. "How are you? How's the nonprofit life treating you?"

"It's been tough as of late. We're expanding, trying to hire team members, and rapidly outgrowing our space," she says. What goes unsaid is how Patrick ghosted her on her workspace. He told me it would be a long-term project. Still, it sounds like she could use it now. "No matter, though, because we're gearing up for our big queer Halloween party, which is going to be spectacular."

"Don't you mean *spook*-tacular?" Veronica says, showing her goofy side.

Kacey's having a cartful of fun, and the ghoulish items make me realize that I have no Halloween plans. "Are you looking for volunteers?"

She pops her lips. "Always. Why, are you interested?"

Within the week, Veronica and I have an email full of details and responsibilities, which help keep my mind off the Christmas wonderland I left behind.

55 DAYS 'TIL CHRISTMAS

On Halloween morning, Veronica texts, I've got the costumes covered.

Fine by me! I send back because I hadn't given costumes a single thought.

I eat my words when she arrives, though, because Veronica comes right from school toting two garment bags. Inside the first is a Santa costume. Inside the second is a Mrs. Claus costume. I resist the urge to vomit.

"I thought it would be funny," she says.

"Too soon," I say dryly. "I'm not wearing that." I don't even let her inside with those monstrosities. I don't need more reminders of the magical life I had to leave behind.

In the bedroom, Veronica marvels at the new accordion-style closet door I replaced the broken one that fell off with. Her compliments wipe away the unease.

We settle on 1950s greasers. Veronica borrows Patrick's leather biker jacket that he bought at a thrift store in New York City but never wore for fear it made him look like a tool. I own a pink satin jacket, which I pair with a black T-shirt and a pair of horn-rimmed sunglasses, which I pop the lenses out of.

We don't have much time to get ready before we leave for Kacey's event, so we're in the bathroom at the lone sink, wrestling for mirror space. Veronica is going for the wet hair, slicked-back look. I find two black clips in Veronica's purse, which I fasten into my curls before grabbing for my liquid eyeliner.

"Are we ever going to talk about what's going to happen with you and Patrick after Christmas? I've been giving you your space and I don't want to pry, but I'm your best friend so I sort of have to."

"I don't know what there is to talk about."

"Have you heard from him?"

"No. Maybe he's not allowed to contact me. Maybe he doesn't want to?" That would really throw salt in the gaping wound of our relationship. I know I'm the one that left, but the memory of that night still stings, and I did it for the greater good. That's hard to remember when it feels like I'm living in a perpetual shock chamber.

Veronica catches my eye in the mirror. "Quinn, Patrick loves you. He built a life with you. Of course he wants to."

"I don't know." I swipe some blush onto my cheeks. "I don't think he built a life *with* me so much as *for* me, and I let him."

"What do you mean by that?" she asks before setting her hair with strong-hold hairspray.

I end up coughing, stepping away so I don't get any more product in my mouth. My tongue is gummy now, yet the words are anything but stuck. "For starters, he built a house for us in the North Pole without telling me. He assumed I would go along with it because, well, I've gone along with almost everything else up until now."

"Okay, I get that." Veronica jumps up to sit on the sink counter so she's facing me. "Do you still love him?"

It's a big question. I grab her closest hand, needing the grounding support to get this out. "Of course I do"—I take a beat—"but *differently*."

"Differently doesn't sound so bad," she says.

"I spent a good chunk of my adolescence letting my mom fill my head with these negative ideas about men and relationships and romance. Then, I met Patrick, and I fell so hard for him so fast. I tried to unlearn all of those things my mom taught me as quickly as possible, which I think meant I never really learned who *I* was on my own," I say with a huff. "Before the North Pole, when we were here, in the same house but living these disjointed, separate lives, I begrudged him for not being around more for me. Whether he can't contact me or he decided not to doesn't matter so much because this time apart has shown me that I'm not Patrick's husband or so-and-so's teacher or the North Pole's Merriest Mister, I'm Quinn Muller.

"I forgot that I'm not just someone to and for others. I have to

be someone for myself, too. Perhaps we were always meant to separate. Maybe two people can't grow properly unless they're apart.
Maybe I have no idea what I'm talking about. Not like I had many
adults modeling strong relationships for me growing up. Especially queer ones."

"Damn, that's a lot," she says, hopping off the counter and hug-
ging me tightly. She gives great hugs and this one is no exception.
"It'll all work out. I promise. Now let's finish up so we can make
it to the rec hall before the guests get there. I want to show off my
look."

"You mean you want to show off your look *for Kacey*," I correct.

"I'm not to be shamed, okay? I'm still single and she's stunning. Let's go before my hair gets messed up."

When we arrive at the rec center, a squat brick building whose
windows could use a good washing, we're surprised to see the Halloween decorations are already at risk of blowing away. It's an over-
cast night, wispy clouds rolling fast across the bright, round moon,
so we rush to save what we can of the garland before going inside
and down a flight of steps.

The ceilings are low, the lights are hazy, and the room is the
size of a postage stamp.

"This has to be a fire hazard, right?" Veronica asks.

"You made it!" Kacey cries. She's dressed as a witch, except
not a green cartoonish one with warts and a pointy hat. More
like she's about to star in a production of *The Crucible*. A Puritan
dress, buckled shoes, a muddy face, and the words TRY AND BURN
ME. I DARE YOU. embellished on the back.

"This look. I'm obsessed," Veronica says.

We're given our posts. Veronica runs check-in. I'm manning
the photo booth.

This place is run-down. Stains and cracks as far as the eye can
see, much like the house before I began my improvements. Clearly,
the township has relegated this queer-centric community group
to the bowels of the building, which is awful, or maybe this is all

Kacey can afford, which is a different kind of awful. No matter, I can see why Patrick's services were needed.

I can also see why Kacey needs to expand her team. Even with the smattering of volunteers, she has to keep the food separated based on dietary restrictions and allergies, run activities, and ensure nobody snuck in any alcohol since this is an eighteen-and-under event.

Overall, it's fun, helping the teens pose for Polaroid photos with paper props before they scurry along to other tables. For the next several hours, I say "Happy Halloween" to gaggles of ladybugs and vampires and Super Marios and hand out miniature candy bars. I think about what it would've been like to have a space like this when I was this age. I wonder if I would have gone to the same college, fallen for Patrick, married him, ended up here.

There's no way to say for certain. The only thing I'm certain of is the stab of missing Patrick that has taken up residence in my chest. I pack it down when another group of kids—this time a bunch of zombies—steps in front of the plastic backdrop.

"Say 'boo!'" I instruct before the flash goes off. It's then that I realize, the scariest part of this evening has nothing to do with the costumes or the decorations, it's the bleakness of the uncertain, Patrick-less future rolled out before me.

MAKING AMENDS

PATRICK

48 DAYS 'TIL CHRISTMAS

Nobody in the North Pole knows I have Quinn's wedding ring fastened to a chain around my neck alongside my own. I wear it at all times.

Nicholas handed it over to me after our run-in the other night in the North Pole Headquarters. It feels wrong to put the ring in a box. The band rests against my chest. Bounces in counterpoint to my heartbeat.

That night and many nights since, I've binged memories like they are seasons of my favorite TV show. Revisiting moments from our past has given me more perspective about our future.

Time has changed us. Viewing the memories like that—switching between my perspective and Quinn's—bolded and circled those changes. Made me realize that we're not the same people we were when we met. We act a little different, we look a little different, and that means we need to love a little differently, too.

At turns, I've been selfish. Offering gestures instead of fixes.

No wonder Quinn wanted space.

On the other side of this revelation, I'm reinvigorated to win Quinn back. His trust, his heart, and then some.

I'm in Toy Maker Tower. Six helpful elves unravel the delicate, hefty scroll of the Nice list across my large desk. We're do-

ing things the old-fashioned way here with a quill pen and ink
canister. I'm making handwritten edits as the magic *still* attempts
to reset itself.

I'm only on the G-names when Hobart knocks before entering
with a large burlap sack filled to the brim with letters. "Time for
a little break from list-checking, Santa Patrick. We've got some
wishes to read over and grant."

The six other elves exit. It's just me, Hobart, and a mountain of
sealed envelopes. It's our job to read through them, cross-reference
the Naughty and Nice lists, and send the approved wishes to production for fulfillment.

Even though it's taxing, and my eyes have to strain, I love it.
There's something calming about going through these. Different
languages magically translate themselves as I read, and misspelled
words rearrange themselves on the page to make more sense. If
I focus hard enough, it's like I can hear the voice of the writer as
clearly as if they were standing right in front of me.

This pile Hobart has brought us takes several hours to get
through. The closer we get to Christmas the more letters come
in and the faster production has to work to ensure no approved
wish goes ungranted. This can mean long shifts, late nights, and
steady streams of coffee with peppermint creamer to keep me
going.

We're about to take a break for the day when Hobart slips me
an extra envelope out from the front pocket of his dark green
overalls. He sets it down on the desk while whistling almost too
casually.

The return address draws my eye. It's my childhood home.
And Bradley's name above it. The handwriting is blocky and
young-looking.

"Bart, what is—"

He's gone. Vanished into thin air. The chair he was sitting in
swivels and squeaks in his absence.

Inside the envelope, there's an old wish letter Bradley wrote from when he was a teen. Mom made us write letters to Santa every year. No matter if we claimed to believe or not. A week before Christmas, she'd set out pens and paper after dinner and demand our undivided attention on the task. Even Dad.

When I got older, I always thought she was stealing them away, reading them, and making sure she purchased exactly what we wanted off our lists. I never suspected she was posting them to the North Pole.

It reads:

Dear Santa,
First off, thanks for the many wonderful gifts you brought
me and my family last year. Every one of them was greatly
appreciated. I hope you had a nice long rest after a busy year of
planning.

I laugh. Even at eighteen, he was cordial. And if he was eighteen, that made me . . . freshly thirteen. The year I began to realize I might not be like all the other boys.

Now for the purpose of my correspondence.
I'm writing to you this year with a wish not for myself but
for my brother.
He doesn't care for me much, which is his right, but I've
started to notice a change in his behavior.

I stop reading for a second. That statement is hard to swallow.

He comes home from school sullen. He shuts himself in his
room. He's grown quieter.
I don't think he'd talk to me if I asked what was wrong, but
I'll admit that I'm worried.
Perhaps this is completely out of your purview, but I was
hoping you could maybe gift him something—nothing flashy—

that shows him how loved he is for who he is. I'm not sure it will
fix things, but maybe it's worth a shot.
   Thanks in advance for your consideration.
Warmly yours,
Bradley Hargrave

I'm out of my chair before I even finish reading the sign-off. In headquarters, I punch in my own name and pull up that Christmas. For the life of me, I can't remember what I got. I scrub the memory for a moment, a look of elation, a shout of validation.

Instead, toward the middle, there is a quiet moment. My hands unwrap a one-hundred-and-twenty pack of artist-grade colored pencils. Up until then, I'd sensed disapproval from my parents over my affinity for drawing. They saw it as childish, a hobby, a time-suck. I glowed, thinking this was from them.

I read the tagline for the brand: THE RAINBOW AWAITS. I was slowly beginning to understand myself as some flavor of queer. My eyes landed on guys longer than girls at the movies or the mall. I knew the rainbow flag as the symbol of pride. At thirteen, I took that as a sign—even if unintended—that if and when I came out, I'd be accepted.

Now I comb back through the memory record. When I turn the pencil set around to show my parents, there isn't knowingness or support in their expressions. But when I zoom in on Bradley's reaction, the side of his mouth tips up slightly in a smile. Like a teen who knows his wish had been granted.

I'm crying now. Fat, salty tears running down my hot cheeks.

Pulling out my phone, I call Bradley. The call connects after a single ring. He must hear the tears before I speak because he asks, "Patrick, what's happened?"

I sniffle. "Nothing. Or everything. I don't know."

He proffers a small apology to someone on the other end of the line. There are muffled footfalls and a door closing and a soft sigh. "Are Mom and Dad okay?"

"Yes," I say. Though, how am I to know? I've been ignoring them since I got here. Chalking up the neglect to a need for my attention elsewhere.

"Are *you* okay?" Bradley asks. His voice is sanded down. But still, it pries me open.

"No," I admit. "Not really." He patiently waits for the blubbering and the heavy breathing to end. "I'm sorry. You're probably at work. Busy. I—"

"Patrick, that's not important. Why have you called? You never call." He doesn't say this to hurt me. He's only stating fact.

"That's why I'm calling," I say.

"I don't understand," he says. But there's an undertone of *I want to.*

"Was I a jerk to you when we were kids?" I ask.

There's a click on the line. Momentarily, I'm afraid he's hung up. "Where is this coming from?"

"I was. It's okay. I know I was. Well, I didn't know until recently, but—" I heave out a breath lodged up in my diaphragm. "I'm sorry, Bradley."

"I, uh— Apology accepted," he says quickly. Like he's been waiting on these words for a while. "But it's really not necessary. I gave you your space because that's what you wanted."

"It wasn't," I say. "You know how Dad and Uncle Luke were always in competition with each other. All those stories Dad would tell about them vying for favorite with Nan and Pop. I guess I thought that's how brothers were supposed to be."

"How brothers are supposed to be?" Bradley asks, confusion audible. "They can barely have a conversation without arguing."

"You're right. I didn't even think about that. I was too busy spending all my energy trying to catch up to you."

"Funny, I always thought you were chasing me away."

I laugh, even though it's not ha-ha funny. More of a sad-funny. "Either way, I was running, and I never stopped long enough to consider how you felt because I was too concerned about what Mom and Dad thought."

"Guess we were both keeping each other at arm's length." He sounds wistful.

I shake my head. "I wish I'd said something sooner. Maybe I wouldn't have been rushing against a clock that was never ticking."

"What's that now?"

"I chose an accelerated architecture program so Mom and Dad would see my career choice as legitimate sooner. I got married to Quinn so they would understand our relationship quicker. All in the name of competing with you and winning their affection," I say. The selfishness bears down on me.

"If it makes you feel any better, you did win that round. I'll never have what you and Quinn have," he says.

"You're young. Don't knock yourself down like that."

"It's not a knock, Patrick. I don't want those things. I've never wanted those things. Not with a woman, not with a man, not with a nonbinary person. I'm ace."

I sit in stunned silence for a second. "That's . . . that's cool. I'm happy you found that out about yourself. How long have you known?"

"A while," he says with a rueful laugh. "I've never told anyone in our family that before. I'm ridiculously surprised the first was you."

I laugh along despite the gibe. "I'm glad it was. Thank you for trusting me with that."

"Of course." Those two words feel like the first bricks laid on a road to a real relationship.

"Say," I breathe, taking my own brick down. "Can I tell you something I haven't told anyone in our family, either?"

"I'd love that. Just give me a minute." It's muffled, but it sounds like he's telling his assistant that he's taking an early lunch.

Before I know it, I'm spilling everything. From the frying pan and the first flight to the dream house and Quinn leaving. It feels good to unload some of this. It feels even better that the person listening and offering advice in response is Bradley.

HERE'S TO NEW BEGINNINGS

QUINN

Thanksgiving is tomorrow.

I park my car in the driveway and let out a sigh.

It's my first without Patrick.

To combat the sadness, I took a trip to the drugstore and picked up face masks and a couple of bottles of nail polish that caught my eye—a deep brown, a dark red, and a buttery yellow. Tonight, Veronica is going to come by, we're going to put on *Carol* (a seasonal comfort watch) and beautify ourselves.

With a reusable shopping bag swinging from one hand, I head for the mailbox, right as my phone starts ringing. It's Mom.

I've received a few texts from her since I returned but they've been brief, from which I can sense an upset she won't admit to. Strange that she's chosen now to call, but I'm not going to miss this.

"Mom, hey! Long time, no talk. What's happening with you?" I ask, keeping my tone light even if I'm hurt.

"Been busy. Work," she says. "Just calling to say happy Thanksgiving before I head up to the mountains with Pete."

"What mountains? Wait, who's Pete?" I ask.

"Oh, right." She clicks her tongue. "My boyfriend."

I lean up against the trunk of my car, setting the bag down on the driveway I salted this morning. There might be snow in the forecast, which I'm happy about. I miss the fluffy stuff. Just like I miss Mom. And I'm more than a little hurt she didn't tell me this sooner. "I didn't know you had a boyfriend."

"There's a lot you don't know as of late." Her tone is clipped.

"I'm sorry I didn't call." I don't add that I've been playing pretend in the land of sugarplums and elves to save Christmas because even if Veronica understood, the improbability here is too high. She'll think I'm making fun of her or something.

I can almost see her shrug and flip her hair over her shoulder like she's so blasé about it. "Yeah. Me, too. Same here."

The silence simmers between us for a second. "Where did you meet this Pete?" She doesn't even chuckle at the rhyme. She must be really pissed.

"The casino." Mom always had a habit of gravitating toward men who ruled the card tables or boasted assurance at the roulette wheel.

"How long have you been seeing him?" I ask. You can miss a lot when you fall off the face of the earth for nine months.

"Seventeen, maybe eighteen weeks?" Mom often relays the length of her relationships in weeks the way a new mother relays their infant's age. She thinks the higher the number, the better it sounds.

These men usually had slicked-back hair, worn leather jackets, and always smelled faintly of cigarette smoke, even when Mom claimed smokers were a deal breaker. They were everything my dad wasn't: freewheeling, partying, gambling men. It's like she never understood that luck on the casino floor usually meant unlucky in love.

Now it makes sense when I think about why I was inexplicably drawn to Patrick when we met in college outside of that clubhouse. He smelled like vodka and he was dressed like Santa and his phone was missing. On the outside, he appeared much like these card sharks my mom brought around the apartment—the masculine ideal I was programmed to want.

But as we got to know one another, Patrick's true nature unmasked itself. His partying, lightly mysterious persona was not a feature of his programming, but rather a bug in his development. It was his way of letting loose, shedding his parents' disappointment over his path of study. Even if I often wondered how true their disapproval was.

The Patrick I started dating barely drank except socially and would rather go to a movie than a club. He was a handsome, stable decision-maker. I sighed with relief and promptly fell head-over-heels in love with him.

Maybe head-over-heels in love isn't a state you can stay in or try to get back to—too much blood rushing to the head all the time, dizzying. Maybe firmly-on-two-feet in love is mature love. The kind we need now.

"Why's it matter?" Mom asks, snapping me back to the conversation.

"A little soon to be going to his family Thanksgiving, no?" I ask without thinking.

"Not like you sent me an invite. I don't even know where you are."

"I'm in New Jersey. Home," I say, sounding salty in the reverb on her end. She must have me on speaker. I temper my voice before asking, "If I had invited you, would you have come?"

"What kind of question is that? Of course. As long as Pete could come, of course." Is Pete there, standing in our old kitchen eating a sandwich over the sink, listening in? That's how it feels.

"Are you sure?" I ask, harnessing some of the forwardness I found in the North Pole. "Because the last few years, the last several holidays, you've bailed."

"I don't bail. I have somewhere else to be." She's failing to spot that there is no difference. That "somewhere else to be" usually only materializes after the fact, after the plans have been made, but I don't want to blame her anymore. There are two people who are a part of this problem. We both have to want to find a solution.

"Mom," I say. "Be honest. The last major event I saw you at was my wedding, and even then, you sulked through the whole thing." I lift my left hand, once again mourning the place where my wedding ring used to be. Before, it felt like a bothersome anchor. Now I feel completely adrift without it. I wish we could split the difference.

"Where is this coming from?" she asks sharply. At least she hasn't denied anything.

I shake my head, unable to find words until suddenly I'm choked up. "It's coming from missing you," I croak.

There's silence and then finally: "Oh, my baby." I hear rustling, the sound of a chair scraping across linoleum, and footsteps down a carpeted hallway that I recognize too well from my childhood. "I don't even know what to say. I miss you, too."

"Then why don't you ever want to see me?" I ask. I wish we weren't having this conversation over the phone while I'm standing in my driveway. But I'm frozen here. Autumn wind gliding over my shoulders. Dead leaves rolling over my feet.

She takes a loud breath that crackles. "Because it hurts too much."

"Hurts? What hurts?" I ask, wanting desperately to understand.

"I had you when I was a teenager, Quinn. Barely an adult. I had plans to go to college and get a business degree. But a couple months after high school graduation I became a wife, and then a couple months after that I became a mother. Gran and Grandpa would've had it no other way. Everything changed for me so quickly," she says, saddened. "I loved you from the moment I found out I was going to have you. Don't mistake my words. I'm only trying to say that one night with your father irrevocably changed the path of my life. I didn't even know if I loved him. All I knew was that I needed to learn how to and fast so that I could be there for you."

"Mom," I say, as if that's worth anything in this moment. I wait patiently for her to continue.

"I wasn't good at it. I tried and tried and tried to make a happy home while I only grew unhappier, so when your father finally served me papers, I flung myself in the other direction." There's a sniffle. I can't tell if it's on her end of the line or mine. I realize now that every relationship is as delicate as a strand of dental floss. Two good tugs in opposing directions could snap the whole thing apart.

"It was me and you, my baby, against the world. That's how I liked it. They tell you in all the parenting books how to make sure your child grows up to be strong and independent, but I liked how you needed me too much. I liked that even in middle school you weren't embarrassed to hold my hand when we crossed the street or to go shopping with me at the mall and then suddenly high school happened and you came into your own. Then, you got into a great college and met this great man with this perfect, perfect family and I know this is selfish, Quinn, I know, but I didn't want to let you go," she says, breaking and somehow also healing my heart.

"I didn't go anywhere," I say reassuringly. "I'm still here."

"It didn't feel that way. It felt like I was being replaced. Again," she says with a sigh. I know she's talking about Dad. Regardless of whether she loved him or not, she depended on him. Her whole life she was told she had to. "But I'm sorry. To protect myself from hurt, I hurt you. That was never my intention. I hope you know that."

"I do," I say. Mom hardened, like Patrick did before we met. They performed "carefree" as if they were being paid to do so. I did the opposite. I was so afraid Patrick would hurt me by leaving that I performed "careful." Careful husband who never says no and is along for the ride.

Marriages aren't one person driving the sleigh and the other playing pillow-passenger in the sidecar.

Marriages are, as silly as it may seem, tandem bicycles. If you can't learn to pedal together, you'll end up tipping or crashing or worse.

"Good," she says, recovering. "Good. So, listen, do you have plans for Thanksgiving? Because if you don't, it's not too late for me to cancel. My car is out of commission but I'm sure I could take the bus up to you or—"

"No, Mom, don't rearrange your plans for me." I wipe a stray tear from my cheek. "I'm going to Veronica's house to celebrate with her mom and stepdad."

"Where's Patrick?"

I sigh quietly, wishing I could tell her the truth after all she just shared with me. "Still traveling," I say instead. I'll explain it all when the time is right. For now, I want this to be about us. Only us.

"That must be tough, my baby," she says. "Being apart like that around the holidays."

"It is." Those two words can't convey even the half of it.

"I'm sorry. I'll tell you what. I've got some sick days saved up I need to use before the end of the year. Why don't I come out for Christmas this year? We'll spend some time together."

I blink back new tears. "That sounds great."

Before she hangs up, she promises to call again when she's on the road back from Massachusetts when the cell service kicks back in. She tells me she loves me. I tell her the same.

Leaving my bag by the trunk, I go to the mailbox, expecting only bills and the odd Christmas card from those families who haven't gone entirely digital. My breath catches when I discover an envelope with no return address.

I don't even need to open it to know it's from the North Pole, from Patrick. The cinnamon scent wafts up off the postage.

My heart turns incandescent.

Inside the house, I sit at my desk in my bedroom, heart beating so hard you'd think I was about to learn government secrets. Which, I guess, being at the North Pole, I kind of did.

The envelope contains two pieces of paper. The first is a letter dated a few days ago:

Dearest Quinn,
My family may not be perfect, but there is one good thing I
learned from them: Hargraves never give up.
> *I made a wish a long time ago, and I won't give up on it.*
> *Not now. Not ever.*
> *Trust in that.*
All my love,
Patrick

The second paper is another letter. This one has the Casola's Christmas Village logo printed in the top right corner. It's from his birthday all those years ago, the letter he wrote to Santa. Only, it doesn't say: *I wish for my degree* like he'd jokingly said to me on the Kissing Bridge. Instead, it says:

Dear Santa,
I wish to love Quinn Muller forever.

REMINDERS OF HOME

PATRICK

25 DAYS 'TIL CHRISTMAS

On my walk home from the workshop after a long day with minimal issues, a light snowfall begins. Barely even a flurry. I have to tilt my head up and stick my tongue out. Taste the flakes to even register it because it's so dark. But it's happening. I hug my coat closer to my body from the sudden rush of welcome cold.

Elves emerge from their homes. Plant themselves on their doorsteps. Excitedly shout to their neighbors, "Come quick! Look!"

I smile to myself as the shimmer of our protective snow globe shell winks in the starry sky. Status quo is returning steadily.

On the mat inside the door of the dream house, an envelope is waiting for me.

Inside the envelope, there's a hand-drawn birthday card. In the pandemonium, I probably would've forgotten all about it had I not received this. I always said I wasn't good with words, and Quinn always said he wasn't good at drawing. Except there's a valiant effort made here, which touches me.

In the center of the paper is Quinn's interpretation of our dream house. *My* dream house?

He's drawn it lovingly and pretty accurately from memory with colored pencil and light shading for depth. The one noticeable difference is that the roof is separated from the rest of the main structure. From inside, dozens of colorful balloons float out between the gaps and up into the sky.

Above the drawing he's written: *It's your birthday, so* . . . Below the drawing: *raise the roof!*

I chuckle at his corny architecture pun before rushing up to my office to read this in comfort.

> *Dearest Patrick,*
> *Happy early, or on-time, or belated twenty-seventh birthday!*
> *(I'm unsure if this will ever make it to you so I wanted to cover all my bases just in case.)*
> *It feels wrong that we're not together to celebrate. I know why we can't be. I accept why we can't be. But hurt can't know or accept. Hurt just is.*
> *I hope the magic is back to normal.*
> *I don't think I made it clear enough when I left, but I'm proud of you, Patrick. What you've done for the North Pole in the last year is nothing short of spectacular. I don't think I've seen you that impassioned or inspired since college.*
> *I guess what I'm saying is that if this truly is your calling, even if it means we can't be together, I'll understand. We had many beautiful years, and it would be selfish of me to demand more when you're meant to be somewhere else.*
> *Wow. This got depressing for a birthday card, but I already spent more hours than I'd like to admit drawing this, so* . . . *sorry for that.*
> *Wishing you a joyous day and a successful run this Christmas.*
> *I love you, Pat. Always will.*
> *Quinn*

I don't even know how many times I end up reading the card. My eyes automatically loop back to the beginning each time I finish. A tear I'm unable to catch falls on the card and smudges the pen ink. That's when I know I have to set it aside or else I'll ruin this wonderful card from a wonderful man that I miss more than anything.

When I shift the clutter on my desk to write back, a hint of yellow pokes out from under a pile of papers. It's my portfolio from New Jersey. I forgot that I sent Hobart after this ages ago.

When I open it, I'm greeted by those blasted toilet partitions and parking plans from Carver & Associates. I'm surprised they didn't confiscate these when they fired me. Doesn't matter, though, because beneath them both are the plans for Kacey's nonprofit workshop.

"Damn," I mutter to myself. I was supposed to have this built and functional for her by September. It's December now. I've missed the mark by a long shot.

The next morning, earlier than usual, after sending off my next letter to Quinn, I return to headquarters, where I key in Kacey Ortega. A photo of her pops up. Tan skin, long black hair, chestnut-brown eyes.

In her saved core memories, there's video of her working alongside her nonprofit volunteers (including, most recently and surprisingly, Quinn and Veronica) in a scrubby recreation center basement with a leak in the ceiling. It's untenable and frustrating. It's visible in the sets of their brows as they put together a ramshackle Halloween party. Not only did I mess up with Quinn, but I did wrong by Kacey.

Quinn's words about my passion lying here assuaged some of my outstanding guilt, but now it's back and uglier.

It no longer matters that I wanted to be the lead designer on a project or head my own firm. I wanted those things because they would be concrete markers of success that would force my parents to realize that architecture is a legitimate career.

As Bradley helped me understand, I'm tired of looking to them for validation. It's time to look in the mirror and find it there instead.

PAGEANT PRINCE

QUINN

12 DAYS 'TIL CHRISTMAS

For almost two weeks, Patrick and I exchange letters.

Beautiful letters. Sweet letters. Sometimes sexy letters.

Today, I catch the postman pulling up to our mailbox right as I'm leaving for the first rehearsal of the Rainbow Connection Coalition's Holiday Pageant. After the success of the Halloween party, Kacey reached out to me via email about doing more work with the group. "Paid this time, of course," she'd said over the phone when we discussed the group's upcoming interest in putting on a holiday production for their parents.

I set the new letter down on my passenger seat like it's truly Patrick, here to visit. I drive over to the rec center buzzing with excitement. I'm eager to work with the teens again and thrilled at the prospect of finding a position at a place that values my unique skill set, allows me to connect and mentor, but doesn't squash my sense of self or mandate me as much.

I'm walking across the parking lot with the letter in hand when Veronica shouts at me from across the way. "Guess what?!" She and Kacey hit it off after Halloween, going out on a string of successful dates. Their dogs have even met. A big step for Veronica when it comes to meeting people. "Ooooh, is that another love letter from your estranged husband?" she asks, eyeing the paper in my hands.

"We're not estranged. That sounds too much like we're characters in a period drama."

"You kind of are," she says. "He's the soldier off in the war. You're the wife character pining away at home, hoping her husband will make it back in time for Christmas. He writes you letters. You write him back. It's all very poetic."

I stick my tongue out at her even though it's childish. Writing these letters has been like meeting a whole different version of Patrick. In his letters, he's clear and precise. He always worried about his way with words, but his words, in these letters, have been having their way with me. At night, I lie in bed, holding them tight to my chest, inhaling the cinnamony scent that some-how clings to the pages even after traveling such a distance. An unmatched intimacy stirs some— "Oh, God. You're right."

"I always am," she says. "And now for my thing. My mom and Noah, as a Hanukkah gift, have agreed to pay the adoption fees for me to bring home a second dog."

"Oh, that's awesome." She's been talking about this forever.

"Luca needs a friend, and I think I've found the perfect one." On her phone, she has an adoption site pulled up. The page features the smiling face of a two-year-old golden retriever named Milo. "Isn't that the handsomest dog face you've ever seen? His family had to give him up because they're moving overseas for work and their housing is no-pets-allowed. I called the adoption agency to see if he was still there, and he is, but apparently, he's so sweet and friendly that there's already a lot of interest in him. The woman on the phone said if I was serious about him, I have to go tomorrow."

"No worries if you can't help me hang the Christmas lights then," I say, already rearranging my schedule in my head.

"Actually, I was sort of hoping you would come with me," she says.

"V, you know I'm not good with dogs."

"I know, but my mom and Noah won't make it home and to the shelter in time before they close, and I just thought since you've been conquering your fears . . ."

"This is a different kind of fear," I say.

"You're good with Luca."

"Because I know Luca."

"You'll get to know Milo, too!" She's smiling at me insistently. "Please, Quinn. It would mean a lot to me."

Veronica has been fiercely there for me these past months. This is the least I can do to repay her kindness and friendship, so I relent before telling her to head inside without me.

On a bench near the double doors, I take a breath and read Patrick's words.

Dearest Quinn,

I knew December here would be busy. I just didn't know HOW busy. I imagine this is what it's like to work on Wall Street or at Vogue. *High-octane, high-energy, all day.*

I don't know how we're going to hit our goals by Christmas. With disruptions and wacky magic, it's been a trip. But a rewarding trip.

I'm exhausted but writing to you always perks me up.

It's weird, isn't it? That we're writing to each other like this?

I sort of love it. I never realized how cute your handwriting is before. It's loopy yet neat, large but never invades on the other lines. It's so uniquely you. Sometimes, I catch myself tracing your letters, imagining that I'm tracing the length of your jaw and the dimple in your chin.

God, I want to kiss you, Quinn.

I know I shouldn't say that since we're separated, but I do. Every day that goes by without you only makes the want grow stronger. One day, someday very soon, the want is going to become a need.

Trust me when I say, I'm working hard to figure out a way back to you.

Will you do me a favor?

If you're willing to, hang a dollop of mistletoe above the fireplace.

*I promise, once I figure this all out, I will land the sleigh
on the roof of our house (careful not to disrupt any of the new
shingles I saw you had replaced), slide down our chimney, and
meet you there.*

*You're not selfish for wanting more years for us, Quinn. I
want them, too.*

No, that want has already become a <u>need</u>.

My love always,

Patrick

I hug the letter to my chest, even if I still have doubts floating
around in my head.

"I didn't know smiles could be that big," Veronica says, poking
her head out the door.

"I can't have one moment to myself, can I?" I ask with an over-it
laugh.

"Nope. We're starting rehearsal. Get in here, Mr. Director."

11 DAYS 'TIL CHRISTMAS

At the dog shelter, I expect to be jittery, but the clank of collars
and the pitter-patter of paws doesn't spark fear like it usually does.
When we're escorted through the hallways, past the cages, where
furry friends bark and wag their tails, I feel light.

They've set aside a special pen for Milo with a water bowl and
some squeaky toys. "Say hello," the friendly volunteer instructs
Veronica, who goes in without hesitation. I, however, hang back,
gripped by an old habit.

"He's very friendly," says the volunteer reassuringly.

"He looks it," I say, shakily, remembering the time my dad
forced me to go up and pet the Morgans' rottweiler at a summer
barbecue, so I didn't look like a scaredy-cat in front of all the other
boys. I think back on the dog that lunged at me and Patrick on our
joyride around the world last year.

But then Milo, after receiving plenty of loving pets from a

trusting Veronica, sees me, trots over to a squeaky toy in the shape of a candy cane, picks it up in his snout, and walks cautiously up to the edge of the pen he's in. With big brown eyes on me, he sets it down like a peace offering.

"He likes you," Veronica says.

"Would you like to go in now?" the volunteer asks.

Hesitantly, I nod. Milo backs up as the gate opens. He's clearly been trained enough to know not to be rough or bolt out. He waits for the gate to close, for me to crouch down and then hold out a hand for him to smell. It takes him one sniff and two seconds to trust me enough to let me pet him.

I decide to take a cue from Milo, who is leaning into me as I scratch behind his ears. I have to have faith and trust that Patrick—the man I've always felt safest with—will figure this one out for us.

AN AHA! MOMENT

PATRICK

Quinn's letter is the most adorable one to date. He documents, in great detail, the thrill of meeting Milo.

I think I might actually be a dog person, he writes. I smile to myself. Quinn's growth is my favorite thing to witness. I only wish I'd been there. Though, this seems like maybe something he needed to do by himself.

Just like how he fixed up the New Jersey house, as I saw in the memories and heard about in his letters.

It's interesting that I made a home for us here, and then he made a home for us there. But the longer we're apart, and the longer our letters get, the more I'm beginning to believe that home is not four walls and a roof.

Home is love.

And my love for Quinn can't be contained by a house or a ring or a place or a time. It's magic.

Speaking of magic, I have handwritten reports from Hobart on productivity, happiness, and love that span from when we arrived at the North Pole, when the redesign launched, and then when Quinn left. Somehow, the magic is working better than ever before. Way past peak performance.

That doesn't make sense.

We're almost a week out from Christmas. Despite our best efforts, we are still ridiculously behind on our production schedule.

Time is of the essence. In one short hour, I'm supposed to present my plan for increased productivity before the council, but with everything so topsy-turvy, I haven't come up with a solid proposal.

I jot all my findings down in my leather-bound notebook, sling on a coat, and walk to the stables. Blitzen comes trotting over from across the field with his head slung low. "I forgot your apples today. Sorry. Scatterbrained." He harrumphs at me, but still accepts apologetic pets on his groomed hide. "I'm in a rush to figure something out and I could really use my best sounding board right now." He playfully kicks up some snow.

"Something isn't right . . ." I almost wish he could read so I could show him my notebook. As I put these data points side by side, I'm reminded of the viewfinder I had as a child. Images of beaches or world wonders gradually moving from grainy into vivid focus with the twist of a knob. "Productivity was up when we arrived, down when the redesign happened due to changes, but then up again around the time of the Elf Extravaganza and the anniversary ball. Then, when I started building the dream house, morale lowered. Productivity did, too." My thoughts grow crisper by the second. "The magic only righted itself and then surpassed itself when . . ." I take out Quinn's first letter to me at the North Pole and, sure enough, the dates match. "We revisited our connection."

Blitzen lets out three quick grunts that sound like *doi, doi, doi.*

At the meeting, Nicholas asks me what's to be done to meet our wish quota. All I do is hold up the letters. There are farcical looks on all their faces. As if they were aware of these letters all along. I proceed with my spiel anyway, showing them the missives and the rings around my neck.

"What do a couple of letters from Quinn and your wedding bands prove?" Ashley asks. She crosses her legs.

"It proves that the separation didn't work the way you all thought it would. Our love can still fuel the magic. Daily, the workshop is producing double the gifts it was when we started here all thanks to these letters. Quinn's and my love didn't need to end. We only needed the space to explore ourselves and our love on our own terms for it to continue," I relay. Loaded silence permeates the room before . . .

"I knew this would work," Colleen says, springing to her feet.

"Absence makes the heart grow fonder," says Yvonne. "The oldest adage in the book. I should've known."

"Wait, this was the plan all along?" I ask, bewildered yet relieved to find I've fallen into a trap.

"Love that overcomes is stronger than love that settles," says Nicholas, imbuing the words with deep sagacity. "The magic is on the mend. Your love has proven itself."

"Does that mean— Does that mean Quinn and I can get back together?" I fiddle with the rings. My fingers itch to remove this necklace, undo the wedding bands, and put them back where they belong.

"Indeed." Colleen touches a hand to her heart.

"And he can stay in New Jersey even if I stay on as Santa?"

Colleen smiles then speaks again. "So long as he spreads cheer and love to everyone he encounters. We've already begun rewriting our bylaws."

"Remember, not all shake-ups are bad," says Nicholas with a wink. "That's our mantra going forward. No more gendered language, no more overly strict expectations, and no more *this is how we've always done it*. Times change. You and Quinn showed us that we need to change along with it."

Hobart yips with glee.

The letters to Quinn, from then until Christmas, pour out of me.

Let's just say a Christmas miracle is on its way, I write in the first one.

What? How? Have I told you recently that you're amazing? Quinn says at the beginning of his reply.

As my days blur into nights and the big ride inches ever closer,

I find time every evening to sit by candlelight, dip my quill into the inkwell, and write to my husband. I'm leaning into the drama of it all.

You're really not going to tell me what to expect? Quinn writes in a later letter.

I'm really not going to tell you, I scribe back. *Can I ask you another favor? Can you tell my parents to stay up until midnight on Christmas Eve? I need to see them.*

Our letters start arriving closer and closer together as the excitement mounts. *Of course. I'm actually seeing your mom this weekend. We're picking out a restaurant for Christmas dinner. Apparently even she's over cooking the ham. She told me she doesn't even like ham! It's just tradition at this point. Suffice to say, we had a good laugh.*

My heart thumps steadily as everything falls into place.

I sign off my final letter to Quinn for the year: *See you soon, my love, when all will be revealed.*

'TWAS THE NIGHT BEFORE CHRISTMAS

QUINN

There's nothing more exciting than watching a festive Christmas movie in your garland-festooned living room at midnight on Christmas Eve.

Scratch that, there's nothing more exciting than watching a festive Christmas movie in your garland-festooned living room at midnight on Christmas Eve when you know, any hour now, your magical husband is going to slide down the chimney and kiss you madly.

I've got hot cocoa to keep me up, kettle corn to keep me fed, and Will Ferrell and Zooey Deschanel to keep me company. I'll never get tired of this movie. Never, ever.

It's the perfect treat after a grueling yet rewarding weekend of performances with the coalition kids. Their holiday pageant went off without a hitch, thanks in large part to me, which is why, in the New Year, Kacey and I plan to discuss potential full-time employment with the nonprofit. I'm excited to ring in a new chapter for my career.

My phone pings with a text from Veronica. Included is a video of Luca and Milo coming in from her mom and stepdad's backyard with mud all over their snouts and paws. *Merry Christmas, ya filthy animals* she's captioned it.

Me: Adorable!

Veronica: Has your husband come yet?

Me: Wouldn't you like to know . . .

Veronica: *rolls eyes into infinity*

Veronica: Off to sleep with the fresh-out-of-the-bath puppers. Keep me posted. Love you!

Me: Will do. Good night. Love you too!

I switch over to my text thread with Mom, which has grown robust since our phone call before Thanksgiving.

Through these texts, I found out that Pete, her new boyfriend and the guy she spent Thanksgiving with, is not some pack-a-day casino card shark like I assumed. He's a veterinarian who was in town for a conference at the convention center and staying at the hotel her casino is in. He was losing miserably at the penny slots when he ordered a drink from Mom. They struck up a conversation that lasted until her shift ended. I'm happy for her.

I pop a gif of a present opening and the words MERRY CHRIST- MAS springing out of the box into the text chain. Wanted to be the first to say it to you! I type alongside it. Really looking forward to your visit.

I set my phone on the end table and press play on the movie, which I know entirely by heart at this point. I'm quoting along, still laughing at every schlocky bit.

Yet the longer the movie plays, the more my excitement wanes and a niggling sense of déjà vu takes over the room. It's almost twelve-thirty. Am I being stood up again like last year?

I started the movie shortly after eleven. I thought, given that he asked me to tell his parents to stay up, he'd be flying through our town right around now.

At the finale of the movie, when Buddy and Jovie hold their baby next to Papa, reunited and happy in their new home at the North Pole, a familiar mixture of anger and worry bubbles up inside me. I tamp it down with more hot chocolate, more kettle corn, and I switch to the Hallmark Channel for some sentimental sweetness to counteract the uneasiness I'm sitting with.

Eventually, I've watched so many snowbound hotties hitch their wagons and kiss before the credits that the predictability lulls me toward sleep. I try to fight it off. I think, *No, Patrick's on his way. He has to be.*

But the last thing I see before I drift off isn't Patrick appearing out of a cloud of gold dust, it's Lacey Chabert kissing a brown-haired man under the mistletoe, just like the one I hung as per Patrick's request.

That should be us, I think sullenly, before conking out.

CLEARING THE AIR

PATRICK

I'm obscenely nervous as I guide the sleigh through the sky.

There's no bad weather on the horizon or hiccups in our flight path. The gifts were packed perfectly. We're scheduled to make every stop on time. After all that practice, the delivering presents part I've got down pat. It's the confronting-my-parents part that I'm freaking out about. No way to simulate *that*.

The reindeer team comes to a stop on my parents' roof. A million thoughts buzz through my head as I shimmy down the chimney. Shrouded in gold dust.

As soon as I'm planted at the foot of the fireplace, in the family room where I spent nights watching sports with Dad and Audrey Hepburn movies with Mom, I hear my mom say from around the corner, "Forget it, Bill. I don't know what kind of homecoming Patrick was expecting, but he's not getting it from me. Not this late. I'm tired. I'll see him at the restaurant."

I set the present sack down with a thud. A hushed "What was that?" echoes through the hall.

"How did you get in here?" It's my dad's voice now. A surly growl. He holds a long, unwieldy umbrella up in the air, ready to swing.

Wow. On the receiving end, this is seriously frightening. No wonder the last Santa quit when we panned him. *Twice.*

I raise my hands in panicked surrender. "No. Dad, stop."

"Dad? What? Who is this guy?" Dad lunges forward. Mom

must recognize my voice because she's instantly there behind him. She wrenches Dad back by the sleeve of his blue cotton robe.

"Bill, don't hit him! I think it's Patrick . . ." She passes Dad. Her eyes squint to get a better look. "In a costume?"

I shake my head. It doesn't matter that I've been preparing for this moment for over a week now. I'm still at a loss for words. My parents have always made my mind go blank and my body tense.

"What's going on?" Mom asks. When I'm wordless for too long, she reaches out and tugs on the beard. Her eyes magnify with shock when she pulls her hand away and it's coated in golden, magical glitter. "Patrick, what . . . what happened to you?" She takes me in. Donning the enchanted cloak doesn't feel like putting on armour anymore. It's an extension of my own body. This power and responsibility are mine to harness.

With the umbrella dangling from his fingertips, Dad approaches. "Pam, what are you talking about? Just because he sounds like our son doesn't mean he is."

"But—"

I don't wait to hear what Mom has to say. She believes. She always has. She sent those letters to the North Pole for years without telling us.

Quickly, I strip off the cloak. For the next sixty minutes, time will stop everywhere but inside this house. I have one hour to tell my parents everything I've been holding back for the last twenty-seven years. My chest constricts.

My parents stumble backward in horror when the gold dust settles. "Hi," I say. As if that simple greeting doesn't completely undermine the magical transformation they witnessed. "It's me."

"Son, I—" Not sure I've ever seen my father at a loss for words before. "I don't understand. Is this some kind of new technology?"

I shake my head again. "No, it's a pretty old technology called magic." I pick the cloak up from the floor. Drape it over my arms. At least it will hide my shaking hands. "Do you remember that job opportunity I mentioned last Christmas?" Their nods of recognition happen in slow succession. "You might want to sit for this next part."

Uncertainly, they shuffle to the couch. Mom sits perched on the edge of a cushion. Dad slumps back.

"This was the job." I shake the cloak. More gold dust falls. "I'm Santa Claus." It feels good to say that again to someone outside of the North Pole. It's legitimizing in a way I hadn't expected.

"What's going on here? Magic? Santa Claus? Have you lost your mind? What am I saying? Clearly, he has with all that world traveling and not calling and gallivanting and God knows what else." Dad's finicky hands move fast.

"Did you miss the whole me-sliding-down-through-the-chimney and the glittery transformation that happened a second ago?" I ask. My dad can't be that dense.

"Let's say, for the sake of this conversation, that magic and Santa are real. How would you have become him?" Mom asks.

I weave the story. The abridged version. Less violence, of course.

They're still stupefied. Still looking at me like I've grown a second head. Suddenly, their attention is caught by thumping up above us.

"What is that? Is there someone on our roof? This little prank of yours has gone too far, son." Dad hauls himself to his feet and out the back door. He walks across the back deck in near darkness. He tilts his head toward the sky. "Holy Mother of— Are those reindeer?" He doesn't notice he's inched too close to the railing. He bumps it, loses his balance, and falls over the edge.

Good thing it's only a few feet and that there's several inches of fresh, fluffy snow on the ground.

"Bill!" Mom rushes out after him.

Dad's okay. Just cold, wet, and shaken. We get him inside, dry him off, and sit him at the kitchen table wrapped in a towel. Mom turns on the electric burner and places the filled teakettle on it before coming back to us.

"I don't expect you to understand everything tonight because

I don't have much more time left." I check my pocket watch. "But I came here because Quinn and I were living at the North Pole for the better part of the year, working with the elves to grant wishes and spread Christmas cheer."

Dad shakes his head fast but blinks slowly. "I assumed Carver & Associates had sent you on some special project to get ideas from around the world."

"Actually, Dad"—I square off to him—"I got fired from Carver & Associates right before Christmas last year."

"You what?" The teakettle begins to whistle. I imagine it's the sound of steam pouring out of Dad's ears as he lumbers up to standing and drops the towel.

Mom doesn't say a word. She's pouring the hot water and steeping the tea, not looking over. I get the sense she's known this part but didn't want to bring it up.

I stand to meet my father eye to eye. "I got fired. I'm sorry I lied. But I don't regret any of it. I don't regret studying what I love or pursuing it, because I'm not you. Dad, I know you wanted me to be a lawyer and, Mom, I know you've always wanted a daughter-in-law because you never had a daughter. I've made concessions every day to try and be myself while still pleasing you both, but I don't think I can do that anymore. I have to choose me."

"I don't understand," Dad says.

"That's okay," I say. "Because I understand now. I'm your son, and I'm wired to want you to be proud of me, but you know what? I learned that it's just as important that *I'm* proud of me. And I am. That's enough."

The three of us stand in tenuous silence. My pocket watch vibrates to remind me that I'm running out of time to put the cloak back on.

"I have to go now, but I'll see you both for Christmas dinner, okay?" I ask, edging back toward the fireplace. Unburdened, at least a little. "I love you both."

I transform back into Santa. Growing and widening. I heft the sack up over my shoulder.

Right as I'm about to disappear up the chimney, Mom calls after me. "Patrick?"

"Yeah?"

She clears her throat. "Those things you said— We never, well, we never wanted you to be anyone other than who you are. We only nudged you in certain directions because we wanted to ensure you'd be happy. Happy and loved. That's all we ever cared about. That's all we still care about."

"That's right," Dad says after a beat. Which is as close to sentimental as he's ever going to get.

"We love you," Mom says. "We love you lots. Always will. No matter what."

"Thanks for saying that. Oh, and here." I pull a wrapped gift out of the bag and tuck it under their nearby pre-lit tree. "Merry Christmas."

Feeling lighter, I slip back into the driver's seat of the sleigh and fly off to make a massive, custom delivery close by before returning home to Quinn.

HOLDING OUT FOR A HERO

QUINN

Bzz. Bzz.

I wake up on Christmas morning to my phone vibrating noisily on the end table. I fell asleep on the couch last night. My neck is stiff. Across the room, the Hallmark Channel is still playing on the TV. It's another Lacey Chabert movie. How does she have the time? And the *range*?

My unwashed mug of hot chocolate still sits on the coffee table next to the open bucket of kettle corn. That's when it hits me: *Patrick never showed.* The devastation is immediate.

Fighting for energy, I pick up the call without checking the caller ID. "Hello?" I say blearily.

"Quinn? Hi. Sorry to wake you so early." I recognize Kacey's voice. "Is Patrick there? I tried calling him, but it went straight to voicemail."

"No, he's not." I elbow away my feelings about being stood up. "Is everything okay?"

"Oh, yes. Sorry. Should've said that from the get-go." Her voice brightens. "I just . . . um. A building appeared in my backyard overnight?"

At first, this doesn't compute. "Wait, what?"

"Yeah, that was my initial reaction, too," she says.

Then, it clicks. This could be the Christmas miracle Patrick was alluding to in his letters. "I'll be right over," I say before hanging up.

I scoop Veronica on the way. I call her from the car and give her very little context, which is probably why she gets in with a duffel bag filled to the brim.

"What is that?" I ask, already pulling away from the curb outside of her mom's house.

"My go-bag."

"Why do you have that?"

"From your tone, I assumed you committed a crime, and now we're going on the run together," she says with far too much seriousness.

I honk out a laugh, thankful I have a friend as ride-or-die as Veronica. "What I'm about to tell you is shocking but not *that* shocking."

When we arrive at Kacey's house, the place is swarmed with neighbors. They all stand around and talk to one another with wonder and confusion and amazement. "Where did that come from?" one man asks an older woman still in her Christmas pajamas. "Beats me," she says. "I live next door and I'm a light sleeper. I didn't see or hear anything last night."

The entire neighborhood is abuzz. A news van rolls down the street. A pristine-looking woman in a bright red coat pops out with a cameraman in tow. This is a lot.

Kacey spots me in the crowd and tugs me through. "It's a madhouse." Everyone else lingers at the curb, but Kacey cuts a path across her driveway, into her garage, and through the house. I'm flabbergasted when we reach her backyard.

The building stands somewhere between a large shed and a quaint cottage. It has a blue exterior, a sloped, tiered roof, and plenty of windows. The inside is spacious, and it's even decorated with Pride flags and quirky chairs in a complementary color palette. It's markedly a Patrick Hargrave design.

"Wowza," Veronica says, walking toward the back and looking out onto the tall, snow-dappled trees that line Kacey's property.

"It's everything Patrick and I talked about when I commissioned him for the project," Kacey says. "You're sure he's not around?"

I deliberately avoid Veronica's questioning gaze. "I'm sure."

Kacey nods as silent contemplation falls over us. My heart is bursting that Patrick did this. On the other hand, I'm nervous about how I can explain this away. Then, Veronica grabs for a piece of paper thumbtacked to a corkboard over the desk in the corner. "Have you seen this?" she asks, passing it over to Kacey.

"No," she says. "I saw the building from my bedroom window, ran out here, and then immediately called Quinn. I didn't exactly look around."

The note reads:

Dear Kacey,
Your organization makes a world of difference to the many
lives you touch. I hope this new headquarters helps expand and
strengthen your mission.
With love,
Mr. C

Kacey's puzzlement gradually shifts to understanding. Tears speckle the edges of her chestnut-colored eyes.

"I, um—" I stammer.

Kacey stops me with an upturned hand. "I was raised not to question the gifts of angels. Weirder things have happened, right?"

"Right," Veronica and I say in unison.

Back on the street, the news reporter runs up to us.

"Miss Ortega, Miss Ortega, what can you tell us about this mysterious building?" the eager journalist asks. She pushes a microphone into Kacey's face.

Kacey stops for a second, looks straight into the camera, and says, "I can tell you that today of all days, I firmly believe in miracles."

The house isn't as quiet as I left it.

After I hang up my coat and slip off my boots, a rustling coming from our living room makes my heart skip several beats. That's where the Christmas tree I put up is, so I'm not totally surprised when I find Santa Patrick standing there, waiting for me.

No matter the anger I felt last night or the disappointment I felt this morning, I'm lit up with delight to see him. "I thought maybe you'd forgotten." My voice is meek, but my stomach flutters.

"I could never," he says certainly. "Sorry I'm late. I was just saving the best stop for last."

I beam, sensing my center of gravity lurch toward him. "Kacey's workshop looks incredible."

"Oh good," he says, almost bashfully. "We assembled it quickly in the cover of night. I'm glad it's nice in broad daylight."

I inch farther into the room. "So, what's the verdict? Have I been naughty or nice this year?"

He chuckles, eyes roaming up to the ceiling. "Nice. Very nice. In fact, so nice that I have a special present for you."

I'm expecting a kiss. Not an envelope. "More letters?" I ask, only a smidge disappointed as I accept it.

"Open it and find out."

What I find is way more than a letter. I think it's a decree from the Council of Priors.

Addendums to North Pole bylaws Article 25, Subsections 11 and 12.

Subsection 11. Santa's ~~wife~~ spouse automatically fulfills the role of ~~Mrs. Claus~~ Merriest Mister/Missus/any such moniker they so choose and all the duties that come with that role.

Subsection 12. The present ~~Mrs. Claus must reside along-~~ ~~side the present Santa in the North Pole for the present Santa's~~ ~~tenure.~~ spouse may reside wherever they choose so long as they spread love and Christmas cheer to every soul their life shall touch.

*Addendums effective immediately as ruled by the Council of Priors and Santa Patrick

"What does this mean?" I ask, still jumbled from all the commotion this morning.

"It means that the magic in the North Pole didn't need us to be married and in one place," Patrick explains, "it needed us to love each other fully and without expectation."

An overjoyed sigh saws out of me. "That's wonderful, so for us that means . . . ?"

"It means I'll send the sleigh for you on weekends. I'll start delineating responsibilities better so that I can take time off to come visit you in the less busy months at the workshop," Patrick says. "And from the twenty-sixth to January first, I'll come here, and you and I will laze and love and rest and just be Patrick and Quinn. Simple. You always said you didn't want a traditional marriage. Would this arrangement bring *our* magic back?"

I nod, elated. "Yes. Yes, of course it would."

"Then . . ." Patrick says. He takes off his cloak. His hair falls flat in his face and his jacket is flecked with golden glitter, but he still looks heart-stoppingly handsome in a sharp, tailored suit.

As I look him over, I notice a simple silver chain around his neck. On it, two rings clang together. He takes the chain off and undoes the clasp to remove one of the rings. It's my wedding band. From the nearby sack of gifts, he produces a single, perfect red rose. "Quinn Muller, will you marry me? Again?" He's kneeling as he says this.

I rush across the room to him, extend my trembling left hand,

and let Patrick put the wedding band back where it belongs. I'm whole again. "Yes. I'd marry you a million times over, Patrick Hargrave."

Smiling, he puts his own ring back on his finger, then stands. "Now let's put this mistletoe to good use."

EPILOGUE

PATRICK

185 DAYS 'TIL CHRISTMAS

My parents look completely out of place in the North Pole.

They stand in front of my house in the village with their hair sticking up, suitcases by their side, and frazzled looks on their slightly green faces. I sent Hobart, in his last task as head elf before attending special-mission training, to bring them here because there are too many last-minute details to arrange. Quinn's and my vow renewal ceremony is somehow more stressful than our wedding.

Of course, that's probably because Mom planned most of the wedding for us on the first go-around. This was Quinn's baby from the start. Every weekend that he has wrestled himself away from working with Kacey and drinking with Veronica and walking the goldendoodle named Kringle that he surprised me by adopting, he is in the North Pole designing outfits with Christa, setting menus with Colleen and Yvonne, and talking logistics with Hobart.

I add my two cents here and there, but for the most part I sit back and let Quinn do his thing. He's refined his planning skills in his new post at the Rainbow Connection Coalition.

"Welcome," I say to my parents, who stand behind the garden gate. "How was the trip?" As part of my changes to the bylaws, biological and chosen family are now allowed to visit the North Pole. My parents, being the people that they are, put off the trip until now. But Quinn's mom has come up a few times to help with ceremony prep, and Bradley has come by, too, for overnights. It's only served to boost the love inside our little bubble of joy.

"It was very fast," Mom says.

"And bumpy," Dad adds.

"Sorry about that," Hobart says. He rolls their suitcases behind him like a bellboy. "It's been a while since I've driven."

My parents are immediately enamored with the house. When I tell them I designed it, they go quiet at first. But then they share a big smile that I suspect they think I don't catch.

I show them upstairs to the guest suite with the big cushy bed and the vintage-style bathroom. It has a mixture of white tile and floral prints in green, white, and light red that Mom will like. Hobart sets their suitcases down in the corner.

"Where's Quinn?" Mom asks.

"Oh, he's working today. He'll fly in tomorrow. He says it's bad luck to see the husband before the vow renewal ceremony." The three of us share a laugh over his superstitiousness. "I figured after you freshen up and get settled, I can show you around the village and we can get some lunch."

They agree, so thirty minutes later, we stroll through town. Elves come up and introduce themselves. My parents glow when people say how much they "love Santa Patrick" and how "lucky they must feel to have such a stellar son."

"I swear I didn't bribe anyone to do this," I say before leading them into the workshop.

I haven't given a tour of the space since the ribbon cutting last year. I'm rusty yet I still find a rhythm. My dad's nods and my mom's small smiles propel me.

We end the tour in my office. The place I feel most at ease.

"That was great, Patrick," Mom says.

Dad's eyes are cast down. Like he's thinking through something. "You manage that whole operation?"

"I do."

He nods. "That's quite impressive, son."

Mom uncharacteristically cups her hands around her mouth to whisper, "I believe he's trying to say he's proud of you." It means a lot, but it doesn't mean everything to me anymore, and that's real progress.

We spend the rest of the day eating good food, checking out the venue, and catching up with each other. I didn't realize how, even when I became an adult, I still considered my parents as sitting on a pedestal above me.

As they talk about new construction going up near their house and health issues and Bradley's constant travels and Nan's assisted living community, I'm reminded that my parents are people, not paragons. And we can connect as such. Not as bricks on top of each other in a pyramid, but as branches extending off the same trunk of our family tree. It's a reassuring thought.

184 DAYS 'TIL CHRISTMAS

The next day, dressed in the tuxedo Quinn designed for me, I stand nervously under the ornate floral archway at the front of the ballroom. I'm there before hundreds of elves; the council; Quinn's soon-to-be stepdad, Pete; Veronica; Kacey; and my parents.

Once again, Bradley stands next to me. This time, I've asked him to be there. And I'm proud of the relationship we've built in only six months. In Bradley, I've found not only a brother but a true friend. "Second time's the charm," he whispers with a smile on his face, jostling me slightly.

I pinch myself, overwhelmed by how I ended up here, and how lucky I am.

Then, I pinch myself even harder. Because the organist begins to play a triumphant tune and, after Kringle the dog trots down the aisle with a basket of flower petals in his mouth, my beautiful husband appears with his mother beside him. She wears a lovely champagne-colored pantsuit with her hair down, but it's Quinn who steals the show.

He wears a green blouse, tucked into a tartan kilt. A red velvet cape creates a train, which drags liberally behind him. There's a string of pearls—my mom's pearls, on loan as a sweet gesture—around his neck.

Arriving at the lip of the stage, Mrs. Muller kisses Quinn on both cheeks and then tends to his train while I help him up. Nicholas, our officiant, stands with us in full Santa garb, ready to begin the ceremony.

"You look stunning," I whisper to Quinn before he takes his position in front of me.

"You don't clean up half bad yourself, Mr. Claus." He bats his long, mascara'd eyelashes at me.

The truth of it settles. My wish all those years ago came true.

I'm going to love this man forever.

I can't wait to declare as much for the second time in front of everyone we care about.

ACKNOWLEDGMENTS

Writing acknowledgments is a lot like making a list and checking it twice, so . . .

Timothy Janovsky's Nice List
(in alphabetical order)

Kasee Bailey

Lisa Bonvissuto

Andie Burke

Alison Cochrun

Char Dreyer

Katrina Escudero

Samantha Fabien

Helena Greer

Olga Grlic

Jeremy Haiting

Kirsten Hess

Tarah Beth Jordan Hicks

Nina Hunter

John Janovsky

Johnny Janovsky

Theresa Janovsky

Anita Kelly

Stephanie Kersikoski

Meryl Sussman Levavi

Gina Loveless

Melanie Magri

Julie Matrale

Ginny Perrin

Chip Pons

Sara Quaranta

Simone Richter

Laynie-Rose Rizer

Lisa Roe

Eileen Rothschild

Mark Sanderlin

Kelsey Scanlon

Heather Shapiro

Anika Steffen

Chuck Stinner

Katie Stinner

Robert Stinner

Sara Stinner

NaNá V. Stoelzle

R. Eric Thomas

Alicia Thompson

Hannah Walker

Sending you all (and the many others I have certainly missed!) the gift of my gratitude.

ABOUT THE AUTHOR

Rebecca Phillips Photography

Timothy Janovsky is a queer multidisciplinary story-teller based in Washington, D.C. He is the author of six published romance novels. To learn more, find him at timothyjanovsky.com or on social media @TimothyJanovsky.